INTRODUCTI

I was born and brought up in I
was. With the partition we moved fr
become Pakistant, to the United Provinces (Uttar Pradesh) which
was to remain as India. As Anglo-Indians, and Christians, we had no
involvement in the political differences between Hindu and Muslim,
but my father preferred to be in a secular State rather than a
religiously based one.

I came to Coventry for an engineering training, and there I
met my Scottish wife, Jacqui, and remained in England. It would
have been interesting to have taken her to see India, but she doesn't
like excessive heat, and the poverty would have upset her. And,
without her, I wasn't going anywhere!

Some of the pieces in this book are from my youth, and some
from very much later. It is thanks to Jacqui that they have been
brought together in one volume. There should be something in it for
everyone, though I must say, I have the unrealistic hope that they will
all be enjoyed.

My thanks go to the Ringwood Writers' Circle who have
given me the benefit of their constructive comments, to my daughter
Lyn for her help in getting this into print, and to Jacqui for her
encouragement in getting the anthology together.

To you, the reader, I wish enjoyment, and the hope that you
will be pleased you dipped into this little collection.

Published and Distributed by K V Coello,
keithcoello@tiscali.co.uk

ISBN 978-0-9522661-2-9

INDEX

Page

1   McClusky

8   Across my Life's Uncertain Seas

9   Advertisement

13   Blind love, blind Hate

19   The Cowardly Whispers of Age

21   Colleen

28   Golden Wedding

29   Meeting Miss Pym

33   Father's Day

38   The Ruin

41   E-Mail

45   The Mortality Syndrome

51   Alone

52   Not Quite Pets

55   Creator

56   Glimpses of my Father

63   Eve

69   Jenny

73   The Face of Korakuya

77   Pebbles of Harnai

78   Mitigating Circumstances

81   The English Teeth

85   Song of the Free

86   At First Sight

90   Tiger

93   Fool's Gold

95   Evidence

97   The Mem

105   Bike

106   Jam and Jerusalem

110   When Darkness Falls

113   When I shall Die

114   Half a Cow

117   Boiled Rice

119   Revelation

120   The Portrait

124   Mother and Child

128	Peace and Quiet
133	What's in a Name?
135	Woody
138	Lines to a Hostel Room
139	The Elizabethan Cottage
141	Hindu Kush
143	Peace
146	Palla
149	The Holiday
152	Patt Desert
168	Bag Lady
169	The Final Birthday
172	Science
173	The Carriage
177	"I'll Look After You"
182	Minor Matters
185	Voices
188	The Otherwhere
192	Nightmare
193	"It Must Have Been Hot!"
196	Seepage and Evaporation
199	The Scan
203	The Painted Board
207	The Oldest Man in Town
211	A Mark upon the Virgin Snow
212	Footprints
213	The Peripheral Man
216	The Lodger
220	The Puppet
221	Impressions
223	The Local Government Officer
225	TheMustard Seed
232	Abandon Ship
235	The Sale
241	Indian Orphan
242	The Eye of the Buddha
248	The Offering
253	The Fiction Writer
255	McConnigan's Wake

McCLUSKY

McClusky was an unimaginative man. In an orphanage from the age of six, and in the army at sixteen, such dreams as he dreamed were simple and uncomplicated. Now, at twenty-eight, he thought of a small house of his own, with a wife to share it, and children on whom he could lavish the parental love which he himself had missed. Most men had at least this much, he thought, but so far it had eluded him. No woman had stirred him into overcoming his shyness, no tender emotions had kept him preoccupied with love. Except.... perhaps.... but that was impossible, and he pushed the thought away.

He was a large ungainly man. His red hair gave a fair indication of his temperament; quick to anger, but just as ready to forgive. He was said to be the clumsiest NCO in the Indian Army, and his fiery impetuousness put him constantly in trouble. His Commanding Officer had once remarked, confidentially of course, that Sergeant-Major McClusky was a man of thud and blunder.

Whatever shortcomings his senior officers may have thought he possessed, McClusky was idolised by the Gurkha sepoys in his command, and especially by the Naiks, the Indian rank of Corporal. Lance-Naik Senling in particular, felt a genuine friendship for the big man. They had fought many skirmishes together against the tribesmen of the Afghan border. On two occasions he had saved McClusky's life, and on one, McClusky saved his. Of such events were built the bonds which bound them.

The Afridis and the Waziris took advantage of the army's preoccupation with the war against Germany to press their own interests on the north west frontier of India. As a result the Fourteenth Gurkha Rifles was stationed at Fort Sandeman to maintain the peace. They champed at the bit. They would rather have been in the fight against the Germans or the Japs, but if they thought the frontier tribesmen any less dangerous they were soon to find that they were not. On only their second sortie the Gurkhas lost three men, brought down by snipers hidden in the

1

hills. One of the casualties was their young Subaltern, inexperienced in the rigours of war. Thus it was that McClusky found himself leading the excursions into the tribal territories.

Moving in single file among the rocks the platoon found themselves being fired on by tribesmen in the hills above them. "Get down! Take cover boys!" McClusky rapidly surveyed the scene, then ran across to one of the sepoys, followed by a hail of bullets. Grabbing the young Gurkha he pulled him to the ground. "Keep your head down you bloody fool," he yelled, "them's bullets out there, not popcorn!"

The young man gave a wide smile. "O.K. Sarge. I get them!" He started to pull his kukri from its sheath.

"Get your head down sepoy! That's an order!" He wasn't going to have this young man running amok, brandishing his kukri and getting himself killed by the Afridis firing down from the hills. He strained his eyes for any tell-tale signs of movement, but the tribesmen were in their home territory, they knew every inch of the country and made full use of every bit of cover. He could see no signs of them.

To his left Lance-Naik Senling was crawling forward, low to the ground. McClusky heard the slight sound of boots against the rock, the occasional stone being dislodged. He strained to hear other sounds, sounds which may have indicated the whereabouts of the enemy, but there were none. Spasmodic firing from the hillsides kept him pinned down. He tried to spot his men, and was relieved to find that he couldn't see them. At least they had the good sense to keep under cover.

He saw the movement out of the corner of his eye. The Afridi was almost on him before he could swing his rifle butt against the man's head. "Christ that was close! How did he get so near without me hearing him?" But it was no time for speculation. He threw away the man's rifle and knife and left him lying unconscious on the ground. A quiet grunt came from his left. He was just in time to see two men carry away the unconscious Senling. They moved like ghosts among the rocks, fading into the landscape without trace and then reappearing somewhere else.

"They have the Lance-Naik. Come on boys, let's get him back!" To let Senling be captured was to leave him to torture and a slow and terrible death. That was never going to happen to one of his boys. "Catch them!" he cried, rising from his foxhole.

"Ya-eeh". The sound was bloodcurdling as it echoed among the hills. "Ya-eeh" cried the Gurkhas as they unsheathed their kukris and leapt across the rocks. Taking no heed of the flying bullets they chased the two men, who soon dropped their unconscious burden and fled. McClusky lifted the wounded man and, slinging him over his shoulder he hurried back to shelter. The sepoys gave him covering fire, but bullets were everywhere. He felt the shock as the Lance-Naik was hit twice and then a searing pain in his shoulder reminded him of his own vulnerability. Another bullet hit his arm and as he scrambled for his foxhole a third hit his leg and he fell into the safety of the rocks, unable to move.

His return to Fort Sandeman was on a stretcher. On the way Senling died, and McClusky felt a fierce rage against the tribesmen who had killed him. It was a new emotion for him. War was his profession, and there was little place for sentiment.

For two weeks surgeons fought to save his leg. The bullet had shattered the bone and it could not be set. A steel rod and a plate were pinned to the parts still left, and three months later McClusky was able to walk with a stick. He would always need the stick, they told him. He limped away from the hospital, and at the same time he limped away from the army. His soldiering days were over.

He said a last farewell to his sepoys, then paid a final solitary visit to the Fort Sandeman cemetery. Many old comrades were there remembered. Outside the hallowed ground was the Gurkha cemetery. Lines of small uniform headstones. No graves, for they preferred cremation, but reminders of sepoys he had known and respected. New amongst them was the name of Lance-Naik Senling. He stood in silence for a few minutes before this tiny monument to the man who had twice saved his life. It looked so insignificant against the surrounding mountains. Then he squared his shoulders and holding his stick firmly, he limped

3

away.

Up in the Nepalese village he again faced Senling's daughter, repeating once more their first sad encounter. He had met the girl two years before, when her mother had died. The Lance-Naik had asked McClusky to attend the funeral, and it was a sign of their mutual respect that the Sergeant-Major had agreed without hesitation. It meant travelling the breadth of the country but as they journeyed through the night Senling told him something of the home life of the Gurkhas, of the villages high in the Himalayas, of herding cattle and goats, or occasionally Tibetan yaks, and of gathering sparse crops in the short season. It was a hard life, with few prospects of betterment, and that was why so many joined the army, or risked their lives as sherpas for the mad foreigners obsessed with climbing the mountains.

Senling rambled on, talking to hide his grief, and McClusky let him ramble. He had an immense regard for these stocky hillmen with their legendary courage. He had served with them for most of his army life and needed no telling of their qualities. "You're a better man than I am Gunga Din". He recalled Kipling's verse, and knew it to be true.

From the railway station they walked twelve miles, straight up the mountain it seemed to McClusky, to Senling's village. It was not till they reached it, and his daughter flew into her father's arms, that the Lance-Naik broke down and wept. Unused to shows of emotion, McClusky stood uncomfortably by, until the corporal gathered himself together and introduced the Sergeant.

"How do you do, Sergeant-Major. My father has spoken so much about you that I feel I've known you all my life. Thank you for accompanying him on this sad journey. It's extremely kind of you." The accent was noticeable, but the English was carefully correct.

McClusky had no veneer of sophistication. Even the sixteen year old village girl was aware of his surprise. She smiled through her grief. "I was educated in Calcutta," she explained quietly. "Many of the army fathers send their children away to school. Perhaps it is due to the influence of the west."

4

He could not decide whether she was gently mocking him, but in this time of sorrow it was more likely that it was simply a statement of how she saw things.

"I'm sorry about your mother," he mumbled awkwardly as he took her outstretched hand.

"She has been ill for over a year. I left school to take care of her, but ..." the words tailed off as she reached for a hankie.

The next day Senling and the girl stood dry-eyed and composed as the pyre was lit and the flames consumed the woman's body. McClusky admired their fortitude. He was not a religious man, but he prayed then, that somewhere, some god would find a way to comfort them.

The girl's name was Sho-han. "Sharn. Now there's a fine Irish name for sure! As Irish as McClusky, which, by the way, I wish you'd call me, instead of Sergeant-Major."

"McClusky then, but not Sharn, it's Sho-han, a Nepalese name."

"What does it mean?" he asked.

"Nothing as far as I know, it's just a name. What does McClusky mean?" Again he had that slight feeling that she was making gentle fun of him. She was just a child, but she was growing up fast. He looked at her closely once more, but he saw only the child again, with hurt in her eyes. He wished he had the power to make it better.

Facing her again after two years, that wish was repeated. She had grown up, a young woman now, just turned eighteen. The eyes were full of pain, but the smile was warm and welcoming, and she seemed genuinely pleased to see him.

"How are you coping?" he asked. "I would have come sooner but I was in hospital."

"I know. When they sent the news of my father, they also told me what you did. You would have been safer if you hadn't gone after him."

"It was my duty. Besides, he was more than a comrade, he was my friend. What will you do now? Who'll look after you?"

"My husband. My father would have arranged my

5

marriage, this year or next. Now," she gave a little shrug, "I shall have to arrange it for myself. Another legacy from the west!" He thought there was a touch of bitterness in her voice.

"Will you let me look after you? I have a small pension, enough to get a little house, and to live in a modest but comfortable fashion."

She looked up at him, eyes ablaze. "As your.... your... 'housekeeper'! No thank you! I'll stick to my goats. I'll get by."

"No; as my wife! If you'll have me, that is."

She sighed and her shoulders slumped. "I'm sorry McClusky, I misunderstood. Forgive me, I'm not quite myself. My father always said you were the finest man he'd ever known. If you were to marry me, he would approve, I know."

"And you, my dear, would you approve?"

A touch of pink crept into the coffee and cream complexion as she lowered her eyes. "My father always led me to admire you. Yes," she said softly, "I could approve too, but it's not possible. British soldiers aren't allowed to marry native girls, you know that."

"I'm not a soldier any more. I can marry who I please. Will you have me?"

She hesitated. "There are difficulties. I don't want to give up my god and become a Christian."

"I'm not a religious man. Besides, your god, he made all this, did he? The mountains and the rivers?"

"Yes, and the sky above, and the stars that shine in it."

"Then he can't be so different from my own, who made the hills and lakes of Ireland. I don't think we'll be squabbling about God, my little Sharn."

"Sho-han," she chided gently, "I told you!"

"Sho-han then. But will you; will you marry me?"

"Yes, McClusky, I'll marry you, and I'll try to be a good wife."

"And will you be wanting children?"

"I'll want my husband to love me."

"I'll surely do that. I've loved you since the first day I saw you, and I'll love you till I die."

6

"Then the children will follow, won't they?" Suddenly, she seemed older and wiser than her years, and as the big man gathered her in his arms, he saw his dream take shape. McClusky's orphan days were over.

ACROSS MY LIFE'S UNCERTAIN SEAS

Across my life's uncertain seas
My Father spreads His arm,
And makes my world a haven
Where I cannot come to harm,

For He has made this universe
From His infinite powers
And it is my inheritance
To walk among the stars.

I'll shed my veils of ignorance
As I approach the dawn,
And my unfettered soul will cross
The threshold of the morn.

I have no need to fear
How my future may unroll
For I am in my Father's care,
And He is in control.

ADVERTISEMENT

It was Marian who bought it, she was the one who claimed to be artistic. The small silver plated wine cooler stood on the sideboard, and he had to admit it was a nice looking object. Four inches high, heavily silver plated, it was a classic shape, delicately fashioned. No good for ice, of course, but then that wasn't its purpose. It was a model, not a real Georgian wine cooler. It was unashamedly an ornament, and no more.

He recalled the advertisement. "Do not have anything in your home unless it is useful or beautiful." He had to admit it was beautiful. He also had to admit that it wasn't the least bit useful. But that wasn't the problem. No, the problem was Marian. Every time he looked at her he couldn't help remembering the advert, "do not have anything in your house unless it is useful or beautiful."

He must have seen something in her to have married her, but that was some seven years back. Looking at her now he realised that she wasn't beautiful. Well, she couldn't be blamed for that, he was no oil painting himself. Unfortunately she wasn't useful either. At least he brought in a decent income for them to live on, an income which she managed to squander in less than half the time it took him to earn it. Yet she wasn't really bad. She was easy to talk to, occasionally she had sensible opinions, but why, why, why did she have to be so bloody incompetent? It was that which got up his nose.

His gaze fell on the miniature wine cooler. He thought of the advert, and suddenly it became clear. He didn't want her in his home. She was neither beautiful nor useful. She would have to go.

He was a man of action. As soon as he got to his office he picked up the phone. "Mr Carmichael? Rogers here, I would like to see you when it's convenient. I want to get divorced. Yes, as soon as possible. OK, tomorrow afternoon, three o'clock."

The offices of Carmichael, Carmichael and Rubens were in a well appointed block in the better part of town. Bill Rogers strode in confidently, nodded briefly to the receptionist who

9

motioned him towards the senior partner's door. A quick handshake and he got straight to the point. "Arrange a divorce, reasonable terms, of course, but get moving on it."

"On what grounds are you basing your petition, Mr Rogers?"

"Grounds? She's bloody incompetent, that's what!"

"I'm sorry, but incompetence isn't sufficient grounds for a divorce. You must have a better reason than that."

"But that's the reason. I'm not going to lie about it."

"Is there any evidence of infidelity?"

"I doubt it, I doubt anyone would want her."

"You wanted her once, Mr Rogers, why shouldn't someone else?"

"That was a long while back. Would you want to make love to someone who dressed like a sack of potatoes? No, she must go, but with a fair settlement, she's not a bad person, not really, but she's completely useless."

Long discussions followed, but the bottom line was always the same. He couldn't petition for divorce on the grounds of incompetence. "Would she be prepared to divorce you?"

"She doesn't have any grounds!"

"Talk it over with her, if necessary give her grounds. It need only be a formality. A young lady, a hotel room, nothing needs to actually happen."

Rogers left Carmichael's office seething with anger. The law was an ass. He'd heard it said often enough, and now he knew it for a fact. Here he was, a perfectly upright hardworking citizen, not wishing to have his money frittered away by an incompetent fool, and according to the law there was nothing he could do about it! Well, that couldn't be right. He'd sort something out. But first he'd do what Carmichael said, he'd talk to her.

"Marian, I'm going to divorce you."

"Yes dear." she said mildly. "Why?"

"You're incompetent, that's why."

"Am I dear? When is this divorce going to happen?"

"As soon as I can arrange it."

10

"Have you found someone else?"

"No, I'm not looking for anyone else."

"Poor darling. You do sound fed up. But if there's no one else there's no hurry is there? Now come and eat your dinner."

Dammit he thought, how could he get through to her? He toyed with the ill-cooked food. It was no better, no worse, than she usually dished up. "This is tasteless rubbish," he grumbled. "Can't you do better than this?"

"You know I can't cook," she replied. "I do try, but it never comes out right."

"Then bloody well learn!"

"Now keep calm, dear, you know what the doctor said, getting worked up isn't good for you."

He had to make a positive effort not to scream at her. Clamping his jaw shut he took a few deep slow breaths, then reluctantly resumed his desultory chewing.

When the meal was over she put the two plates, cups and saucers and cutlery in the washer. It left the machine practically empty, but she closed it and turned it to the 'Super Wash' programme.

"That's very expensive for just a few plates. And why super wash?"

"We want them to be clean dear, don't want any nasty bugs, do we?"

With a hopeless gesture he rose to get a drink from the sideboard.

"You sit down dear, I'll get it."

Handing him a whisky she sat down opposite him, knees primly together, hands on her lap. "Now tell me what's bothering you. And what's all this about divorce?"

"I want you out of my life. You waste all the money I earn, you keep the house like a pigsty, you always look a mess, I'm just fed up with it. I want a divorce."

"But you've no grounds. I've never done anything to give you grounds for divorce."

"You've never done anything, full-stop. You're the most useless person I know, and I want shut of you. I'll see that you get a fair settlement, I don't hate you, but I want you out of my life. Is that clear?"

"Yes dear, quite clear. I suppose you'd better set things in motion."

"You don't mind?"

"If it's what you want. What grounds will you cite?"

"That's the problem. There are no grounds, no legal grounds anyway."

"No, I see that. Perhaps it's best to leave things as they are."

Her calmness infuriated him. "Don't you care, doesn't it matter to you that I don't want you any more?"

"Of course I care, dear, but you must stay calm. You know what the doctor said."

"I don't want to stay calm, I want to rant and rave and get my life back together, without you messing everything up all the time. I want to have a meal that I can enjoy, a shirt that I can put on without creases all over it, a chair that I can sit on without moving your damned magazines. Damn you woman, I want a life!"

"Of course you do dear, but you mustn't blame me. You know I do my best."

"Your best is bloody pathetic, that's all I ...." His words stopped as he gripped his chest and sank to the floor. Marian looked at him. What should she do now? She didn't want to upset him further.

She took his glass and, adding it to the few things in the dish washer, she started the machine. That should leave it really clean. "I know it's expensive," she thought, "but we don't want dirty dishes, do we dear?"

When she returned Bill still hadn't moved, and she called the doctor.

There are now two miniature wine coolers on the sideboard. 'Have nothing in your home that isn't beautiful or useful'. Well, they are useful, she supposed, but one just wasn't big enough to hold Bill's ashes.

BLIND LOVE, BLIND HATE

"Here, let me help you."

The deep voice was reassuring, the strong hands gave her confidence as she regained her balance. The white stick was placed in her hand and she was led to a seat.

"My handbag, I've dropped it."

"I know. I'm afraid most of your things have fallen out. I'll pick them up and put them back. There's nothing too personal I hope."

"Thanks. I feel a bit shaken. What was it?"

"A dog. It bumped into you and knocked you over. It's all right, it's gone now. People should be more careful, they shouldn't let their dogs run loose in the park." She detected a slight note of anger in the voice. "There, I think that's everything." The bag was put into her hand.

"Thank you .... er.."

"John, John Morton."

She held out her hand. "Susan Oestler. Thanks again." His grip was firm, and once more she felt reassured.

"Hadn't you better check your bag, make sure everything's there. Your accent Susan, Australian?"

"South African. Johannesburg. I'm at the University here. You're American aren't you?"

"Yes, from New York, and I'm at Aston University too. It seems I've come halfway round the world to pick you up when you fall!"

"Just as well too, but I'm not at Aston, I'm in Birmingham University, at Edgbaston. Oh John, my keys. I can't find my keys. The ring's got a tag with my name on it."

"Hang on, I'll look for it." After a few moments searching he found the ring and gave it to her. "You look a bit shaky," he said. "Perhaps I should take you home." There was a quiet note of humour as he added, "No, I'm not trying to pick you up, even if I did talk about coming halfway round the world!"

She laughed. "I didn't think you were. Men don't make passes at girls who wear glasses, especially not dark glasses!"

13

She started walking to the park gates, the white stick held at an angle before her. His hand took her arm and guided her from the grass to the path and then, through the gate, to the pavement.

"Where now?" he asked. She turned right and after a hundred yards stopped at the pedestrian crossing "Just across from here. Number 53, I have a room there, a bedsit."

"Not on campus then?"

"No, this is adapted for me. It's comfortable. Everything's right for someone who's blind."

When the lights changed and she heard the bleeps she strode confidently across the road and up to the door of the house. "Come in for a coffee?" she asked.

As she made the coffee he looked around the room. Good quality furniture, rounded corners wherever possible, and a Braille clock beside the bed. "Have you been blind long?"

"All my life, I was born blind. Spoiled rotten mind you, Mum couldn't do enough for me. Special school, special care from Dad and her. It was nice, but a little stifling when I started to grow up. Coming here has been good for me."

It was the first of many visits. She felt attracted by the warmth in the voice and the total lack of false sympathy. Real sympathy was there, she knew, but in the room he never pushed to help. It was her place, and she coped without assistance. He seemed to realise that she preferred it that way. On her twentieth birthday he gave her a gift. She thanked him with a friendly kiss. It was the first of many kisses. Three weeks later he stayed the night.

She phoned home about this man she had met. How kind he was, how strong and reliable. She felt safe with him, she said.

"Be careful," they warned, "remember how vulnerable you are," but she was convinced she was in love. "Finders keepers," she laughed, giving him the key. "Now you can come to see me whenever you like."

"Tell me about yourself, I want to know all about you," she added.

He told her of his childhood in New York. "It was just a tenement building, and Dad was the janitor, but it meant a roof

14

over our heads. Mum worked evenings to send me through college. I won a scholarship, that's how I'm able to be here."

"Move in with me," she said, but he wouldn't. "I told you, I'm here on a scholarship. I haven't your sort of money."

"Move in, please, there's no sense in me being here and you on Campus. I'll fix it with the landlady."

Next day she spoke to Mrs. Morris. "I'd like my boyfriend to move in. We'll pay a bit extra for the room, of course, but we want to be together."

"Well, it's your business, my dear. I know lots of you young ones don't bother with getting married these days. There's s couple on the top floor, I don't think they're married. They're coloured too, so your boyfriend may make friends with them. Yes, it should be all right, my dear."

Lying in bed that night she was happy in the knowledge that now he had to reason not to come. "They're coloured too, so your boyfriend may make friends with them." That's what Mrs. Morris had said. She had been too excited to take it in. Recalling the words she suddenly took in their meaning. She must ask Mrs Morris, but she felt certain what was meant. John must be black!

Oh, God! She had kissed him, lain with him, wanted to share her life with him! Suddenly she felt soiled and dirty. All the old prejudices flooded over her, all that she had learnt at her mother's knee. She lay there crying, wanting the man, but helpless against her inbred revulsion for the colour she had never seen.

"Susan." She stopped uncertainly. Blindness prevented her from knowing whether the call was for her, but there was a memory of the voice, blurred by time, yet still with a sense of familiarity.

She moved towards the back of the pavement to get out of the bustle and waited.

"Susan. It is Susan Oestler, isn't it?"

"Yes, I'm Susan Oestler. I'm sorry, I feel I should know you, but…"

"It's John, John Morton. From Aston University. It's

15

been a long time, ten years, you probably don't remember." His voice sounded unsure now, and she thought she could detect a note of regret.

"Oh, John! Yes, of course I remember. How are you?"

"I'm fine. Got time for a coffee? We can catch up on things. What are you doing now?"

"I'm with a bank, I look after Credit Control. I have to get back now, I'm late, but yes, it would be nice. Here," she took a card from her bag and handed it to him. "That's where I live. Give me a ring."

She felt him take the card and as she hurried away she heard him say, "Thanks, I'll phone you."

All that afternoon she thought of their University days. Happy days! What rubbish, she thought. They were the worst days of her life. Stupid, juvenile decisions. Well, she'd paid for them. But now he was back. She looked forward to his call, if he did call, that is. It would serve her right if he thought better of it. She had treated him badly she knew, but that was in the past, and he seemed willing to forgive. She hoped he would.

When the phone did ring she was uncertain what to say. Could he see her, dinner perhaps? She agreed, reluctance and eagerness confusing her emotions even as she answered. She felt sure he would want to know why she had suddenly stopped seeing him, and she wasn't quite sure how she would explain. Susan was an honest straightforward person, and decided that, however painful it might be, she would tell him the truth. Then it was up to him.

Dinner started awkwardly, but things eased a bit as they chatted. He was now a successful architect, partner in a small practice. No, he wasn't married, he said. "Too busy studying and then working up the business. Anyway, the right girl hadn't come along."

"And what sort of girl would that be?" She tried to keep her tone light, but felt her chest tighten as she held her breath.

"One just like you." There was nothing flippant in his reply. Then he added, "What went wrong, Susan? Why did you

16

suddenly stop wanting me around?"

She paused for a while. Taking a deep breath, she said, "You're black, aren't you? I was young, South African, and I couldn't handle it when I found out."

"I see." He spoke slowly, deliberately. "I'm sorry. I wasn't trying to keep it a secret from you, it just never seemed relevant. So what now? You're still South African, and I'm still black."

"It's different now. Things have changed, even in South Africa. It doesn't matter so much now. We can be friends."

"I don't want to be friends. I love you Susan, I never stopped loving you. Friends isn't enough, but I can't change my colour." With a touch of bitterness, he added, "And I wouldn't want to, not even for you."

There was a long silence while she tried to think of something to say. Then she heard his chair being pushed back. "I'm sorry Susan, this was a mistake. I'll order a taxi to take you home. It will be paid for, and tipped, so don't worry about finding change for the driver."

"John, wait," but it was too late. She heard him walk quickly away. A few minutes later the waiter told her that the taxi was waiting. She was grateful for the dark glasses, which hid her tears.

After a sleepless night she knew what she would do. "Directory Enquiries? I'm looking for the number for Morton, John Morton, Architect."

"Sorry, I have noone under that description."

"Are you sure? John Morton. It's a partnership, so maybe it's Morton and Something, or Something and Morton, Architects."

"Nothing under Architects. If you know the partner's name I could look under that."

"No, I'm afraid I don't." She replaced the receiver.

It was a setback, but Susan wasn't the sort of girl to give up at the first hurdle. Coping with blindness had given her an emotional strength that belied her delicate features and slender frame. She was determined to find him again, to explain her

17

actions all those years ago, to show him she had changed.

She asked her colleagues, her friends, even her boss, but all they could suggest was either the electoral register, or a private investigator. She decided to try both.

Her local librarian was helpful. "What district does he live in?"

"I don't know."

"Then I doubt we'll find him through the register, especially if he retained his American nationality. An architect you say?"

"Yes, in partnership, but I don't know the partner's name. Directory Enquiries couldn't find him under Morton."

"Let's try the Trade and Professional Directories."

The woman brought some large books, but after a while said that she could find nothing helpful.

"Can you give me the name of a private investigator?" asked Susan. It was as well that she couldn't see the raised eyebrows as the librarian thought that here was someone very determined. What had this Morton fellow done, she wondered. Got the girl pregnant and run off? Inveigled her out of some money? She hoped the girl caught up with him.

Clutching the piece of paper with two addresses on it, Susan found a taxi rank, and showing the driver the paper said "Take me to the first of these."

The small office smelled musty. A woman, a young woman judging by her perfume, asked Susan her name and what she wanted.

"I want somebody found. I don't want to go into it further until I see ..." her voice tailed off as she realised she didn't know the investigator's name.

"You'll have to wait a bit, I expect Mr Collins in about ten minutes."

"Does he undertake this sort of work?"

"What, finding people? Yes, it's his specialty, he's good at it too. He'll find your bloke, if anyone can."

"I didn't say it was a bloke."

"Bless you, love, it's always a bloke. More trouble than

they're worth if you ask me. What's this feller done?"

"He hasn't done anything, I just want to find him."

"Joe… Mr Collins, will find him, don't you worry. It's as good as done!"

THE COWARDLY WHISPERS OF AGE

When the cowardly whispers of age
            grow suddenly bolder,
When the summer of life is gone,
            and the days seem colder,
Why then, I'll remember I once
            had your head on my shoulder,
The touch of your hair on my cheek,
            and you in my arms.

When the morning of youth has gone
            and is past regretting,
When the evening has come and the sun
            of this life is setting,
There'll still be one memory, my darling,
            too sweet for forgetting -
The memory of your dear kisses,
            and you in my arms.

COLLEEN

She sat wide eyed, as the story teller told his tale. The flickering oil lamp sent furtive shadows scampering into the corners of the room, adding to the tension. He told of the wreckers on the coast. how the lights were set to lure the vessels to the rocks, the screech of shattered timbers, and the cries of drowning men.

The ghosts of bygone seamen rode upon his words, and the keening of gulls as they swooped upon the debris at first light. She sat, wide eyed, enthralled.

The story told, the child was sent to bed, to dream of vessels bound for distant lands; China, India, America, exotic places far from the little Ulster farm on which she lived. She lay awake, savouring still the excitement of the tale, sorrowing for the drowned men, and marvelling at the rich cargoes taken by the wreckers.

Of course, there was the radio. Heavy with the weight of the battery, it sat on the kitchen shelf. There were story tellers in the radio too, their crackly voices telling of the war, of German U-boats and sunken convoys, and aeroplanes bombing London.

"Serves the bastards right." Granddad remembered the Black and Tans, and had no love for the English. "Serves them bloody well right."

The child knew nothing of the English. They lived across the water with motor cars and factories and they kept their curtains drawn for fear of the aeroplanes. This she had heard from her mother, but who they were, and why they were fighting she did not know, nor cared to find out. In any case the stories on the radio were very dull and uninteresting. The news readers did not include any of the exciting details which made the story teller's tales so fascinating.

She rose early, and washed before the fire in the big farm kitchen. Face scrubbed and gleaming, with thick black stockings and heavy tweed coat, she plodded through the snow to school. School was enjoyable. It opened the window on the world beyond the small farming community in which she lived. The village had no electricity, no gas, and each home drew its own water. Her father had installed a pump, a heavy cast iron pump with a long brass handle, but her friend Kathleen pulled buckets from a well It was 1941, but the village had scarcely changed since the turn of the century. She was nine years old, bright, innocent and uncomplicated. For her, change was something yet to come.

When it came it did so in a dramatic way. The plane flew in from the east, engine spluttering, smoke trailing behind. The pilot left it, just in time, for within seconds the plane had plunged to the earth. There was a bang, a flash of flame, followed by the crackling sound of fire. The pilot floated down in his parachute.

It wasn't like the films she had seen. He didn't stand up, furl his 'chute and walk towards the farmhouse. Instead he lay where he landed, half covered by the folds of fabric. Her father and brothers ran to the man and carried him to the cart.

"English pig," said granddad, "you should have let him lay".

"He's only a lad, can't be more than twenty. Jesus! some war this, when young lads get into their fancy machines to kill each other."

"Do you think they care, when they drop their bombs on women and kids? D'you think he cares?" Granddad wouldn't let it drop.

"Oh shut up Da. Put him on the table. Anyway he flies a fighter, doesn't drop bombs on people. Martha!"

Clothes were cut away. Her mother washed the wound in the young man's chest. "To the post office, John," she said. "Telephone for the doctor. Tell him it's a bullet through the chest."

By the time the doctor had driven from the town and bumped his way to the farm the pilot had been bandaged with strips torn from an old sheet, and was lying in Colleen's bed. Being the only girl she had a bedroom to herself. Now she would sleep on the mattress in the attic.

"You've been lucky, my lad." The bullet had nicked the shoulder, but missed the lung completely. As he restrained the arm the doctor said "I'll have to inform the authorities of your arrival. Meanwhile, Mrs. Innes, can you keep him here in bed? It won't be for long, just till I arrange a bed in the hospital."

"To be sure, doctor, it'll be no bother."

The girl stood in the corner of her room, silent in the face of this drama. "He's a real pilot," she told them at school. "He flies this fast plane and shoots down the Germans, to stop them dropping bombs on London. He's killed hundreds of them, hundreds I'm sure."

All the village knew of the plane, but she had the inside story and revelled in her new found importance. "He's been put in my room," she boasted, "in my bed, and he's a real pilot."

She went to her room to hang up her coat. "Hello" he said, "What's your name?"

"Colleen." She was shy.

"I'm sorry; it seems I've pushed you out of your room. It won't be for long though."

"It's all right." She wanted to say more, to ask him thousands of questions, but stood tongue tied in front of this stranger.

A week went by, then two. The doctor came regularly but for some reason the patient was not removed to hospital. Every day, when she came back from school and put away her things, they talked. She asked an endless stream of questions, and he told her about his home in Warwickshire, and how he had not been a pilot very long, and had not really shot down any Germans at all, not even one.

Gradually a friendship sprang up between the young man and the child.

The time came when he could get up and walk about. She showed him her favourite calf, and the pigs in the yard.

"Colleen," said her mother, "you get on with your chores, and stop being a bother."

"I'm not," but she left, and became more reticent. Saying less she dreamed more, refusing to believe that he was not some glamourous wartime hero, an air ace, and bound to get the VC for being so badly wounded.

23

A month passed, and he left as suddenly as he had come. An official envelope arrived and two hours later two uniformed men took him off in a car.

"Is he being arrested?"

"No, of course not," scoffed her mother. He's going back to his squadron, that's all."

"Thank you Mrs. Innes. It was very good of you to put up with me. Thank you for all your care. G'bye Colleen."

She ran to him. "You be careful now, and don't get yourself shot again."

He smiled. "I'll try not to! But if I do I'll make sure I come down in your field." She stood and waved till the car was out of sight.

The room was hers again, but it was strangely empty. She came in from school to put her coat away, but there was no "Hello, how's my Irish Colleen today/" There were no more stories about Coventry, no exciting exploits of the skies above England. Life was dull and flat.

He wrote to her parents, thanking them again for their kindness, and there was a note for her, with a photo of him beside his plane.

She wrote back to say that she missed him, that life was uninteresting without his stories of England and flying. She said that he was more interesting even than the story teller. When was he coming again?

"Some time" he wrote back, humouring her, and not realising that she believed he meant it.

She found a snapshot and sent it to him, and with a smile he stuck it in his plane. His little mascot he called her.

She wrote again, asking him to promise that he would visit the farm, and once more he replied, "Of course I will, some time. Maybe after the war."

He didn't come of course, but he kept writing, and his letters became a regular feature of her life.

The years went by. The war was over; the child became an adolescent, and then a young woman. There was no work in the locality and she went to England to become a nurse.

"I'm coming to nurse in England," she wrote, "and I decided to train in Coventry. It will be great to see you again." It did occur to her that he was eleven years her elder, and that he would have a girlfriend, maybe even a wife. No, not a wife, he would have written and told her of that, she felt sure, but a girlfriend, almost certainly. She sighed. It would still be good to see him.

She got off the train clutching her suitcase. The busy platform was confusing, but she took her time to read the notices and decided that her best bet was to get a taxi. It was easier than trying to find her way around this strange town. There was a queue at the taxi rank and she had to wait her turn. The cars pulled away and others edged forward, but when the last taxi left there were still two people before her in the queue.

"Will there be any more taxis?" she asked the woman before her.

"Any minute now, I dare say." and sure enough more cars arrived even as the reply was made.

"General Hospital, please," she said to the driver, and watched as she was driven through streets full of shops, down a steep hill, to slow up outside a tall dingy building. It didn't look very prepossessing she thought, but it was going to be home for the next few years, while she was training. Suddenly she felt very homesick for the old fashioned little farm she had left.

"Take me to the Nurses' Home, please." The car had almost stopped but now picked up speed again and went around the next corner to pull up at a more modern building which was obviously not a part of the hospital itself.

"There you are, Miss. Hope you get on all right." It was the first comment he had made. So much for the friendly taxi drivers she had heard so much about!

She reported to the Matron and was shown to her room, a tiny box of a place. Matron gave her a host of instructions, things she could and could not do, and then abruptly left. She sat on the bed and suddenly felt tears trickling down her cheeks.

He hadn't come to meet her. That was the over-riding thought in her mind. He knew she was coming, she'd written and

25

told him so, but he hadn't come to meet her. She felt very young, and very lonely. Obviously she wasn't as important to him as she thought she was. The friendship, started as a child and cemented over the years of letter-writing, had been the main reason for her choice of hospital. She had put too much store by that, she could see that now.

Two days passed in hectic activity, finding her way about the long corridors, all of which seemed to look alike, and lessons about nursing and things about the human body which were never spoken of at home. Good job she'd lived on a farm she thought. Some of the others who were from the cities didn't know how to hide their embarrassment!

"Innes, Colleen Innes, phone for you!" She went to the payphone on the wall of the entrance hall. "Colleen, that you? It's Peter. Sorry I couldn't come to meet you at the train, but I've been up in Manchester for the past few days. How are you, are you settling in OK? Look, can we meet? When do you get some time off?"

She was too confused to think straight. "Tomorrow evening, no sorry, Saturday, yes Saturday."

"OK, I'll see you then. I'll come and pick you up. Where exactly is it? Nurses Home, Gosford Road? Right, ten o'clock on Saturday. Look forward to seeing you."

She stood holding the phone a long while after he rang off, lost in a world of her own. Saturday! Saturday took an age to come.

He roared up in a red MG and came to a skidding halt. There was an embarrassed silence as she got in the car. She hadn't seen him for ten years, since she was just a little girl. It was the same for him. The nine year old child who first wrote to him, was now a young woman, and he wondered what sort of woman she was. Pretty, he could see that, but what was she like as a person?

"Shall we go to Stratford? Take a look at Shakespeare's cottage and then feed the swans? What do you think?"

"That would be lovely." She had no idea what the area might have to offer, and in any case she was far too occupied looking out of the corner of her eye at his profile as he drove. He hadn't changed so much. She could still see traces of the young pilot she had first met. He had matured, of course, and for the better she thought.

Stratford was wasted. Shakespeare's cottage was little more than a distraction for her thoughts. Lunch was better, sitting across the table and talking. Feeding the swans was better still, that was when she relaxed and they laughed about old times. He hired a skiff and rowed her up the river.

"It's lovely to spend time with you again. I've missed you."

"I was only a child. It was ten years ago. You must have had dozens of girl friends by now. I thought any time you'd write and say you were getting married."

"Never met the right girl. What about you? Some handsome Irish lad waiting at home?"

"Never met the right man," she mimicked. "Kept your photo though, the one by your plane, I guess that held them at bay!"

"You kept that, all these years!"

"And your letters. You were a fighter pilot remember, a hero!"

He laughed. "Hardly that! But there's something I'd like to show you." He took out his wallet and handed it to her. "Open it!"

She hesitated, and then as she unfolded the wallet she saw the picture she had sent him when she was nine.

His kiss was slow and gentle, but definitely worth waiting for.

GOLDEN WEDDING

Half a century, gone so soon,
And sometimes tears dimmed the laughter,
But still we struggled for the moon
And aimed for 'Happy ever after'

Now I can face the autumn years
Without regrets or sorrows,
You've shared with me your yesterdays,
And promised me your tomorrows.

MEETING MISS PYM

'Prudence Pym was a frumpy middle-aged woman.' The words showed up on the screen of his computer.

"Do you mind!" said a voice. "I'm certainly not frumpy!" He looked around his study, but there was no-one there. The bookcase, the desk, his computer work-station, there was nowhere to hide. He turned back to the screen only to find that behind the words there was the picture of a face. "I resent you calling me a frump," said the woman in the screen.

Well, he had to admit she wasn't frumpy at all. About fifty years old, she had well-groomed grey hair, a cheerful smile which showed fine even teeth, and hardly a wrinkle in sight. What little he could see of her jacket seemed well cut and expensive. "Who are you?" he asked in surprise.

"Prue Pym of course! And by the way, it's Prue, not Prudence. Prudence is far too old-fashioned."

"But, but," he stammered, "what are you doing in there? How did you get in my computer? This doesn't make sense."

"Of course it makes sense! You've just typed me in, haven't you, so where else would I be but in your computer? Mind you, you haven't got me right at all. I'm nothing like the woman you're going to describe."

"How do you know what sort of a woman I'm going to describe?" His nervousness made him aggressive. "Anyway, you're just a piece of fiction, you don't really exist except in my imagination. My story needs a frump, so that's what you'll be."

"Oh no I won't! What's more, young man, if you're going to be so arrogant I won't be in your story at all. You'll just have to find someone else to play your silly little charades," and with that, the few words he had written cleared from the screen.

"But listen," his voice was more conciliatory. Frankly he was rather scared. "You must see that all this is a bit of a shock, you taking over my computer like this. It's not natural; all a bit unnerving."

Her look of irritation passed. He got the impression that she wasn't the type to stay angry for long. In fact, once he got

29

over the first shock of fear, he found her very likeable. "This kind of thing has never happened to me before," he continued, "and I must confess I find it rather scary. I've always been terrified of ghosts and things like that."

"Ghosts! Good heavens, I'm not a ghost! You know that. You're the one you thought me up, so you should know, if anyone does. But now that you've brought me here you can't expect me to just disappear. I'm here now, and I've a life to lead."

He was taken aback by this. Did she mean that every time he wrote of a character it really came into existence, and carried on living, even after he had finished the story? No it couldn't be!

"But listen Prue," he used her name hesitantly because it seemed overly familiar, "I may call you Prue, may I? My story needs a frump. I can't write it without."

"What's it about? When is it set?"

"About twenty-five years ago."

"Twenty-five years! Well I certainly wasn't frumpy then, or middle aged either!" She fumbled about somewhere below the screen, out of sight, and then held up a photograph. "See, that was me twenty-five years ago."

The photo showed a young woman, slim and remarkably attractive. Well cut clothes enhanced a good figure, slender legs were shown off to perfection by just the right length of skirt. She looked as though she had stepped from a fashion magazine.

"Well?"

"No," he replied, "you certainly weren't frumpy, then or now. But what do I do about my story? My editor's screaming for it, and now you've put me in a spot."

"Why not just find someone else? Sarah Jones won't mind. She's an actress, and plays all sorts of parts. Give her a good ending and she won't mind acting a frump. Actually she's very smart, but she's a good actress and will probably welcome the challenge. Mind you, if you write her the rotten sort of tale you had in mind for me she'll probably turn you down too."

He was just about to ask her more about Sarah Jones when she exclaimed, "Good Heavens! look at the time. I must dash. 'Bye!" and he was left facing a blank screen.

'Sarah Jones was a frumpy middle-aged woman,' he wrote. The words showed up on the screen of his computer. He altered the plot, so that the middle aged lady turned out to have a great deal of courage, and ultimately won the hearts of the readers. The story was a huge success and his editor was delighted, but he was left wondering just what had really happened. It wasn't something he could easily forget.

It was five weeks later that he saw her again. Across the road was the young woman he had seen in the photograph! Slim and remarkably attractive, her well cut clothes enhanced a good figure, her slender legs were shown off to perfection by just the right length of skirt.

"Prue!" He rushed across, dodging cars as he raced to catch up with her "Prue."

"Yes?" There was a question in her tone.

"It is you, isn't it; Prue Pym?" He was gasping, as much from surprise as from running.

"Yes. Do I know you? I'm sorry, I can't recall where."

"Yes, you know me." He stopped in confusion. "No, perhaps you don't, but I know you. You were in my computer." It sounded stupid even as he said it.

She raised her eyebrows slightly and gave a little smile. "Is this some sort of a pick up? It's a new line, I'll grant you that. Perhaps you'd better explain before I get the wrong idea."

"It's a long story. Have you time for a coffee, or maybe lunch?" She shrugged a tentative acceptance, and they sat down at one of the tables in the near by pub. He went to the counter and brought over some sandwiches and then told her of the strange encounter with the woman in his computer. "But the photo was of you Prue, that's how I knew you. Prudence Pym."

"Prudence!" She gave a light silvery laugh. "My name's not Prudence, it's Prunella. Prudence! It's pretty old-fashioned! My mother's name was Prudence, but even she wouldn't use it."

"But it was you, Prue, honest it was!"

He wondered how to make her believe him. She had a warm, captivating smile and a lovely laugh. And she was good to be with. Now that he had found her he didn't want to lose track of her, but he had to admit that his story sounded a bit thin. "Will you have dinner with me? I must try to convince you. Maybe we were meant to meet, isn't that a possibility?"

"My mother was always trying to find me the right man, so it may once have been a possibility," she agreed, "but she died a couple of years ago, so she could hardly have arranged it; and I've never gone chasing men, by computer or otherwise."

He could believe that. With her looks and her charm she didn't need any help from computers. "Dinner?" he asked again, "please!"

Dinner was wonderful. Two days later they went to the ballet. He had known her a month when he asked her to marry him. They were in her flat, having coffee after a show.

"Marry you? Are you serious? You've only known me a few weeks, you know hardly anything about me."

"I know more than you think. I know what you'll be like at fifty, and I want to be there. That's good enough for me."

She hesitated, searching for the right words, for exactly the right way to answer.

"Please think about it Prue. Please don't say no, not yet."

She leaned back in the settee. Her hair touched his cheek, and his arm, across the back of the seat, went around her shoulders. She turned her face towards him, and gave that lovely smile of hers.

"I'm surprised, that's all," she said, "and I will think about it. I wasn't going to say no. Whatever made you think that?"

FATHER'S DAY

It would be nice to go out for lunch on Father's Day. Jacqui could do with an outing, she needs a break, but it is not to be.

After several months we have at last found a carpenter to fit the kitchen. He starts on Monday. Saturday and Sunday will be taken up with emptying all the kitchen units, ready for him to take them out and put in the new ones. He estimates the job will take a week.

I console myself with the thought that lunch is a daily event, and some other day can be chosen for eating out.

Our daughter, Lyn, brings cardboard boxes in which to put tins and packets, so that some semblance of order can be retained during the transition. We prepare ourselves to face the chaos.

"Hello". It is Dr. Shaw on the phone. It is Thursday afternoon. He has the results of my blood test. He wants me to go into hospital at 10 a.m. on Friday.

"Is it just for the day?" I ask, remembering that I wish to be home for the weekend. There are tins to be put in boxes.

"No, you'll probably be there till the middle of next week."

"Can it wait till later?"

No, he wants me to go in urgently, so Friday morning it is.

Rapid family discussion takes place about overnight bags, pyjamas, towels, and the general utilities of everyday living. In spite of her anxieties about me, Jacqui sorts things out.

We recall that there is an electric cable behind one of the kitchen units. It is faulty, and needs to be removed before the new units block all access. I get down to it. Jacqui washes, irons, and packs. She doesn't want to be ashamed of me when I arrive at hospital.

It is midnight before we go to bed. We don't sleep. The doctor says anaemia, but why the rush? Jacqui worries about leukaemia, cancer, all the things which might be shown up by a

33

blood test. It is speculation. We don't know, and we can't judge.

We talk about what we do know; our lives together, our love, our anxieties. Eventually we fall asleep.

Morning comes, and Lyn in her BMW. If one has to travel to hospital, one might as well do it in comfort.

Outpatients? Emergency? I thought I was to be admitted. We sit in the waiting room and wait. It is what the room is for. In about an hour I am called. Jacqui comes with me. She wants to hear at first hand all that is said. She is pale and very tired. She needs reassurance, which I can try to provide, but can't convince.

They take a blood sample. My GP has already taken two armfuls, but they want to see for themselves. Strangely, they find the same results. It is difficult to decide whether this is a good thing, since the results aren't particularly satisfactory.

By now it's lunch time. "They won't do anything till Monday," says the doctor. "You may as well go home for the weekend."

"That would be more convenient," I reply, thinking of the tins which are to be put into the cardboard boxes.

"I'll just talk to your GP. Wait here."

I am wearing only a hospital gown which is slit all the way up the back. I have little choice but to wait!

When he returns I do not go home. I go instead to an admission ward. It is a lovely ward. Single room with en-suite toilet. Three star at least. All the nurses are very pleasant and caring, and this continues throughout my stay. They work a twelve hour shift, and at the end of it they are just as pleasant as they are at the start. It is only fair that I should record my praise for their dedication.

Jacqui goes home, relieved that at least I shall be comfortable and well looked after.

"You should have a transfusion. With your blood count I'm surprised you haven't had one already." To establish my blood group the nurse needs to take a blood sample.

The consultant and his entourage arrive about four o'clock. He takes a quick glance at my notes. "You should have a blood transfusion," he announces. The consistency is reassuring. He goes on to tell me that later in the evening I shall be transferred to one of the medical wards. In the Thoracic Department, because I was an outpatient there about a year ago. "It's the best place," he adds, "they know you."

They do know me, if they remember a year ago, and they know about my asthma, but do they know about anaemia and other blood disorders? I assume that they do. Anyway, nothing will happen till Monday.

The nurse comes back to arrange my move, but before that she tells me that a silly thing has occurred. The lab. has misspelled my name. As a result the analysis of the blood sample can't be relied upon. "I shall need another sample," she says. I have the absurd impression that my arm is beginning to sag.

Including the investigations done by my GP, this seems to be about the twelfth sample in quick succession. It is with some relief that I remember I am to have a transfusion. At least it will replenish some of the loss, and will not be a wasted exercise.

I don't wish to appear selfish, but I am hoping that the fictitious patient with my misspelled name is found to have the same deficiencies in his blood as myself. In matters such as this, even in bad news, one looks for consistency.

I am moved to one of the Thoracic wards. There are two people in the ward who are really ill. It makes me feel a fraud. Meanwhile, the fictitious patient with my misspelled name is nowhere about. Presumably he has left. This augers well for my recovery.

The real me is still here. Jacqui worries about me, and I worry about her. How will she cope with the kitchen?

Fortunately our son, Kevin, is on hand to help. He deals with the heavy things. He also finds another electric cable which goes to a connection strip, but appears to do nothing. It may, however, do something drastic if not dealt with, so he promises to make it safe. The carpenter assures Jacqui that he will manage all right, and despite the difficulties, all is still on track for Monday morning.

The night nurse tells me that my blood analysis has

arrived, and she will prepare me for a transfusion. I am glad she has oriental features, for with a racial heritage of acupuncture, preparing me for a transfusion should be no problem. "Be positive," she says, "be positive."

I feel that I am reasonably positive, but I am nevertheless grateful for the encouragement. Then I realise that she is not exhorting me to show courage in the face of adversity. She is talking of my blood. "B positive," she says again. "It's an unusual blood group."

A needle is inserted in my arm. The transfusion has to be into a vein. There are some quite distinct veins in sight, but she doesn't seem to consider them satisfactory. She chooses one which is almost invisible. The needle is taken out and tried again.

"Almost there." I feel the entry of the probe, and the pressure as it goes further in. It pushes the vein aside!

"Oh damn!" says the nurse. "Must try again."

Again. And again, and again. The veins, she says, are tough. To me they seem rubbery. Either way, they resist the probe, moving adroitly out of the way just as success seems assured.

She calls for a doctor. It is late on Friday night, and the duty physician is stretched. He cannot be spared for such minor matters as a simple transfusion. I agree with his decision, but it doesn't please the nurse.

At the seventh attempt, when she is full of apologies and embarrassment, the veins relent. She tapes the needle in place but decides to quit while ahead. She leaves the transfusion for the morning.

The probe is an interesting piece of medical engineering. A solid metal needle, about a millimetre in diameter, is encased in a plastic sheath. This, at least, is how it looked to me. The pointed needle carries the sheath with it, and is then withdrawn, leaving the tube and its connections in the vein. The outer end has a screw cap to close it off, which is just as well, for the idea is to put blood in, not to drain the system. For the transfusion the cap is removed and blood fed into the vein through the plastic tube.

I am given real blood, not plasma. It drips slowly in, but there are four units of it. By the fourth bag it is late into Saturday night. At one thirty the drip stops. This is because the blood has coagulated in the filter. There is hardly any left, however, and the nurse decides to call it a day. After seventeen hours of transfusion I feel that her decision is justified.

The tubes are disconnected and I can get some sleep. The plastic insert, however, is left in place. My arm is bruised, and the insert hurts, but it took so much effort to put it in that one might as well keep it there as an investment for the future.

Father's Day dawns and I can move about freely. No longer do I have to drag my pole with the bag of blood wherever I go. I walk outside to see the ducks. They are nice ducks, friendly ducks, and they come right up to me. I have no bread to give them, but they forgive me this and nibble grass at my feet.

The sky is blue, the sun shines, and the weather is warm. The ducks nibble grass. In the absence of one's family, what more can one ask of Father's Day?

THE RUIN

The Ordnance Survey Department was no doubt unaware that in Goat it had a dedicated, though unexpected, ally.

Looking at an O.S. map, at grid reference SU 196109, I discovered that the point is marked as a ruin. This disturbed me considerably, since it is the site of my garage. I had only recently moved into the property and wondered if I had been cheated, but no, as I inspected the garage carefully I found that though the timber building was of unusual construction it was far from being a ruin. It was a rustic but serviceable assortment of partitions which comprised a store, a garage, a carport, and a donkey stall. I concluded the map was out of date. That was before the coming of Goat.

Goat's real name is Woody, and he arrived some years ago in the back of a battered Estate car. He had with him, as an accessory, a tea chest in which he slept, much like a dog in a kennel. He was 17 weeks old. It was a sad tale, but the couple who rescued him from the Livestock Market, when he was only a few days old, could no longer keep him in their flat, and he would have had to be put down. Rather than have that happen my wife agreed to have him.

The first task was to find him a place to stay. The carport was the answer, and, to restrain his tendency to wander, it was necessary to put a fence across the front of it. Our ancient hatchback took up residence on the drive. It was in fair condition at the time, but it lasted only two more years before the depredations of damp and rust caused it to be consigned to the scrap yard.

The second task was to fence off a portion of the paddock so that he had somewhere to run, other than the open acres of the New Forest. Blossom, the donkey, did not take kindly to this, but Goat had horns, and Blossom did not. As a result of this evolutionary difference the possession of the top part of the paddock was resolved. Goat took up residence, and in the two years it took for the car to steadily disintegrate, he established his right to stay.

Because he still had his horns he loved to butt. He butted everything, including the walls of the carport. It was where he slept, so perhaps he felt it was his right to butt it if he wished. He eventually knocked out the back wall, and the following morning was wandering about the donkey's paddock.

By a fortunate coincidence I had booked a day off work. The butting out of the supporting wall had caused the roof to sag, but with the help of a car jack and a stout length of timber this was lifted sufficiently to enable the wooden struts to be restored to their vertical position and the roof rehung. The wooden panels of the wall could then be replaced. The repairs took most of the day, and the trip we had planned to Brownsea Island did not take place. Perhaps there is a lesson to be learned, for even now, many years later, that trip has not yet been taken.

I was relieved that he had not also knocked down the paddock fence and taken to the garden. The roses were in bloom, and on the few occasions he had been in the garden he had ruthlessly pruned the pyracantha. It is unlikely that he could have resisted the roses. Such an eventuality may well have led us to abandon our vegetarian principles.

Goat soon outgrew his tea chest, but until he did he was small enough to come for rides in the hatchback. He stood in the back, looking out of the window, causing considerable comment among passers-by. We took him to different parts of the Forest for his walks so that he had a change of scenery, and I am sure he enjoyed it. In the manner of the Kabuki theatre, his pleasure was clearly demonstrated by his total lack of expression. Goats do not have the most expressive of faces, but even so, I am sure he enjoyed it. If he had not, he would surely have let us know!

Time went by and Goat grew too big for the car. The point was largely academic because by this time it was little more than a rust heap, but Goat now took his walks locally. Meanwhile, his onslaughts caused the condition of the garage and the carport to hang precariously between the hope that it would survive, and the probability that it would not. I designed a more permanent structure. Our book on goats suggests that they will not butt brick walls, so we now have a new building containing a goathouse, a double garage, a donkey stall, and a hay store, all built of dense concrete blocks. I have also taken considerable trouble to familiarise Goat with these new materials. The author of the book maintains that goats will not butt such a structure because it jars their heads.

I do not want to have to rebuild the whole thing yet again, so I am fervently hoping that although Goat has not read this book, he will be just as keen to uphold the reputation of the author as he has been to support the accuracy of the Ordnance Survey Department in listing my garage as a ruin.

e-mail

"Hi Jill. You don't know me but I reckon you pressed a wrong key, because your message to your mother came through to me instead. I think you'd better send it again, and never mind, your secret's safe with me. My name's Jack. You'll find me in Ringwood at beanstalk@btinternet.com. Hope to hear from you."

"Jack! Are you for real? Just 'cos I'm called Jill is no reason for you to be Jack, and what's all this beanstalk rubbish? Are you into fairy tales?"

"No fairy tale Jill. Your e-mail got here, so this must be a proper address, mustn't it?. And I am really called Jack. John on my birth certificate, but Jack in practice. Talking of fairy tales, are you serious about your secret? Maybe I can help. I'd like to."

"Thanks, but you promised my secret would be safe with you. I hope you'll keep to that. I worked up the courage to tell my parents, but somehow you got the message instead, and I chickened out of sending it again. They're terribly disapproving about things like this. You and I are the only ones who know about it, and I'd like to keep it that way."

"I promised didn't I? Don't be so suspicious. I would like to help if I can, honest."

"O.K. then Jack, tell me how to get two thousand pounds for an abortion. If you're some philanthropic millionaire then that's one of the problems solved, otherwise I don't see how you can help. Thanks anyway."

"Hey, you must have given up on me! Sorry Jill, I've been away on business for over a month, but I didn't run out on you. I wouldn't do that. I'm not a millionaire, but there must be something I can do. I'm an architect, and I'm trouble shooting on a project in the States, so I'm back and forth all the time. I've been so tied up that I haven't picked up my personal mail, only stuff sent by the office. I won't be so lax in future. Anyway, what's the present position? Is your Mum with you, or are you still all on your own?"

"Good to hear from you Jack. Yes I did think I'd frightened you off. Present position is that I'm on my own. I told

41

them about the baby, but not about the real problem. They say have an abortion. I'd have agreed a month ago, but it grows on one, you know, and in the last month I've begun to want it, so no abortion. 'Unmarried mother, aged 25 seeks company for self and coming baby to fill long hours of loneliness'. If you see that in the personal column spare a thought for your fairy tale friend!"

"Now cheer up! I never read the personal columns, anyway. Why don't you give me your address, or let's meet and talk about this. There must be some better prospect than the lonely hearts pages. I'm off to the States again next week, but I'll pick up my messages this time, so keep in touch."

"Thanks Jack. I felt really down when I didn't hear from you. In a way you're the only friend I have. When the baby begins to show I guess I'll lose my job. Can hardly model swimsuits and lingerie with a bulging tummy. And then there's that other thing too. Got some serious thinking to do."

"Hi! Project nearly finished. Two more months and I'll be back in England, for good I hope. So you're a model. Have I seen you, up on billboards maybe, or glossy magazines? Give me an autograph so I can tell people I know you!"

"No billboards. Mail order catalogues, that's where you'll find me. Not as glamorous as you imagined I'm afraid, and that'll be stopping soon too."

"Don't be so glum. We're pals remember. I'll be back on the tenth. Now let's stop beating about the bush. You've got a problem, and I'm in the problem solving business. I think of you as a friend, so I want to help. Tell me where I can meet you, so we can have a proper talk about the situation, and see what ideas we come up with. It can't be much fun facing everything alone."

"Jill, why don't you write? Are you O.K? It's over three weeks since I sent you a message, and each day I look for an answer. Please write, at least to tell me where to find you, if nothing else."

"Jill, I'll be back in England next week. Please, tell me where we can meet. Your friend, Jack."

"Jack, thanks for all your messages. Been in hospital, and only got my computer on line today. I'm going into the Royal

Bournemouth Hospital, Ward G3. Name's Gillian Stanton. Looking forward to seeing you. I need to talk to someone. Be nice if it was you."

He was startled to see the pale thin figure in the bed. He walked towards her, carrying a huge bunch of flowers. "Hello Jill. So we meet at last! I'm Jack, Jack Foster. How are you feeling?"

"Not good Jack, but it's nice to meet you. This isn't your problem you know, but I need all the help I can get. It's good to have at least one friend."

She told him of the miscarriage which was only just prevented, the high blood pressure, the fluid swelling her ankles, and most of all, of her depression. "So I have to lie here till the baby's born. I've lost my job, my flat, my parents, everything!" Tears welled up in her eyes.

He leaned forward and gently put one arm around her. "Don't cry, Jill, we'll sort it out. Where's the father? Have you thought of getting the CSA onto him?"

"I don't want that devil anywhere near my child. I don't even want him to know there is a child."

"Why ever not? Anyway he should pay towards it."

"I don't want him to, he's evil. I don't want him to have any access to my baby. Jack, he's a drug dealer, that's why we broke up, that's why I don't want him to know I'm pregnant."

"And after? Who'll look after the baby?"

"I was hoping you'd take it to my parents. It's a lot to ask, but you're the only one who knows, and I can trust you, I'm sure.."

"I don't know Jill, it's a big responsibility."

"I know it is, but please do it for me Jack. I'm dying you know. The drugs that swine got me hooked on are killing me. It's too late for treatment, and I've only a few weeks left. It might even come to a Caesarean after I've gone. Take my baby to my parents. I've written this letter for you to give them. It tells them what happened, about the drugs, and all the things I was afraid to tell them before. Mum and Dad are so bitterly opposed to drugs that they wouldn't even speak to me if they knew, but though she won't be thrilled, Mum just may look after the baby once she realises I've gone. More probably you'll have to put it up for adoption. Please Jack, you're the only one I can turn to."

"beanstalk@btinternet.com. Regret to tell you Miss Gillian Stanton died yesterday. She gave no next of kin, but said to inform you of the birth of her daughter. The child was four weeks premature, and will be in the intensive care unit for some time yet. She said you would know what to do. For registration purposes can you tell us, are you the father?"

He sighed. That one visit to the hospital had done it. Seeing her lying there, frail and defenceless, he knew he couldn't let her down. It wasn't love. It was something else, pity perhaps, or maybe his own loneliness, but it would change his life. He couldn't help Jill, but by God, if her parents wouldn't help, then he'd see that her daughter was taken care of!

"royalbournemouth/uk.com   Yes. I'm in America at present. Will be returning to England in three weeks, and will see you then, to take charge of the child. Please register her as Jill Foster, mother's name Gillian Stanton, Fashion Model, father's name John Foster, Architect. Will ratify the formalities when I return."

MORTALITY SYNDROME

Julie Whiteman lay still, looking up at the ceiling, silent tears threading their way slowly down her cheeks. Beside her lay her new born child, a horrible travesty, so ill formed as to be scarcely recognisable as human. Mark sat beside her, equally horrified, and quite unable to offer any comfort.

A nurse entered and quietly beckoned Mark towards her. "Doctor wants a word," she said.

"Mr Whiteman, I don't need to tell you that your son is badly malformed. I'm sorry, but it seems unlikely that he can survive for long. Forgive me if I sound rather blunt, but experience has taught me that it is better to be factual than to offer false hopes. What we need to establish is what went wrong, so that when you try again, there won't be any difficulties."

"Difficulties? What difficulties? Julie had a perfectly normal pregnancy, and a perfectly ordinary birth. There were no difficulties."

"Your wife is a little old for a first child, forty one is she?"

"Forty three."

"She doesn't look it. If I hadn't been told she was in her forties I'd have put her at no more than twenty five. And you, Mr Whiteman, how old are you?"

"Forty five."

"Indeed. The same goes for you, you look no more than twenty five."

"That's because of the modification."

"Do you mean gene modification? That's not approved, you know, in fact there's talk of making it illegal as soon as the Government can get round to it."

"They assured us there weren't any side effects, so we went for it. They took away the gene that causes ageing. They were right, too, we've both been fine, there are no side effects."

The doctor shrugged. "Till now."

"What do you mean, till now?"

"This is just a personal opinion, Mr Whiteman, but you

45

can't fool around with genes without paying a price."

"We paid all right! Fifty thousand to the company holding the patent, and another twenty thou. for the treatment. But as you can see, in the past twenty years there've been no signs of ageing."

"I don't mean money, I mean in other ways. Thirty years ago, from 1999 to 2003 there were a lot of genetic patents taken out. Everyone was cashing in on the fact that big computers could crack the genetic code and isolate which genes did what. The human genome contains billions of combinations of letters in the DNA chain, and no computer can really tell whether there will be side effects or not."

"They say you're an authority on genetics. What do you think is the problem?"

"I don't know for sure, but my opinion is that by removing the ageing genes from both your wife and yourself, your baby could not inherit it from either parent. I believe that if you prevent ageing, you also prevent development, so the foetus has no means of developing normally, with the tragic results we have just seen."

"But they said ."

"I know, they said, 'No side effects', and there haven't been any, either on you or Mrs Whiteman. But the child can't inherit what isn't there. Of course, this is all speculation. With your permission I'd like to take DNA samples and check it out properly. It would be worth finding out, because if ever you are to have normal healthy children, we need to know."

He was right, of course, the baby didn't have the genes for ageing, but the lack meant that it couldn't go past the earliest stages of embryonic growth. Development stopped prematurely, and survival was impossible. Two days later the baby died.

Mark and Julie felt little regret when it did. It was almost impossible to love that grotesque, misshapen "thing" which Julie had borne, but there was acute unhappiness at the loss of their dreams of a child. They comforted each other as best they could.

Test after test only confirmed the initial theory. Cultures tried out in test tubes, information gleaned from other laboratories, one or two rare cases observed in other hospitals, all led to the same conclusion. Without the gene the embryo could not develop normally.

"What alternatives can you offer? They were desperate for a child of their own. Money they had in abundance, but it couldn't buy them the future they dreamed of. They had slowed the ageing process, maybe even stopped it, but for what? If they couldn't have a child then what was the money for? They had prolonged youth, and the means to enjoy it, but they had already had over twenty years of that. Without a stake in the future life was pretty flat.

"We can put back the missing gene. It's never been done before, the reversal of a gene modification, but we can try. Of course, it will mean that you will lose your constant youth. You will age, just as though you never had the modification."

"Can't the missing gene be put into the embryo just after conception?"

"We tried that Mrs Whiteman, but it didn't work. You know that." Julie did know, but she was clutching at straws.

"Try it again!"

They did, and again it didn't work.

"No, Mark, no. I'll not give up my youth. After twenty years I'm not going to suddenly grow old. We'll just have to adopt."

But Mark wanted a child of their own. Because it was a deprivation, where wealth had previously prevented deprivation, it took on an added importance. Julie was more philosophical, but with Mark it became almost an obsession. He read every article, followed up every lead, consulted every expert he could find. It was the trigger of Julie's fiftieth birthday that made him change his mind.

"I"ve been thinking," he said, "If we can't have a child that's a bit of each of us, then I want one like you. Let's have a clone! You're fifty, but you still look only twenty five. If we have another, just like you, she'll still be twenty five years younger than you."

"Or maybe she'll be fifty years younger," said Julie.

47

"I thought a clone would be exactly like you, in other words she'll seem about twenty five. But even if she's an infant, would that be so bad?"

"No, maybe not, but it's illegal, isn't it?"

"Not in South America. We could get it done there!"

Dr Alvarez pursed his lips. "Mr Whiteman, Mrs Whiteman, please understand, this is an extremely delicate procedure. The fact that it was successfully done in a sheep, forty years ago, does not mean that we have advanced. There have been very few trials since then, and none on humans. I hesitate."

"Can it be done?"

"Yes, I believe it can."

"Then we want it!"

Alvarez shrugged. "Very well, I'll do my best. Mrs Whiteman, can you come to the hospital on Tuesday? You will be admitted for three days. We will make certain tests, and then take some cells. After the cloning process has started there are two options. I suggest we play safe. Keep one clone in a laboratory environment, that is to say, in a test tube, and implant the other in the uterus. If all goes well, you can then give birth to your daughter in, what one may regard as, a normal confinement. In the event of difficulties, there will always be the other as a safeguard."

"Difficulties,"said Mark. "I don't want anything which puts Julie in any sort of danger."

"She will be in no danger. She will donate some cells, that's all. Once the clone is implanted everything else will be like an ordinary pregnancy. But it has never been done before, that's why I want the laboratory back up.

It was agreed. The tests were done, the cells were taken, the cloning was started. And there the matter stopped. Without the relevant gene there was no cell division, Mark recalled what the doctor had told him years before, "You can't fool around with genes without paying a price."

After several unsuccessful attempts, Mark reluctantly conceded that they could never have children of their own. "We'll just have to adopt. They still looked twenty five, but he was fifty six, and Julie was fifty four

At the adoption agency the Chairman was apologetic. "Under the new international agreements, to be considered as suitable adoptive parents, you must both be under fifty. I'm very sorry, but you don't qualify."

"There's no way out!" wailed Julie. "We'll just have to have it reversed. Oh Mark, I don't want to be old."

"You won't be old! We look twenty five now. In say, two years we'll look as though we're twenty seven. Then we'll have the gene taken out again. Twenty seven isn't old, now is it?"

"Suppose not. It'll cost the earth, won't it?"

"It'll cost, sure, but hell, we can afford it!"

"It's never been done Mr Whiteman. Gene reversal isn't something which people go in for. After all the counselling they go through before any gene modification is done, it isn't likely people will want to reverse it, besides which the expense would stop them."

"I'll stand the expense. We want it done. We want to have a child!"

So it was done. Julie and Mark went into hospital in the same private room. They spent seven hours under anaesthetic, and they woke within half an hour of each other. They gazed at each other intently, looking for tell tale signs of change, but there weren't any. Jubilant, they returned home. They wanted to make love right away, but had been warned to wait for some days.

Impatiently they waited. In any case, they felt tired, so waiting was less difficult than it might have been. A good night's sleep was what they needed. In the morning Julie woke to find Mark staring at her, an odd expression on his face. He looked different. Tired, no not just that, different. She smiled up at him, still half asleep "Hello, darling."

"Hello," he replied.

"What's the matter?"

Silently he brought her a mirror from the dressing table. A fifty four year old Julie looked out at her. She was still a good looking woman, but she had never seen her face with wrinkles. The tell tale puckering of the top lip changed the curve of her mouth, and the crowsfeet at the corners of her eyes dismayed her. Laughter lines, some called them, but to one who was used to looking a smooth, radiant twenty five there was nothing to laugh about. "Oh God! What's happened?"

"How old are you?" he asked.

"Fifty four, you know that."

"And how old do you look?"

She hesitated, and then, flatly, but with a wealth of sorrow, "Fifty four, I guess."

"Exactly! And I"m fifty six. More to the point, women can"t have children at fifty four, they're past child bearing! Hell, it's all been for nothing!"

Words echoed in his memory, "Mr Whiteman, you can't fool around with genes without paying a price."

ALONE

Alone, day after day, always alone,
With one vain hope, to which I blindly clutch;
But there's no hope, you're gone and I'm alone.
I watch the shadows creep along the walls,
And watch the windows darken, still alone.
Then in the dusk an unseen shadow stirs,
A trembling sigh, a soft caress, I turn,
The window has been left ajar, the breeze
Blows in, it's just the breeze, and I'm alone.

NOT QUITE PETS

It is always a doubtful matter as to how far one should tame wild animals. One argument is that it isn't safe for wild animals to trust humans. This, I fear, is very true, but that is more a criticism of humans than of animals.

The average human tends to think he is in some way superior to any animal. I question this supposition. We are more intelligent than most animals, I grant you that, but let's look at the wider range of abilities. Most animals, size for size, are stronger, can run faster, and fight better than we can. Without the aid of weapons we could not match them. The average huntsman could not chase and catch a fox, and if he could, he would probably be unable to despatch it with his bare hands. Even less would this apply to a leopard, and not at all to a lion or a tiger.

Could we summon the strength of a gorilla, or the speed of a horse? No, but we don't have to. We can work in unison with others, and a group of men can capture a horse, or even an elephant. This makes us superior. However, a few dozen wasps can kill a man quite easily. Does this make the wasp superior? Not if we apply the usual standards, and these standards are to compare man and his technology on the one side, and the animal without any technology on the other. Not surprisingly the man comes out on top. Strip the man of his technology, and then ask the same question. Will the answer be the same?

To go back to the huntsman. He requires thirty dogs and several fellow hunters on horseback to chase and kill one fox. A more equitable sport would be for one huntsman, with no weapons, no protection, no technological help, to pursue one fox. It is, after all, a small animal, and is therefore, by definition, very unlikely to do any harm to this superior creature! The wolf is still fairly light in comparison with man, so it will, at worst, inflict only minimal damage before being overcome. The leopard, about the same weight as man, should be able to give a fair account of itself, but I don't think many humans would care to test their superiority in this way.

We are the superior species, the top level of creation.

This, we are told, is God's decision, or Jehovah's, or Allah's, or Bramah's. But what if we came across a more superior species? Would we then be content to be second class, to be farmed, or culled, or bred for meat? Why not, if technological superiority is our sole measure of worth. We have already seen in our own history, how Europeans thought that Africans were inferior, because they were technologically, but not necessarily intellectually, less advanced. They were therefore enslaved, transported, and treated as less than human. More recently, Nazis considered themselves superior to Jews, though it is not clear to many of us where this superiority lay.

It is interesting that for eighty million years the top level of evolution was the dinosaur. Eighty million years! Presumably they were not static years, and changes must have occurred, but generally it is reckoned that some sort of dinosaur ruled the roost for a very long time. They, too, might have thought it was by divine right of some reptilian deity. Reptilian, because we all seem to be arrogant enough to believe that any Creator must be like ourselves!

We've been around for two million years or less. This, we claim, makes us the final product of evolution. Such presumption amazes me, particularly when displayed by a so-called intelligent creature. In eighty million years will it still be humans who rule the roost? In eighty million years will there still be a roost to rule, or will we have destroyed it ..... intelligently, of course.

I think the decision as to who, or what, is the end product of evolution, is a decision which should be made by God, not by man; and if we sincerely believe that man was made in God's image, then we need to explain the poor quality of the copy. If we don't, or can't, then we risk having to explain shortcomings in the original! The Genesis explanation is to say that man was created perfect, but given free will. He used his free will, and thus became imperfect. Logically then, the giving of free will was an error on the Creator's part, which led to our downfall. Not quite as simple as it at first appears! It would be easier to believe that we are simply another animal, slightly brighter than the others, or maybe just slightly brighter than some of the others.

I would like to think that somewhere along the line we will realise that we are one link in a chain which leads from the creation, and continues until we join the Creator, whatever route that evolution may take. It will surely not take the same route among the myriad of planets, circling the billions of stars.

As far as image goes, the whole of creation must obey the Creator's plan, and therefore must be made to His specification, and in His image, including the imperfections which we think we see. I can personally see no merit in midges and mosquitos, but it is decreed that they exist, they are part of the plan, so they presumably have their purpose. So do the fox, the wolf, the leopard and the lion. They inhabit the same small, insignificant lump of rock as we do. For the moment at least, it is the only home we have, both for them and for us. They may not quite be pets, but they could be friends. We manage it with dogs and cats, and with horses and rabbits, even hamsters and gerbils, so why not with the others? We claim to possess the immortal souls. We claim to have the free will. The decision therefore, must surely rest with us.

CREATOR

Lord, thou art all of everything,
Above, about, below;
All that is, is part of thee,
And was, and will be so.

No reasons can we offer thee,
No merit can we show,
Yet take us to thy bosom Lord,
We've nowhere else to go!

GLIMPSES OF MY FATHER

The boy was ten.

He thought he could remember his mother, but of course he could not. She had died when he was two. What he remembered was an old sepia photograph, taken in the eighteen-nineties, of a woman seated at a piano. An oval face looked out from the picture, and the boy thought it was beautiful. It may have been, but the photo was faded and creased, the emulsion cracked and stained, and there was no real indication of the lady's features, except in the eyes of the boy. The photograph was one half of all his treasures.

The other half was the silver locket. It had been his mother's. It was the only thing of any value which he possessed. It opened by means of a clip on one edge, and inside was a photograph of his father. Black hair, black beard, wide forehead and piercing eyes. The boy was proud of his father. If his mother was an angel, then in the boy's eyes, his father was a god.

He was alone in the dormitory. The school was closed and all the pupils had gone home for the winter. It would be March before they returned for the next term. Until then he would be the only person in the school. He, and the Headmaster, whom he hated.

The boy lay on his string bed, staring at his treasures and longing for his father. His bottom hurt where he had been caned. There were weals on his legs, and on his stomach too. He had not thought the Head would cane him on his stomach, so he had turned, but the Head was in a fury and had not stopped. Twenty, twenty-five strokes? The boy had lost count.

At first he used to cry, but now he was past crying. He got beaten, and he never left the school. It was the way of things. He had cried, and he had prayed, but neither had brought about any change. Now he simply accepted what came, and in his heart he stored up his hatred for the Head.

Yet, though he hated the Headmaster, he knew he should also be grateful. It had all happened a year ago, when he was nine, when his father had died. The boy could remember his

56

father's death. He had died of cholera, and the boy had sat beside him, occasionally placing a small piece of ice between the dying man's parched lips, or wiping his brow with a cold cloth. When the man died the four children were separated. As far as the boy knew his brother and his two sisters had also been sent to school, but no one school was prepared to support them all. His eldest sister, Evelyn, was only fifteen herself, but she wrote to each of the others. "We are a family," she had said, "and we must always keep in touch." But the boy got no pocket money, so he could never buy stamps to reply to her letters.

After his father's death the boy had been brought before the Governors of the school. He was told that he was an orphan, there was nowhere for him to go. The Governors would keep him at the school and he would be fed and clothed and taught, all out of the charity in their hearts, and in return he must do well and must come first in his class, and he must perform odd jobs in the holiday, and he must at all times do as he was told. If not, and the Governors shook their heads sternly, if not, then surely he would not be allowed to stay; and since there was nowhere for him to go, he would end up as a street urchin, a "chokra".

So the boy studied hard and came first in his class, and in the holidays he did the chores which were given him to do. If, like today, he spilled some milk he got beaten. Sometimes, especially if the Head was in a bad mood, it seemed to the boy that he was beaten anyway. Once he ran away from school, to some friends of his father, but they brought him back, explaining that his education was a very important thing. The Head locked him in a store-room and he was beaten every day for a week. He did not run away again, ever. But he wet the bed!

He was publicly caned and called a filthy beast. He was made to stand in his soiled pyjamas while the whole school filed past, and as each one passed the boy had to say "I'm a filthy beast, I wet the bed."

It was a nine days' wonder, and those who called him a "wet-ninny" soon stopped, but the boy did not forget the humiliation and hated the Head even more. His bed was replaced with a string "charpoy" and his wet mattress and blankets were taken away. Winter or summer, he had only two sheets. Every morning he had to rise half an hour earlier than the others and wash his pyjamas and sheets. "But sir," he once said, "I didn't wet the bed last night." He was beaten for disobedience and a lack of proper gratitude.

I have lived all my life in an atmosphere of care and affection. I have never ceased to wonder that the boy did not grow up with a warped and bitter personality, yet he did not. He hated the Head, but as he grew bigger and stronger, so the beatings lessened, and eventually stopped. He lived, of course, always under the cloud of the Governors' words, always under the threat of expulsion if he did not come first in his class; but since he had the brains, and nothing to do but work, he was able to come first in all his exams. At last, when he was still not old enough, he lied about his age and joined the army. It was during the nineteen-fourteen to nineteen-eighteen war, and he was sent to East Africa, where he was mentioned in despatches, and where he nearly died of blackwater fever. I am glad he did not die, for if he had, I would never have known him. If he had died he would not have had a son, he would not have become my dad, and I would not exist!

He was a logical man. In fact, he was logical to the point of eccentricity.

When I was four and a half years old he took me into a large department store. I saw a model train and I wanted it, but the set I wanted was the display layout. It was not for sale, and, if it had been, he could not have afforded it. Being a thoroughly spoiled young brat I threw myself on the floor and began to scream. For a few moments he looked at me pensively, and then continued his shopping in various other departments of the store.

I caused a fair amount of commotion, eventually attracting the attention of the store manager. Having failed to silence me, he was at last able to find my father, to whom he explained that he did not want this disturbance in his store. My father agreed that it was undesirable, and suggested that I be put out on the pavement! At this the manager was horrified and said that he was a very hard man.

58

Mildly pained by this accusation my father explained that the man had not grasped the crux of the problem. He was, he said, a soft and gentle man, who loved me dearly. I wanted the model train layout, but he was unable to give it to me. As my second alternative, I wanted to kick and scream. This, he pointed out, he was able to let me have!

Needless to say, I gave up kicking and screaming, not because I became well behaved, but simply because it didn't work!

This type of logic continued throughout my childhood. I was treated as being an intelligent and rational human being, and was allowed to make my own decisions. The main constraints I can remember were that these decisions must not hurt other people, and that I must accept responsibility for the consequences. This was enhanced by that fact that I was in boarding school from the age of five, and then at college, till I was eighteen. It tends to make one self-reliant, an attribute my father strongly encouraged. Because he had been an orphan, in a country with considerable poverty and no welfare state, he regarded self-reliance and independence as necessities rather than virtues. It was not, he said, a father's main duty to look after his children; rather it was to teach his children to look after themselves.

When I was five he put me on a train to school. It was the norm for Anglo-Indians to go to boarding school, besides which, he would comment, tongue-in-cheek, that bringing up children was a serious matter, and should not be left to amateurs!

It was about nine p.m. and past my normal bedtime. "Tomorrow morning, at Lahore, go to Platform 8 and get on the train to Kalka. Can you do that?" Of course I could! I had been brought up on the Railway, and was quite familiar with trains. Not quite so familiar perhaps with the fourteen platforms at Lahore Junction. Yet I had no difficulty. If I had I am sure that every Driver, Guard, Conductor and Station Master on the route would have come to my rescue, but it wasn't necessary. I arrived safely at Kalka, nine hundred miles from home, and then changed again for Simla. There I found a "coolie" to carry my tin trunk to school. As my father had pointed out, the porter would know the

59

way, so I didn't need to. It seemed a great adventure for a boy of five, and it wasn't till I was alone in bed after "Lights Out" that I felt lonely and homesick. It would be nine months before I saw home and my parents. I cried myself to sleep.

Some years later, when I thought the House Master was picking on me, I wrote a sorrowful letter to my parents. It was 1939 and my father was most sympathetic. He was not going to stand for people misusing their authority. It was unfair and unjust. Look was what happening in Germany. Justice must be upheld at all costs. There was a foolscap page of typescript, much of it above my understanding, but the gist was that something needed to be done. However, he was a long way away, and he was rather busy just at present. Since I was on the spot, would I be a good lad and deal with it for him?

I took the letter in my grubby little hand, knocked on the House Master's door, "Please Sir, my Dad says it's got to stop!"

"What's got to stop?"

"You've been picking on me!" When I explained how I felt, we went through the punishment book, and, in fairness to the House Master, I was not being picked on. I was simply being punished for more than the usual number of misdemeanours, and he took the whole incident in good part.

Another example was that when I decided I wanted to change schools, the response was, "Find out the fees, and if it doesn't cost any more you can go." How does a ten year old 'find out the fees'?

I wrote a letter addressed to "The Boys' School, Murree" In reply I got a prospectus which told me that the school was, in fact, the Lawrence College, at Ghora Gali, near Murree. The fees quoted were slightly less than my father was already paying so he asked if I still wanted to go. When I said I did, his answer was, "OK then, fix it up."

After I had filled in the enrolment form and placed it in the envelope he offered to post it on his way to work. Of course, he opened it, wrote a covering letter, and enclosed the required cheque; at least I suppose he did, for I realised later that the school was unlikely to enrol me without these formalities! When

I arrived, however, I was quite sure it was all my own doing.

Life went on in this vein. Only once can I remember being chastised, though for what I can't recall. "Yes, my son, I am a firm believer in freedom. You MUST feel free to do as you want, but please remember that I shall feel free to belt hell out of you if I don't like it!" And on another occasion he asked me about my school results for some years back. "Oh, that's really quite a good record. Well done! I've been looking at some of my old reports. You'll see that I came first in all my exams." He handed over the documents. There was a pause while I looked at them, followed, very mildly, by the question, "So what makes you think you're so bloody clever?" I don't remember what made me think I was so clever, but at that point I stopped thinking it!

Yet he always treated me as being intelligent. He never forbade me from doing things, just pointed out that there might be consequences. When I wanted to see the rioting during the partition of India he simply said "Yes, that should be interesting. Of course, you could get yourself killed!"

At eighteen I decided to come to England. "I'll get my secretary to arrange your flight if you like." There were letters to write, formalities to fulfil. It was a big help. After some weeks he returned from work and gave me an air ticket. "You can have that as a present from us. By the way, are you going for good or are you thinking of coming back?"

You may think this cold and unfeeling, but let me explain the logic. If a young man, who has just become an adult, decides to go halfway round the world, he either has a good reason or he is a fool. To question the reason would be to insult his intelligence. To regard him as a fool would be an even greater insult. This, my father would never dream of doing.

He came to England after he retired. The man who got off the ship at Liverpool looked old and ill, and suffered from a nervous tic. He did not show the brilliance I remembered. I doubt if this old man could have guaranteed to finish a Times crossword in twenty minutes, or play a game of three dimensional chess. No, the man in my memory controlled all the movements on a railway with thousands of miles of main line track; and during the partition of India he had taken personal charge of the railhead near the border. Muslims travelled north through Amritsar's platform 1 and the 'up' line, Hindus fled south through platform 2 and the 'down' line, and the Sikhs attacked both sides indiscriminately. The two platforms and the two tracks were littered with corpses. There was disease, and shooting, and massacres, but despite this, he moved millions of refugees through the station in only three weeks. The man I remembered could do that, and he could walk along a station platform, past the band, and up the red carpet, to say quietly to the Viceroy of India, "I'm sorry, but you can't go, I've just cancelled your train!"

EVE

The capsule came down not more than a mile from its target. But there was no debriefing party, no pick up vehicle, as had been planned, for Megan Williams, eleventh British astronaut, was the only human being alive.

For a moment tears sprang to her eyes, but she brushed them away impatiently and let her training take over again. How often had they been taught to "expect the unexpected" and to cope with it. She had been in space for nearly nine weeks, but had encountered nothing unexpected there. It was here, down on earth, that the unexpected had happened.

She recalled the last few radio messages from Adam. A disease, a man-made disease, had rampaged through the world. Maybe it was the result of bombs on Iraq, maybe it was an accidental escape from one of the world's weapons laboratories. Nobody knew, and anyway, it didn't matter any more. It had spread like wildfire. There was no known antidote and no-one had been known to survive.

"It's some adaptation of anthrax, specifically tailored to humans, but it doesn't last. Ten days they reckon, and when there's no host population left it just dies out." Adam's voice was factual, emotion kept firmly in check. "Stay up there, Meg, as long as you can. You've got oxygen for five weeks, six if you're careful, so don't come down till you have to. Maybe, with a bit of luck, it'll have cleared by then."

The computers controlled the rockets, but Adam had rewritten the program so that the return rockets wouldn't fire until Megan pressed the button. "When the oxygen gauge reads zero-seven, press the switch. The computers will guide you down, you won't have to do anything else. Just strap yourself in, and keep your fingers crossed that I've got this ruddy program right. There's no chance to test it, you see."

"Thanks, Adam."

"All part of the service, Meg." The voice was light, but there was concern behind the words. There had been a bit of a thing between them, a year or so ago, but it had fizzled out, neither of them quite knowing why. The program would work, she felt sure of that. Adam was the best.

She landed safely. Adam was the best. Yes, and in more ways than one. A lump came into her throat.

"Well, this is it. Either the anthrax is still around or it isn't. Either way I have to get out of this buggy before the air runs out." Opening the capsule, she scrambled out onto the soft sand of the beach.

She could see the outlines of buildings in the distance. After the zero gravity of space it took her about an hour, and a lot of effort, to walk to the town. A small place called Heronsfield. She'd never heard of it, but there would be a car there, and a car was needed if she was to get to Cambridge, where the British space program was centred. The town was deserted. She knew it would be, of course, but to actually see it, to feel the emptiness, came as a shock. At first she had expected to find bodies lying about, but she soon realised that sick people went home to bed, or else to hospital, they didn't just keel over in the street. There were signs, of course, uncut lawns, blown litter, and animals foraging for food; but it was less dramatic than her imaginings.

She would have been more uneasy had she known that packs of stray dogs had cleaned up any carcasses, and killed most of the remaining animals. In a bigger town she may well have been pulled down and eaten, but unaware of the danger, she took no particular precautions, walking painfully to the first garage which came in view.

She took a few deep breaths and straightened herself before she took the keys from the office and chose a car from the small selection at the local garage. Luckily the fuel pumps still worked and she filled the tank to the brim. Helping herself to a road atlas, she sat in the car and planned a route to London, thinking that the largest city would also be the most likely to have any survivors. Quickly realising that she was being illogical, she changed her mind and decided to go straight to Cambridge. At least she knew her way round Cambridge, and all the space technology was there. More

64

importantly, the Space Centre had huge solar panels, so she would always be able to use the computers and the radio transmitters. She wasn't prepared to accept that no-one had survived.

Absorbed in the map she didn't notice the dogs until one jumped up against the window, causing her to give a startled cry. Luckily it was closed, but the barking of the others as they came around the corner and began to jump up at the glass made her realise the danger. Turning the key in the ignition she drove off quickly, with the pack in pursuit, but once she was able to pick up speed, they soon gave up the chase.

Out of town the roads were empty, but she took care not to drive too fast. Stray dogs might still cross her path at any time. No point in surviving space only to kill herself on an almost empty road. Even so, without any traffic to delay her, the journey was quick, and she was soon facing the gate of the Centre. She hadn't considered the possibility that it might be locked. What now? Clambering over the fence was impractical because of the barbed wire at the top. She had no key for the gate, and knew well enough that without the key she'd never open it. Yet she had to get in, she hadn't come all this way to give up now.

She walked thoughtfully to the car, then checking that there was an airbag, and strapping herself in, she drove straight at the gate. There was a tearing of metal as the car slowed, wheels still spinning, and finally came to a halt. The airbag pressed her momentarily against the back of the seat before it deflated.

The front of the car was a mess, crumpled to half its original size, but she was unhurt. She pushed herself free and tried the door. It was stuck fast in the twisted body. The passenger side was no better. Crawling over the front seats she found the back doors pushed tight against the half demolished gate. She was trapped in the vehicle.

"Like hell I am!" She was damned if she'd let this happen to her. Somehow or other she was going to get out of this bloody tin can. Going back to the front seats she kicked against the broken windscreen until some of the shattered glass was cleared away, but the internal safety layer of plastic was still in place. Forcing open the glove box and rummaging among the oddments she came across a lady's manicure set. "Good girl" she commented to the unknown owner of the car, as she used the little scissors to prise off pieces of broken glass, and cut a hole in the tough plastic.

Forcing her way through the opening she slid down over the bonnet of the car. "Expect the unexpected." It had turned out to be good advice, and it still was. She went through the inner gate, and made sure to bolt it behind her. There were no dogs in the Centre, but she didn't want any to come in from outside. Tired, she walked slowly to the training wing. In her room she removed her overalls and had a leisurely shower, trying to collect her racing thoughts, then flopped on the bed. She needed to rest, but sleep wouldn't come.

Remembering her training, she tried some deep relaxation, but even that didn't come easily. She got up, and took her favourite dress from the wardrobe. She had worn it for her first date with Adam. Damn, she was being stupid. It was over a year since she and Adam.....the tears came unbidden. Drying her eyes, she put on the dress, and applied her make up carefully. She knew it was irrational, there was no-one to see her, but she was an attractive woman, in a desperate situation. She needed all the reassurance she could get. The image in the mirror looked good.

Tired and dispirited as she was, the little ritual had given her some semblance of normality It made her feel a little better.

She started to explore the Centre. As expected, it was empty. Strangely enough there were no bodies, not even in the barracks. She concluded that in an epidemic they had disposed of the dead as quickly as possible, but they couldn't all have gone.

She found them in the Control Room. As the door opened the smell made her retch. Bodies, partly decomposed, were slumped by the instruments. Those who had been last had stayed by the radios, trying to contact anyone still alive, trying desperately to bind together the last remaining threads of civilisation. With a choking sob she saw that one of them was Adam, the features, bloated in death, still just recognisable A message was on the computer screen, and later she found it on the printer as well. Addressed to her, it detailed all that he had been able to find out about the disease.

There had been time in the capsule, time to think about how she would tackle this thing. She knew exactly what she intended to do.

With a promising career in microbiology she had had no incentive to raise a family. Perhaps that was why nothing had come of her affair with Adam. Too late now, he was gone, and not just Adam. Everyone it seemed, was gone.

She wept her tears, and said her goodbyes, then made her way slowly to the Medical Wing. The first cupboard she opened was filled with standard medicines for the common ailments which occasionally disrupted the work of the Centre. She left it, and moved to the next. It was marked "Poison" and the door was locked. She found the keys in the supervisor's desk, but it wasn't poison she was seeking, it was something far more important. She was looking for one particular locker. She had never seen it, but she knew it existed, and from Adam's vague description she had some idea of what it might look like. It took over an hour of searching, of trying keys in locks, before she found it. Then she had to find the records. She was not prepared to take a chance on this. She had to be sure. It was late evening when she found the information she needed. It was on the computer! Why hadn't she realised that earlier!

Punching in her password she prayed that it would give her access. It did, and displayed on the screen was the data she needed. Returning to the locker she searched through the phials to find the particular one she was looking for. Exhausted from her search and the tension, she took the phial, and a small syringe, and returned to her room.

Megan was not a religious woman, but flopping down on her bed she prayed that this would work. She was twenty eight years old. Too old for sentiment, she told herself, but she felt too young to carry the burden of all humanity.

She hadn't wanted children, but it was this, or wait millions of years for evolution to catch up. She had, maybe, fifteen childbearing years left. With a deep sigh she filled the syringe and inseminated herself.   She could easily find fifteen different donors, but the first must be Adam, the one she loved.

JENNY

"Will Jenny come back?"

"No Emma, Jenny's gone, she won't be coming back."

The wide eyes looked up at me, tears glistening on the lashes. "Emma won't cry, Jenny doesn't like Emma to cry." The four year old was being as brave as she knew how, looking at me for a lead. I tried to remain dry eyed, for Emma, for Jenny, for my own sanity too, I guess.

Jenny. It was like a wailing in my thoughts. How could Jenny be gone? How could someone so vibrant, so bright, be snuffed out like a candle? It couldn't be, yet it was.

I had only known her a year. She had arrived in the small village, a young girl, with her four year old daughter. No wedding ring, no partner, it had been hard for her. Small village mentality had blocked her out. They didn't want unmarried girls and their bastard children in the prim little streets of the village. She couldn't find a room to rent, so she lived in a caravan on a disused field. She couldn't find a job, so she helped out on the farm when there was fruit picking or haymaking to do. For the first long months she couldn't get Social Security benefits because she didn't have a proper home.

One day she walked into the village store for some milk and as she was paying Emma ran out. I saw the child stop at the kerbside, and seeing the road clear she dashed out after her ball. Coming out between the parked cars, she hadn't noticed the delivery van coming towards her. There was a blaring of the horn and the screeching of tyres, but it was too late for him to stop. I rushed out and swooped her up just in time.

That was how I met Jenny.

"She should look after her child. Irresponsible, that's what I call it." Jenny got no sympathy from the locals. I was the only one who accepted that she couldn't be counting out the pennies from her purse, and keeping her eyes on Emma at the same time.

She took the child from me, and I could see how her

hands were shaking. "She's all right," I said, "no real harm done."

"Shh.. Emma, it's all right. Now say thank you to the nice man who saved you."

"Thank you," Emma's voice was choked by sobs, and as I looked at her mother I could see that she was very close to tears too. She didn't look very steady on her feet either. "Come on, I'd better walk you home, you don't look too good. You've had a shock."

"Thank you so much. I was just getting the money out of my purse when I heard the noise outside. If it hadn't been for you..." her voice broke, and her hand reached out and gripped my arm so tight that it hurt.

There are few secrets in a small village. I was aware that she lived in a caravan, that she was on her own, and that the good folk of the village didn't like her. More than this was said about her, but it was gossip and speculation, not knowledge. She insisted that I have a cup of tea, but she was shaking so much that I sat her down and made the tea myself.

"You'll be talked about," she said. "People don't like me hereabouts."

"Well, that's their problem. All I did was pick up a little girl who ran into the road. If that's so wrong then to hell with them. Anyway, what's to not like about you?"

"They think I'm an unmarried mother, and they despise me for it. And Emma too."

"They can hardly blame Emma for that."

"I was married," she said. "He died two years ago up near Aberdeen."

"Just show your wedding ring, that'll stop any gossip."

"I pawned it. I didn't want to, but it was that or watch Emma go hungry. I'll get it back some day I hope."

So that was how we met. Next time I saw her she just smiled but Emma came running up and took my hand. "Look Jenny, it's the nice man." Well, she couldn't just walk on by, so we went down the High Street together, and we could both see the heads turning.

70

"Would you like some ice cream, Emma?" She looked up at her mother before replying. Getting a small nod, she said, "Yes please."

Inside the store I asked Emma what flavour she'd like. She gave me a blank stare. "She doesn't know about flavours, we haven't afforded ice cream since she was two, she can't remember. Just get her Vanilla, it's simplest."

"And you? What flavour for you?"

"Oh, nothing for me, thanks," but I bought her one as well. She was a proud little thing was Jenny, wanted to pay her way where she could.

Then, when the ice cream was finished, we walked back to her caravan, Emma hanging on to my hand as though I was her dad. More stares down the street, more whispered comments.

"Will you come to dinner one day? A sort of a thank you for accepting Emma and me. It's not been easy, these past few years." There was a tremble in her voice.

"I'd love to, but tell you what, let me bring a take-away, and a bottle of wine. I insist."

Dinner was a sparse little affair, made as pretty as Jenny's budget would allow. There were some wild flowers in a glass tumbler, and a candle on the table. She unwrapped the take-away and put it out on three plates, the chipped one for herself, and we drank the wine out of tumblers, "I'm sorry, I don't have wine glasses," she said.

"Why should you? I don't expect you drink much wine!"

I had brought some lemonade for Emma, so she could join in the toast. "To you," I said, "to you and Emma."

"To Jenny and me," said Emma, taking a sip like the adults, "and to the nice man."

"Yes and to the nice man, too. His name is Bob."

"Bob," said Emma, her brown eyes looking at me over the top of her glass.

It went on for a year. We became the best of friends, and the scandal of the village. We shouldn't have been, mind you. Jenny was twenty-one, and I was forty-four, she was beautiful, and I was balding, with middle age approaching fast. There was

71

no romance, nothing for the gossips to shout about. But when we walked down the street with Emma holding my hand, or up on my shoulders, people jumped to their own conclusions, When I visited the caravan, or took Jenny out to dinner, people made two and two add up to five.

I loved her, oh yes, I loved her, but like a daughter, not a lover. And she? Well, I don't really know, but I think I was just a friend, her only friend perhaps, certainly one she needed.

The fire engine roared past, sirens sounding its urgency. It was the caravan. The flames spilled out and the wooden frame crackled and smoked. I just got to the edge of the field when the gas bottles exploded.

I ran forward yelling for them. "Jenny, Emma!" Arms held me back. "Stay back, stay back."

Emma was standing dazed, and I could just see Jenny lying on the grass. Her clothes were singed, her lovely brown hair half burned away, and her face ... Oh God, her lovely young face disfigured with burns. I forced myself through and knelt beside her.

"Emma?"

"She's all right. Don't talk Jenny, they'll get you to hospital."

"Bring Emma, I must see Emma."

I ran and brought Emma to her mother's side. She sat down and kissed her Mum's blackened face, and then put her ear to Jenny's mouth.

She was brought away by the medics, and came running back to me, arms outstretched. I swung her up and held her close. The blanket was pulled over Jenny's face. It was over.

"Jenny told me," Emma's voice was broken with sobs.

"What did she tell you, Emma?"

"She said I was only little, and I need a big person like you to look after me. She said it would be OK."

"Yes, it'll be OK Emma, I promise."

THE FACE OF KORAKUYA

John Vandell was missing. So was the ninety-fourth frame of the film.

When an image analyst at NASA disappears, it causes concern. When a high-security film goes missing, it causes concern. When both happen at the same time, all hell bursts loose.

There was no announcement in the news, no paragraph in the press, but there was excitement of an order unknown to either of these. National security was at risk, and forces more powerful than ever imagined by the supposedly free population, moved swiftly and silently into action.

"Find him!" The Controller was angry. Vandell was his most senior analyst. He had appointed him, promoted him, and now it seemed, he may have taken a traitor into the fold. Already the weekend had passed. Vandell could be anywhere by now. "Find him!" The voice was menacingly cold.

What exactly was missing? That was the question to which everyone wanted an answer. What made frame ninety-four different from the others? The spy satellite had made seventy-eight orbits of the earth, before splashing down in the north Pacific. It had been photographing all the way. Normal photos by day and infra-red photos by night. Where had it been when frame ninety-four was taken?

That was no problem. It had been midnight. The satellite had been over Polynesia, directly above Korakuya, a small volcanic island about five miles long, apparently no different from many other small uninhabited islands in the group.

It took just over two hours for the investigators to discover that Korakuya was sacred to the Polynesians. It took three more hours for a team to fly to the island. But they found nothing unusual. A hunk of volcanic rock, thrown up quite recently as geological time-scales go, about five miles long at sea level, and stretching out to nearly fifteen under the water. The volcano was inactive, but there were warm currents around the island, and up, near the top of the steep northern edge were two pools of water. Why there should be springs at the highest part of the island instead of at a lower level remained a mystery. Heat from the substrata was forcing water up through internal crevices, that was the first tentative theory.

But they were not there to theorise about the island. They wanted to know what was special about it. Divers looked for hidden military bases. There were none. Scientists searched for signs of radiation. There were none. Psychologists talked to the natives on nearby islands, and got only a garbled tale which they did not believe.

Korakuya was the goddess of Polynesia, sacred to the people of the islands. "Mother Goddess?" asked the psychologists, but no, not mother, they were told. She was a virgin goddess, a maiden saviour. "Not mother," said the priest, "Sacred One of Realisation. Not mother."

It took six more hours to gather the team of anthropologists, and fly them to the island. They asked more questions and got more answers, which they too, did not believe. The two pools were the eyes of the goddess, and at times they filled with tears, tears of joy when she found love.

The island, they concluded was the place where the goddess lived, but again the natives said no. The island was the goddess. She was the most beautiful being in the world, and the most compassionate. When she chose to show herself, to gaze on her was to love her; and for those who followed that love, her eyes filled with her tears of joy, and she promised reward beyond compare. So the investigators gazed, but they saw only a volcanic rock, with two pools of sulphurous water near the top. Korakuya did not show herself, they did not see her beauty, and they did not learn to love her.

While one investigating team scrabbled its way about the island, another was busy tracing the movements of John Vandell. After his shift he had spent a short time in the photo-lab, and then left for home in a state of considerable excitement. No-one knew why, and he hadn't discussed it. They easily broke into his bachelor apartment but there was nothing there to help them. A few clothes seemed to be missing, but that was all. At the airport they found that he had gone to Hawaii, and from there it was easy to track him to Manila. He had made no attempt to hide his movements, and that puzzled them. It made them suspicious, and suspicion made them cautious. They wasted hours because of it. Had they been less careful they might have caught up with him sooner.

From Manila he had hired a fishing boat to take him to Korakuya. The second team followed, and joined the investigators already on the island. Pictures of the rock were analysed, searched for tell-tale signs of military bases, missile sites, underground bunkers, anything which might explain the disappearance of a secret photo and a senior member of NASA. The pictures, clear, and taken in the best of light, showed nothing suspicious. The top of a volcanic peak stood above the sea. There seemed no particular features to connect it with the legend of Korakuya. It was not shaped like a goddess, nor like anything recognisably human, yet the islanders insisted that the two pools were the tears in her eyes.

Temperature tests showed that the water was warm, so the volcano was not entirely dead. There was heat seeping out into the ocean, causing a pattern of warm currents. This was common enough in the area, and gave no reason for suspicion.

It was the pilot of the search helicopter who first saw something in the water. He radioed it through, and those on the island clambered up to the top. There, in one of the pools, they found the balding, middle-aged body of John Vandell. The steep climb had been too much for him, and his heart had given out.

He was face down in one of the shallow pools. When they dragged him out they saw that he had a peaceful smile on his face. No, it was more than that, it was the look of utter contentment of one who, at last, has found his perfect joy.

In his wallet was the missing negative, frame ninety-four of the film, and clutched in his hand the print he had made before he left. In the pinkish-brown colours of the infra-red image, they could see the pattern of heat which was generated round the island. But then, when they smoothed the crumpled paper, and looked at the photo, the pattern that they saw showed the features of a young Polynesian woman; the pure, exquisitely haunting beauty of the face of Korakuya.

PEBBLES OF HARNAI

Pebbles of Harnai upon your dried up river bed,
Burnished bronze and yellow by the dawning of the day,
I don't believe you really are inanimate and dead,
And I think it was by living that your edges smoothed away.

For if you had not lived at all, you could not understand,
You could not lie so friendly in the hollow of my palm,
You could not speak so clearly by your smoothness on my hand
Of our universal searching for contentment and for calm.

Since the fires of your conception long ages you have spent,
A million years, or more perhaps, your heartbeats have been
                                     stilled,
And yet I think you are not dead, but merely lie content,
In the bliss of your nirvana, with your destiny fulfilled.

For I think your prayers were answered by the spirits of your
                                     time,
And I think you found salvation with whatever gods you know,
But here, here is my destiny, who slips her hand in mine
And here is my nirvana, with her shining eyes aglow.

MITIGATING CIRCUMSTANCES

Henry Ollerenshaw was a mild and self-effacing man, pushed deeper into obscurity by his overshadowing wife. She was an uncompromising woman, and, if she felt a grievance falter, she would doggedly and diligently nurse it back to strength. Since most of her grievances were directed at Henry, he did not lead a comfortable life.

His weary expression and thinning hair made Henry look considerably older than his forty one years. Martha was two years his senior. They had been married for ten years. When she accepted him, in preference to being left on the shelf, it had been from desperation rather than affection. She had promised to love and honour, and staunch in her principles, she did her best, but if she found the first difficult, she found the second impossible. She submitted to his cautious demands with dutiful reluctance, and eventually even gave him a son, who alas did not survive.

It confirmed her suspicion that the pleasures of the flesh were an unwholesome digression from God's real purposes. She moved out of Henry's bed and thereafter devoted herself to caring for his spiritual welfare, overlooking entirely that in her efforts to ensure his happiness in the next world she considerably diminished his happiness in this.

"Hello dear, I'm home." It was the standard ritual of Henry's return from work. A dull man, returning from a dull job in a dull office, he tendered the usual greeting as he replaced the key in his pocket and pushed the front door shut. There was no reply. He had learned not to expect one. Placing his hat and scarf on the dark wooden hall-stand he unbuttoned his black overcoat and hung it up.

"I suppose you forgot the stamps."

"No dear, I have them here. I could have posted your letter," he added.

"You would have forgotten. You never remember anything I ask you; you'd have forgotten."

"I didn't forget the stamps!"

A sound of disparagement, somewhere between a snort

and a sniff, came from the kitchen. "Your dinner will be five minutes."

Henry slowly climbed the stairs, washed his hands, and returned to the dining room. A plate of Shepherd's pie awaited him. He had once praised her Shepherd's pie, and she had taken him up on it. Now it appeared three or four times a week. He ate it without enthusiasm. She didn't dine with him, her excuse being that he didn't get home till seven-thirty. It was another of her grievances. She liked the theatre but, because of Henry's work, with his office on the other side of London, he returned so late that she was deprived of going.

"You can go with a friend, or even on your own," he had once suggested, but she had no friends. As to going on her own, she said, it was ludicrous, and he only suggested it to annoy her. Was he unaware of the murders and rapes which occurred almost nightly, and did he want her to be murdered? "You never did care about me. If something happened you'd consider it a blessing. Then you'd find some young floosie and try to behave as though you're twenty again."

It washed over him, the same as all her other tirades. When Martha decided that he was in the wrong it rapidly became a proven fact as far as she was concerned. He tried to shut out the shrill recriminations, some going back ten years or more, to the very start of their acquaintance. There was no point in protesting, but even his silence was wrong.

"You never talk to me," she complained. "You're a deep and secretive man, and that's the sign of a guilty conscience. Oh! you've a lot to hide I'm sure. I don't suppose I know the half of what you get up to."

"I don't get up to anything."

"Well, you would say that, wouldn't you? You'd hardly admit it, but I know you too well, Henry Ollerenshaw. I know what you're like. They warned me, my friends, they warned me not to marry you. Not suited they said, not suited. I should have listened to them."

"Yes, dear." It occurred to him that he, too, wished she had listened.

The Shepherd's pie consumed, he took his plate to the kitchen and washed it. Pouring two cups of tea he went through to the sitting room. Martha sat facing the television, though it was hard to tell whether she was interested or not.

"Tea, dear." He passed her the cup. She took it silently, and began to sip. It was just then that the television broke down. There was a blinding flash, a loud bang, and smoke began to pour from the back of the set.

Henry put down his cup and ran to the socket on the wall, pulling out the plug. Then he rushed to the kitchen, wet a towel and threw it over the smoking set. In the excitement he didn't notice that Martha's cup had fallen from her hand, and she was choking, trying desperately to get her breath. Her sharp, surprised intake of breath when the television exploded had drawn a mouthful of tea into her lungs. When he did at last notice her gasping on the floor, his first instinct was to slap her on the back to try to get rid of the obstruction. But the thought of physically striking Martha was too much for him. He hesitated indecisively as her face turned blue.

She looked up at him as she struggled for breath. She tried to speak but could not, and on her face there was an expression of baleful impatience with his dithering. It was at that moment that he made his decision. He turned and left the room. He waited fifteen minutes before he phoned for an ambulance. When it arrived, he was told sympathetically that it was too late. He accepted the brandy they poured. Then he accepted another. He felt he needed it. It had been an eventful evening.

THE ENGLISH TEETH

Dafyd Jones had come from a poor family, and as a result he treated money with a respect which bordered on reverence. Except for the home of some mythical Shylock, it is hard to imagine where a shilling might find a warmer and more affectionate welcome than in the household of Dafyd and Blodwen Jones.

A true Nationalist, Dafyd had no time for the English tourists who crowded into Colwyn Bay each summer, cluttering up the local streets and causing miles-long traffic queues along the coast road. Besides, he spoke no English, preferring to use Welsh, with its musical lilt and its rich Celtic heritage.

All through the winter Dafyd could leave his home, in the village of Llysfaen, up above Old Colwyn, and drive his ramshackle Morris along the main road into Colwyn Bay or Llandudno, with Blodwen sitting starchily upright at his side. But now, at the height of summer, he left his car at home and took Bus Bach, the little bus, which ran along the upper road and dropped down into Colwyn from the hill road above.

The bus never actually entered the main part of town, and Dafyd would alight and walk the last part of the journey, loping along with the long bouncy stride of a man who is used to the hills; through the residential streets, sloping steeply towards the sea, thinking in his mind of the enormous cost of these houses, inflated by the influx of the English, who had bought up all the better parts of town, either for retirement homes or as Guest houses, where yet more English came for the summer.

Dafyd was a thin man, or perhaps scrawny would have been a more accurate description. Tall and angular, with a thinning crop of brownish hair, and gaunt, hawk-like features, he was an unprepossessing soul, and his physical unattractiveness was heightened by a potent halitosis. When this was added to his natural reluctance to put his hand in his pocket, it is not surprising that, as far as the social graces were concerned, Dafyd lacked practice.

It was in the summer of eighty-three that Dafyd was

81

persuaded to learn English. The persuasion was effected by Blodwen, in spite of the fact that she herself could not speak English either. "Look you," she intimated, "whether you like it or not, the English will come, and when they come they bring money. Because we can't converse with them we don't get our hands on any of it, so we are left with all of the inconvenience and none of the profit."

It was a powerful argument to one such as Dafyd. The logic was irrefutable, but the overwhelming reason was the lure of English pounds. He determined there and then that he would master this hated language, which had so unfairly been foisted on his native land. He would master it, and he would play them at their own game. After all, one did not need to love the English to take their money. Indeed, he persuaded himself, there was a certain justice in the thought of it.

He and Blodwen enrolled at the College in Llandudno. He assiduously tackled the grammar, the parsing, the strange and varied vocabulary of this polyglot of a language. But try as he might, he could not master it. The English, paupers as they must be in all things cultural, seemed to have taken words from almost anywhere, and according to where the root word originated, so the rules of its usage seemed to alter. To form a plural one added "s", but only sometimes. Child became children, formula became formulae, gateau became gateaux, and others seemed to go their own way too. The multiplicity of sources was too much for Dafyd, and he had no success with his studies.

Blodwen fared better. Devoid of Dafyd's staunch nationalism, she accepted that English was not Welsh. There was no reason for it to follow the same rules, or indeed, to follow any rules at all, so she absorbed what she was told without preconceived ideas of the rightness or wrongness of it, and in her fashion, she mastered some of the intricacies of the language. Enough, at any rate, to converse with the English tourists, whose knowledge of correct English was not necessarily any better than her own.

It was in that same summer that the source of Dafyd's halitosis was established. Receding gums had allowed teeth to become exposed below the enamel. The resulting decay caused them to break off, and Dafyd found himself with fewer and fewer teeth in his head. There was no cure but to have a set of dentures.

"How much!" he exclaimed when told the price. Even under the National Health system Dafyd had to pay exorbitant sums of money, or so it seemed to him.. Money which would go into the coffers of Westminster. No, he would not do it. The dentist argued that without the dentures Dafyd would find difficulty in chewing his food. This could cause problems with his digestion, and all in all, it really was advisable to have a good set of false teeth, properly fitted.

Unfortunately the dentist was English. Despite a thorough search of the Yellow Pages Dafyd had not located a single dental practitioner called Owen, or Jones, Thomas or Williams or Evans. Haythorne-Thwaite was no sort of name to be paying good money to, but he was the only one who gave treatment on the National Health. The others were equally English, and private; and hence even more expensive.

Dafyd had the extractions, ignored the smiles of the receptionist, who incidentally, was wholly Welsh, and refused the advice that he should be fitted with dentures. In the pawn shop in one of the side streets he had seen some false teeth. Four pounds was wanted, but Dafyd haggled, and few could haggle like Dafyd. He pointed out that the bottom plate had much less material than the top. It should cost less he argued, besides, who would buy second hand dentures? He thrust his face close to the pawnbroker to emphasise his argument. The pawnbroker put up a brave fight, but the halitosis drove him back from Dafyd, and when he had retreated as far as he could, and was pressing against the counter, the man capitulated. The teeth were bought for two pounds fifty.

They didn't fit, of course, that would have been too much to expect, but they sat in his mouth and gave an impression. The sort of impression would no doubt depend on the observer, but to Dafyd they were a triumph of good sense. So many pounds saved! False teeth, after all, were false teeth, and no-one expected them to be real. He continued his studies, and Blodwen was helpful and encouraging. Suddenly, he began to get the hang of it. Words began to make sense, structure became less obscure, English began to flow from the mouth of Dafyd Jones.

When he spoke, the teeth would perform two or three circuits of his palate, until they found a place to settle, and then would follow a flood of words. Sing-song in lilt and style, sibilant with air hissing through the ill-fitting dentures, occasionally of doubtful grammar, but clearly the language was English.

Acquaintances were surprised that after so many months of failure there should be such a sudden transformation. They sought an explanation, but none was forthcoming. It remained a mystery.

The rumour, however, was that the teeth were the cause. They had been found in a hotel room where they were accidentally left by a particularly garrulous English tourist!

SONG OF THE FREE

Give me a bike and the open road
As far as the eye can see,
Where the desert wind on the plains of Sind
Is singing the song of the free.

Or give me a pack and a mountain track
High up in the snow country
Of the Hindu Kush, where the waters rush
In their quest for the distant sea.

Come ride with me on the unmade roads
Where the tyres crunch gravel and dirt,
Where the joy of life can be so intense
That it almost seems to hurt.

Come north with me where the mountains rise,
Come south to the rolling sea,
But wherever I ride, be by my side,
And sing me the song of the free.

AT FIRST SIGHT

She seemed to walk right through the closed door. That's what made me take notice. I couldn't figure out how she'd done it.

"Hello," I said. "How did you manage that?"

She looked at me oddly, looking through me rather than at me. Then she shook her head slightly and looked again.

"Oh, hello. I didn't see you there at first. Have you been here long?"

Her voice was quiet, delicate, a well educated voice, with a faintly old fashioned air about it. Her clothes looked old fashioned too, but they suited her, and these days when anything goes, they didn't look at all out of place. In fact she looked stunning,

"I got here about four hours ago. I'm visiting my aunt for a holiday. She didn't tell me there would be other guests." I held out my hand. "I'm Harry, Harry Roberts."

She took it, murmuring something polite, and then said hurriedly, "My name is Amelia Marsden. I think there's something wrong. I had better go."

"No, please don't rush off, it's a cold night, and it's getting late. Auntie won't mind, I'm sure, there's plenty of room. You'll be welcome as my guest, so please stay."

She looked around, puzzled. "I don't know. I'm not sure I should be here. It doesn't seem that I'm expected, it might be better if I went."

I didn't want her to leave. There was something quite captivating about her, and her old fashioned courtesy was charming. I urged her to stay, and eventually she agreed, but reluctantly it seemed. "How did you get in?" I asked. "I didn't see you open the door, it looked as though you walked right through it."

She gave a nervous little laugh. "Of course not! That would be impossible, wouldn't it? You didn't expect anyone, so you formed the wrong impression."

"Yes, that must be it. Anyway, come on, I'll introduce

86

you to my aunt. Don't be nervous, you'll like her. I'll tell her you're a friend of mine, and she'll like you too. Oh, I'd better explain, after my parents died my aunt brought me up, she's more like a mum to me." I led her through to the other room.

"Auntie, this is Amelia, I didn't expect her, but she popped in just now and it's such a cold night that I've asked her to stay. You don't mind do you?"

My aunt was a bit taken aback, but too polite to ask any questions. I would have to make up some story, but it could wait a while. She showed Amelia to one of the spare rooms, and told the maid to make up the bed.

"Have you no luggage, my dear?"

"No, I wasn't expecting to visit, and I'm afraid I'm quite unprepared. Harry persuaded me to stay, and I agreed. I must apologise for any trouble, but he was quite insistent."

"Yes, Harry can be insistent, but it's no trouble, really it isn't." She was putting a brave face on it, but she was puzzled, I could tell.

After a drink we said our goodnights and went to our rooms. There was a quiet knock on my door and Aunt walked in. "Where did you find her? She didn't just turn up, I know that, so come on, what's going on?"

"She did just turn up, honestly. It's late and she obviously hasn't anywhere to go so I asked her to stay. It's all right isn't it?"

"Yes, but who is she? What do you know about her? Goodness Harry, she might be anybody, and now here she is in the spare room. You must be more careful you know, you're always picking up waifs and strays, but animals, not pretty young women."

"Her name is Amelia Marsden, and she doesn't look like a waif, does she?. She's all right, I'm sure. She seems a really nice girl, you must admit that."

She didn't comment, and for the moment that was that, but the subject would come up again I was certain. It did, over breakfast the following morning. "Where are you from, Amelia?" asked my aunt.

"From here. I was born in this house. I've been away in Europe for a few years, but I've always thought of this as home."

"And now you've come back. How nice. Where are you stopping?"

"Oh, I can't stop. I tried to explain to Harry last night that I should really be going, but it has been very good of you to give me your hospitality."

"Well, Harry must drive you, it's too wintry for you to go wandering about without a warm coat."

I opened the car door and after the faintest hesitation she got in. She looked around as though everything was unfamiliar, and the quiet hum of the engine surprised her. "I expected it to make more noise," she said.

"Well, it's a pretty expensive car. I'd send it in for service if it made too much noise. Now where to?"

"The Railway Station please. It's just down the road."

There hasn't been a station at Allerton for years, Beeching closed it down. I thought for a moment. "When did you live at the Manor, Amelia?"

"Four years ago. Then I went to Europe to finish my education. I've just got back."

"Four years? You sure? My aunt has had the house for eight years now, so there must be some mistake, you can't have lived there in 1998."

"1998? I left in 1927, and now it's 1931. I didn't know my parents weren't still there or I wouldn't have come."

I pulled the car over to one side. "Amelia, it's 2002. What makes you think it's 1931? Look at the car, this watch, the radio, the electrical gadgets. They didn't have things like that in 1931! What's happened that you can be so far out?"

She turned and put her hands against her face. "I don't know. Harry. I'm frightened. Something's very wrong, and I don't know what."

"Hey, it's all right, I'll look after you, I won't let anything hurt you. It's probably stress. You'll be all right once you take things easy. It's just a delusion."

"No Harry, it's not. I am from 1931, it is 1931. You say

it's 70 years in my future, but that's not possible. It's you who's deluded."

"Then how do you explain the car and the things in it?"

"I don't know. Anyway, I don't know anything about cars, perhaps this is how expensive cars are. I wouldn't be able to tell any different."

We argued about it for a while, her voice growing more agitated, till I had an idea. "You were born here, and you lived here most of your life?"

"Yes."

"Come with me to the local church."

"No Harry, I'd rather not, there's something odd going on. I'm frightened," but I drove there anyway. We searched around. It didn't take long to find. An angel with wings outspread stood above the headstone. "Amelia Beatrice, beloved daughter of Sir John and Lady Beatrice Marsden, 1909 - 1931"

She was trembling as I held her to me. She had died seventy years ago, but she was here, in my arms, young, beautiful, and real. I couldn't explain it. I didn't try.

"I knew something was wrong," she said. "I really must go." She gave me a quick kiss. "Goodbye, Harry," and then she walked forward.

"No!" I cried, gripping her hand firmly. "You can't go, I've only just found you. I couldn't bear to lose you now."

There were tears in her eyes. "I'd love to stay, Harry, but it isn't possible."

"Stay," I pleaded, "we'll work something out, there must be some way. Please stay."

She shook her head sadly and turned away. Still holding her hand tightly, I followed, merging into the headstone. I didn't know where she was leading me, but I knew I couldn't let her go.

Love at first sight, it doesn't happen does it? But then a lot of other things don't happen either, or so we are led to believe.

TIGER

India is the Land of the Tiger.

I was born and brought up in India, yet all the time I was there I never saw a wild tiger; lots of wild leopards, often at close quarters, and on two occasions wild elephants, also at close quarters, but never a tiger.

In fact the only tiger I have ever been close to, without any bars between us, was one that escaped from a zoo.

Late one morning, word went round that the tiger had escaped. There was great excitement among the young men. Those who had guns grabbed them and went out to hunt it. If they spotted the tiger then for sure they would bring it down with a single shot and become the heroes of the day. Such are the aspirations of young men who don't know what they are talking about. A more likely scenario was that had they actually come face to face with the tiger, they would have been rooted to the spot with fear, or run a mile; but it looked good in front of the girls to join the throng who were so keen to make the town a safer place.

Most of the guns would be quite unable to bring down a tiger, most of the young men would be quite unable to hold their nerve if facing one, and if anyone had been stupid enough to wound the animal and fail to kill it, it would probably have been a fatal mistake.

I did not possess a gun, not even an air rifle, so I didn't see myself as a likely executioner of runaway tigers. None the less I joined the throng at the zoo, and I also went out searching for the beast. Strangely enough, I wasn't afraid. As I have said, I had been at close quarters with wild leopards in the Himalayas. At night they roamed the playing fields at school, or wandered the road to town, and they had never hurt anybody. After a few years of this acquaintanceship I had grown a little blasé about leopards, they were after all only overgrown pussy cats. "Here Pussy, here," we often called, but the response was a quiet growl, a swish of the tail, and the leopard went off.

This tiger could only be like an oversized leopard, and in

my experience, leopards didn't hurt people, so why would the tiger, unless of course, someone was fool enough to upset it. I wasn't going do that, so I wasn't afraid, just curious to see where it had gone.

I was with a group of friends, on our inevitable bikes, and we cycled around all afternoon, dismounting at every clump of trees to see if the tiger was there. We had no guns and it wasn't our intention to harm the animal in any way, but if we spotted it one of us would have pedalled like mad to report the sighting, while the rest kept track of it. This might have been a silly thing to do, and maybe it was not just an oversized leopard, but our theory was never put to the test. No clump of trees that we explored concealed the tiger.

The afternoon wore on, and we grew weary. We had been cycling rapidly for about five hours, going quickly from one likely hiding place to another, and it was suggested that we return to base to see if anything, had developed. We got back to the zoo but there was no news. The sun began to set, and gradually the armed members of the search came back. Like us they wanted news. Unlike us, their intention was to blast hell out the poor creature. Given their aggressive attitude, they may have expected reciprocal hostility. I suspected that they didn't wish to be out in the dark with a tiger wandering free, and their return for news was an excuse to avoid this eventuality. I'm not sure that I can put my hand on my heart and say that it wasn't the same for us. Maybe our group wasn't quite as sure of our theories about tigers as we claimed to be.

Whatever the truth of our sentiments, at dusk almost everyone was back. No-one was going to admit that it might have been fear that brought us back, and none of us was in any position to criticise the others.

There was a stir at the gates of the zoo, and there, walking calmly through enough armament to have converted the tiger to a colander, came the keeper. He had his turban tied loosely round the animal's neck. It followed him in a very subdued fashion, while he harangued it mercilessly. "You stupid animal, what do you think you're doing going off like that? Where will you sleep?

How will you eat? Who'll look after you and keep you safe?
What sort of a silly prank was that?" and so it went on. If a tiger
can be said to have a hang-dog expression, this tiger had it.

I still believe that animals will not attack unless
provoked. In the New Forest our visiting badgers could have
bitten our fingers off quite easily, but we didn't really think that
they would hurt us. We still allowed them to gently scrape cat
food off our fingers. Similarly, hornets nested in one of our bird
boxes. Practically eye to eye when I was painting the eaves they
looked at me warily, one even settled briefly on my hair, but they
never tried to sting me.

It may just be age, or it may be that I have grown away
from my closeness to wild animals, but I am now less confident
of their acceptance. I am less sure of what they might find
threatening, and I know that animals are bound to be aggressive
if they feel threatened. I have always realised that, even at
school, even when I was calling, "Come pussy, come," to the
leopards.

FOOL'S GOLD

Dawn was lightening the sky, the first faint flush of pink edging the tops of the mountains, and spilling over to the valley below. The stream which etched the bottom had long since gone, and the smooth pebbles strewn along its ancient path gleamed yellow, brown, and pink in the morning glow.

Here and there sparse blades of grass edged the sides of the dried up river, recalling, perhaps, better days when there had been rain and fertile fields. The desert soil was rich and productive where water could be found, but it was long ages since rain fell in this small valley. The dryness was so intense it could almost be tasted. The tiny mud huts were little more than waist high walls, the roofs fallen in, mixed into what had once been the earth floors of simple dwellings.

The village was abandoned long ago, when the rain had failed for years in succession. Now there were no fields, no sign of goats or sheep. Nothing remained of the life of the villagers, driven out by drought and famine. Now only the nomadic Hurs occasionally passed, riding their camels and driving their herds of goats. They shunned the ruined walls, pitching their low black tents of skin on the higher ground. From this vantage point they could better keep an eye on their animals, and protect them from predatory wolves.

The sun slowly rose above the mountains, slanting down the valley, glancing off the pebbles. It brought out the myriad hues and the magical beauty of the various shapes. Some were simply smooth and round, but others had been wrought into mysterious forms by the age old flow of water. There were shiny grains in some of them, silvery specks of some metallic substance, and occasionally the joyous glint of gold.

It was fool's gold, not real. Real gold would have brought half the world to this remote valley, but that had not happened. It remained hidden, and distant, and peaceful, hemmed in by the silence of timeless hills. It was a silence you could almost hear, and a searching solitude which seeped into one's soul, a solitude which was emphasised by the lammergeyer high above, its three metre wingspan reduced to a distant speck.

A soft breeze moved along the valley floor, not blowing, but dropping gently, soundlessly, because it was cooler, and therefore slightly heavier, than the rest. It would drift along the river bed until the shelter of the hills was lost, and then, on the plain, it would get caught up in the flurry and twisting of the wind.

I turned and went back towards the tent. As I looked up, I saw her come out. She stood and stretched, her back arched, her arms towards the sky. Her body gleamed golden in the orange light of the morning sun. Fool's gold? Not so. This was more precious. This was real.

EVIDENCE

Professor Morrison sat at his desk in the University of Belfast, contemplating the two packages before him.

He thought he might open the larger package first. It contained the pictures of the deepest part of the Mariana Trench, taken by the bathyscope camera developed by Morrison. It would take some time to interpret all the pictures, he knew, because this was a region of the earth never before observed. Eleven thousand metres below the surface, untouched by sunlight, what would be revealed in these unexplored depths?

Morrison's hand shook slightly in anticipation.

Inside the package, the photos were quite unlike anything he could possibly have expected. Weird shapes of creatures so unlike anything on earth, that one was tempted to believe they must have come from somewhere else. Extra-terrestrial? No, it couldn't be. How could they have got here, in the deepest stronghold of our planet?

The still pictures couldn't reveal whether the objects were living creatures or fossilised remains. They were a drab greyish brown. This was only to be expected of fossils. It was also to be expected of living creatures at these depths. There was no evolutionary purpose in colour if there was no light, but what were they?

Six creatures with two heads, each with five eyes, and one with tracks where legs might be expected. Creatures? No, this last wasn't a creature, it was an artefact!

Artefacts presupposed intelligence to design them, and factories to build them, and no coincidental chance of evolution could lead to a living creature with tracks for mobility. Atlantis! So, had it existed after all, and there in the dark depths of the Mariana Trench, was this the evidence?

It didn't account for the creatures though, those that really were living things, or had been once. Five eyes! Nothing earthly had ever had five eyes, or two heads! They bore no resemblance to anything in the evolutionary line. Perhaps the vehicle was their means of transport, but transport from where? They were surely not related to anything on earth. From the pictures the vehicle didn't look any larger than the creatures, but the automatic zooming of the Morrison camera filled every frame, so there was no sense of relative size. That was a bad decision on Morrison's part. He had decided that it was the best way to get the detail, but he had overlooked the matter of scale. Now it had turned out to be a serious error. There was nothing to indicate the size of what was photographed.

Yet who ever heard of a space ship with tracks? It didn't have the streamlined aerodynamic shape so necessary for lift off. Unless... of course! Unless it took off from an airless world, a world without atmosphere. Then the creatures wouldn't need air. They may not be fossils after all, they could be present day descendants of long ago visitors, not needing air, and presumably not needing light, and so far down in the ocean that they had never been found. Till now!

Oh the irony, that the camera, with its static images, could give no clue as to whether they were alive, or fossils from aeons ago. But what possibilities would be opened up!

Only, that wasn't the way it happened.

Morrison's hand trembled in anticipation.

He curbed his impatience. He felt that he needed time to savour his discoveries, so he laid aside the larger package unopened, and decided to look at the other one first. As he tore open the wrapping it triggered the device. There was a sharp explosion. It threw the Professor, unconscious, against the wall, it demolished his desk, and it completely destroyed the evidence he would have so looked forward to analysing.

THE MEM

Janet Frobisher was that relic of the days of Empire; a genteel lady of independent means. Living quietly in her small flat in London she reminisced of grander times spent in the tropical heat of Burma.

She had been younger then, of course, but she had always been delicate. In the quaint Victorian language of the colonies she was said to have enjoyed bad health. The heat had always made her feel lightly heady, and too much sun gave her a migraine. In the back of her mind was the vague thought that only the natives, and perhaps the lower classes, were blessed with rude good health. There was something rather unrefined, it seemed to her, about being too fit. It savoured of athleticism and manliness, and she deplored the modern trend of young women aping the male. It was unnatural she would confide, in that curiously theatrical whisper of hers, for women to want to be the same as men when they were clearly quite different.

Yet she had not hesitated to go with her husband onto the plains and into the jungles. It was she who had shot the leopard, when he had been so badly mauled. True she had fainted later, it would have been almost vulgar not to have done so, but she remembered with pride how she had picked up the heavy gun, pointed it, and fired. The shock of the recoil had bruised her shoulder and thrown her against the palisade, but the leopard had fallen, killed cleanly with a single shot.

She had a confused recollection of native bearers shouting and running towards her as she fell. She came to with the sharp pungency of smelling salts rasping her throat. There had been the trek back, down country to the river, and then the long haul in the river boat. Too late alas. William had died of his wounds.

As the widow of the Assistant District Commissioner she was given a grand farewell, with flowery speeches, bouquets and garlands; but it hadn't meant anything. William was gone. This country wasn't hers, the people weren't hers, and she was glad to be out of it. Home. Home was England, with its green fields and rolling downs, its trolley-buses, and busy streets. She walked in the park, slowly and genteelly, the slender pink umbrella held against the comforting English rain, so different from the torrential downpours of the monsoon.

But she suffered the cold. She had been too long in the tropics, and her blood had thinned. Besides, she confided to her friends at whist, she had always been delicate. Almost every week she visited her doctor, with some new ache, or some recurring twinge. He told her bluntly that to withstand so much ill health she must be remarkably fit. The following week she found another doctor. He had no right to speak to her like that. England was not what it had been. The classes were no longer clear cut. Even the natives, as she still thought of them, were now treading the pavements of London, raising families, and buying homes, sometimes as good or even better than her own. It wasn't right, she thought, this disappearance of the proper order of things; and as prices kept rising, so she found it more and more difficult to maintain a decent standard. The fixed pension seemed increasingly inadequate as inflation soared to fifteen, twenty, even twenty-five percent.

A windfall came her way, a small prize on the premium bonds. It was nothing dramatic; certainly not enough to change her way of life, but enough to make a bit of a splash. She decided to take a holiday. A couple of months in Burma, where for so long she had lived the privileged life of a colonial officer's wife.

It was on Tuesday the 17th of May 1983 that she arrived at the Hotel Excelsior in Rangoon. She noticed the change. Obsequiousness had gone, replaced by a professional politeness more on the style of the West. She could not complain of any lack of courtesy, but it was the courtesy of a commercial concern to its clients. She was no longer the "Mem", with all the privileges to which that status had entitled her. The hotel staff addressed her as "Madam", and they looked straight at her, not lowering their eyes as they would once have done, and they accepted the tips without the exaggerated gratitude given to baksheesh.

She took a boat up-river, retracing the journeys of the

past, and vaguely, half unconsciously, making a pilgrimage of sorts. It was on the 21st that the boat tied up at the town of Kusama. Passengers disembarked and made for their homes. The tourists, of whom there were only five, were advised to take a guide, but she had no need of this. She knew this country. The sounds, the smells, the sticky warmth even so early in the season, flooded her with memories. She had not liked it when she was here with her husband, but now it seemed welcoming and familiar, so unlike England which had changed so much.

She walked unheeding, lost in her own thoughts. Spring flowers were in bloom, and insects buzzed, busily collecting nectar. Jacaranda trees in the sidewalks dropped petals as she brushed by them, the smell of their blossom mingling with the other spicy smells of the bazaar. She soaked up the nostalgia.

Suddenly there was a lot of noise and a shout of warning. She looked up to see a lorry careering round the corner. The horn was blaring and the vehicle was clearly out of control. In its path was a four year old girl. Without thinking she ran forward. Her handbag fell from her shoulder, its contents scattering on the ground, and just in time she scooped the child into her arms. She felt a blow to her side and, as she fell, the front wheel hit her leg. She heard the bone snap but felt no pain. Seconds later she heard the crash as the lorry ploughed into the front of a shop.

Willing hands lifted her. Only then did pain flood over her and she fainted. When she awoke she was in hospital, plaster on her leg, flowers beside the bed, and a glass of water with a net to keep the flies off. The grit from the road had been washed from her greying hair, and a clean hospital gown covered her slender body.

A nurse passed by, and seeing that she was awake, came over to her. "How are you feeling now Mrs. Frobisher?" she asked.

"The girl. The little girl. Is she all right?"

"Yes, thanks to you she's all right. Frightened of course, but quite unhurt. You were very brave they tell me. There's someone waiting to see you. Do you feel up to it?"

Thirty years she'd been away. She knew noone here.

Who on earth would want to visit her she wondered. She would have preferred to sleep, but curiosity got the better of her. She nodded slightly.

A young woman was ushered into the ward. Her flattish brown features seemed pure Burmese, and she spoke English hesitantly, with a rather pronounced accent. "Mrs. Frobisher? I came to see how you were," she said slowly, "and to thank you for what you did for Leila."

"Is she all right? Is she your daughter?" The questions bubbled out, giving no time to reply. "I thought she would be run over."

The young woman had difficulty keeping pace. Carefully she worked out the meaning of the words and then searched for the right ones to reply. "She is all right. Safe at home. No, she is not my daughter, she is from the orphanage where I work."

"Oh the poor mite! And the driver, is he safe?"

"The driver was hurt in the crash, but not badly. He will be all right in a few weeks the doctor says."

"The orphanage, have you many children? I didn't know of an orphanage when I was here."

"You know Kusama?" There was surprise in the voice.

"I was here, now let me see, until 1952. Yes, that's when I left Burma. I was thirty then. My husband was the Assistant District Commissioner until Independence, then he was kept on as an advisor, but he died, and I went home." Home; the word suddenly made her think. Did she really feel at home in England? She had always taken it for granted that she did, but she had been very aware of the changes. It was no longer the England she had loved so much, the land she had pined for. That land was a memory. But so was this, she told herself. Burma wasn't the same either. Thirty years had brought changes. Did she still dislike it so much?

The young woman was still talking in her hesitant English, and she had missed the gist of it. "I'm sorry" she began, and then changed her mind. "I'm sorry," she repeated in Burmese, "My thoughts wandered and I missed what you said. Forgive me. Will you please tell me again. I think you'll find it easier if we speak Burmese!"

A warm smile crossed the face of the young woman. "I don't speak English well," she agreed. "I was telling you about the orphanage. My father started it, and since his death, my sister and I have run it. We have twelve girls, Leila is one of the youngest. She is troubled, and runs away a lot."

"Perhaps she's unhappy there." She accompanied the words with a slight, apologetic, shrug.

"Perhaps." The girl's smile held no reproach for what might have seemed a criticism. "We think it is because she is disturbed. Her parents died in a fire, and it must have had a terrible effect on Leila. It may be that psychiatric help is needed, but we can't afford that, so we have to do what we can with love and sympathy."

"May I come and see this orphanage? When I'm out of here, of course."

"I was going to invite you! Leila will want to see you, I know, and we are grateful for what you did, really we are."

After her visitor had left she lay thinking about events. "We are grateful for what you did". Yes, they probably were, but why had she done it? It was not like her to go charging into the thick of things. She was a quiet, shy, English lady, given to minding her own business. She had never liked the social side of William's work, mixing with the other wives, attending soirees at Government House. It was too much effort she felt, for such an ineffectual life, but after William died, life had been just as ineffectual. Whist on a Wednesday, coffee mornings once a fortnight. Yet she'd been content enough in her cocoon, whether in Burma or in the suburbs of London. She had never tried to break the mould; indeed, she felt vaguely disturbed at the modern trend of equality and women's liberation. Yet she would not have missed this for the world. For only the second time in her life she had done something she felt was really worth while. She remembered the satisfaction she had felt when she shot the leopard which was attacking her husband, even though it had been too late to save his life. This time she had been in time. This time she had succeeded.

It was ten days before she was fit enough to take a rickshaw and visit Miss Gadesh at the orphanage. Young Leila rushed to her and hugged her with enthusiasm. "Be careful of Mrs. Frobisher's leg," but the child was oblivious to admonishments.

"Your leg, is it healing properly?"

"Yes, they're quite pleased with me. The plaster has to stay on for a while yet, but I've been discharged from hospital. I telephoned as soon as I knew, and came straight here. Now I must excuse myself and find a hotel. Naturally my booking was cancelled when I had to stay in hospital"

"You have no booking? Then you must stay here. We have plenty of room."

"Oh, I couldn't! Well," she hesitated, " perhaps, if you allow me to pay for my board."

"I wouldn't hear of it," said Miss Gadesh. "Come, let me introduce you to my sister. She will insist I know."

The elder Miss Gadesh was taller and less Burmese looking than her sister. Their father had been a Madrasi doctor who married a Burmese girl. She had died early in the marriage and he had remained in the country, practising medicine and ministering as best he could to the poor of the district. Eventually this had led to the setting up of the orphanage.

Her room was small, but clean and airy, cool after the sultry heat of the May afternoon. A rickshaw was despatched for her cases, which were still in the hotel basement, and by early evening she was comfortably settled. The two sisters made her feel very much at ease, and Leila made such a fuss of her when she found that she was to stay as a guest.

The first morning passed quickly, getting to know the children, and exploring the house and the gardens which surrounded it. The walking stick and the plastered leg made progress slow, but the whole atmosphere was so friendly that she felt no embarrassment about her clumsiness. All the children who were six or older were sent to school but the youngest followed her about, helping her down the garden steps, or opening doors for her. She had no children of her own, and for the first time since William's death she felt part of a family. The children asked repeatedly for stories. She told them about England, about her life in Burma, so long before they were born, but most of all she told them the folk tales of their own country. Her role became that of an adopted grandmother, advising and comforting, and linking their young modern lives with the long heritage of their past. They addressed her as the "Mem", but she knew it was from a real respect and affection, quite unlike the formality of the title she had held as the Assistant Commissioner's lady.

The plaster was removed from her leg, and all too soon the holiday was over. It was time to return home. The sisters embraced her with a genuine warmth, and there were tears in their eyes. She too, found it hard to speak when, each in turn, the children hugged and kissed her goodbye.

England in August was dry and sunny. Her flat was snug and comfortable. Everything was as it should be. But she missed the little feet pattering on bare floors, the childish cries of laughter when she stumbled over some half forgotten Burmese word. In her suitcase she found a bag of boiled sweets. She had meant to give them to the children when she left, but had forgotten. Now there were no children to give them to. She developed a cough, and knowing she was delicate, she took to her bed. A fortnight after her return a letter arrived from the Gadesh sisters. They wished her well, thanked her for the pleasure her visit had given them all, and said how much she was missed, especially by Leila. They were having trouble with Leila. She was running away again.

It brought a tightness to her throat, causing her to cough. She swallowed some of the linctus prescribed by her doctor, and reread the letter. The tightness returned. It occurred to her that she had not been ill during the months of her holiday. Oh yes, she had broken her leg, but she had not been ill, not once.

She decided to dress and go out. There was something she wanted to do, something she felt she had to do. At the Foreign Office the clerk was polite and helpful. No, he did not think that her pension was payable if she left the country, but if she cared to wait he would find out what he could. It was nearly half an hour later that she was ushered into the office of the Assistant Paymaster. If her husband's salary had been paid abroad for more than six years, he said, arrangements could be made for her pension to be paid in the same country. It was a bit of a rigmarole but it could be arranged, and she was certainly eligible. Was that what she wanted?

Yes, she replied, it was what she wanted. "Leave it with me," he said. "It will probably be about four weeks before you hear anything, but call me if there are any problems."

She left the building and went straight to a local Estate Agent. "Always glad to be of service," he assured her. "I'll come round tomorrow and take measurements of the flat. I expect you want to move to a bungalow or a house. What sort of property did you have in mind? We have some very desirable bungalows on our books."

"Oh, a rambling place, with lots of rooms, and jacaranda trees in the garden."

"Jacaranda trees?" He sounded puzzled.

"I'm not buying a property," she laughed. "I'm investing the money I get for the flat."

"Investing it? We can offer some very sound investments," he said. "But where will you live?"

"I told you, in a rambling house, with lots of rooms, and jacaranda trees in the garden. I'm going home; and my money will be safely invested - in my children's future!"

BIKE

We've struggled up the mountain pass,
We've sped across the plain,
Our bikes have brought experience
Whether marvellous, or mundane.
We've seen the Taj by moonlight
And the Temple of the Jain,
But we shared the Sarju ferry
With the cattle and the grain.

We went in all directions,
We travelled far afield,
The land of the five rivers
Has rolled beneath our wheels,
We've taken salt with strangers
Who shared their humble meals
And we learned to love the peasant
In his villages and fields.

Some things we've seen to marvel at,
And some have caused us pain,
But we learned from every journey
It has never been in vain.
So get your bike and sleeping bag
And once more let us go,
And we shall search for Xanadu
Where golden apples grow.

JAM AND JERUSALEM

Mildred Evans was in her fifty-second year. It was three years since Harry died, and only now was the raw pain beginning to lessen. The W.I. helped. It had given her something to do, something to fill the empty void of his absence. She didn't pretend that it was very much, but it had been something, and something, as Harry would have said, was better than nothing.

Gradually the pain eased, and the companionship of the other women, many of whom had been through it too, made it easier to bear. Harry, dear Harry, how she wished he could have been here. He would have loved to see the Orient; India, Singapore, and then on to Japan. The holiday of a lifetime. She had arranged it through the W.I., and got a discount too! She gave a little sigh as she settled back in the aircraft seat.

She must have dozed off, because she woke with a start at the shouts. "Keep your seats. Sit still and you won't get hurt! The man brandishing the gun had a heavy accent, but she didn't know whether he was Jewish, Arab, or even Pakistani.

Another man came out from the flight deck. His English was better. "This aircraft has been commandeered by the Afghan Rebel Army. We are taking it to Kabul where most of you will be disembarked. Please do not cause any trouble, and you will be safe, but we shall not hesitate to shoot if there is any interference with our plans."

"What do you mean, "Most of us. Why not all? It was the senior stewardess. Plucky girl, thought Mildred.

"Some will stay as hostages, but it is not our intention to harm anyone. That is all I can say."

"I must see to the boy in the front seat. He's travelling alone. I must look after him. She began to walk forward.

"Sit down! His voice was icy cold, even colder than his eyes.

"But he's frightened, can't you see that?"

"Sit down, I said." The barrel of his pistol left a red weal on her cheek. She slowly retreated to her seat. The younger stewardess was already seated, her mouth trembling, tears gathering in her eyes.

The plane continued smoothly on its way. Whatever drama there was, was on the flight deck, and in the radio messages. In the cabin there were only the men at the front and rear, both with automatic weapons pointed towards the passengers. It seemed very calm, but Mildred could sense the tension, and feared the inevitable eruption which would come.

She looked out of the window beside her seat. She could see the wing below her, and beyond it, the distant outlines of fields, partly obscured by cloud. Funny how the wing kept flexing. She had never noticed that before, but she noticed it now, when there was so much more to worry about. Just like her, she thought, to seize upon the trivial.

There was a sudden movement as a man in an aisle seat leapt forward towards one of the hijackers. A muffled oath, in some foreign language, was accompanied by a single shot. The man slumped to the floor without another sound. A trickle of blood began to form a pool on the floor. The stewardess immediately got to her feet to go to him, but she was waved back with the gun barrel. She sat down again, but not without a protest. "Shut up," said the gunman, "Or I hit you some more."

Mildred lost track of time. She had her watch, but she didn't know what time this had all started. It seemed to be a long while before the Captain's voice came over the intercom. "Ladies and Gentlemen, this is your Captain. As you must know, this flight has been hijacked by members of the Afghan Rebel Army. They demand that we divert to Kabul. In twenty-five minutes we shall be reducing altitude over Kabul Airport where we are awaiting permission to land. Please do as they tell you until we have landed. A bullet could pierce the skin of the aircraft, causing decompression, and possible break up of the fuselage. After landing the ground authorities will take over."

Several minutes later the lights flashed a warning to fasten seat belts, and the Captain spoke again. "We are now approaching Kabul runway. Extinguish all cigarettes, and fasten your seat belts. We shall touch down in a few minutes."

The stewardess again got to her feet, only to get the back

of a hand across her already bruised face, and be pushed back into her seat. "Put on your seat belt," said the man who had hit her. She looked at him with such revulsion that Mildred was surprised he didn't hit her again. How plucky the girl was!

The landing was perfect. Smoothly the plane put down and taxied to a halt. It was almost immediately surrounded by armed men, guns pointed at every window. Loud hailers were brought into use, and dialogue which Mildred couldn't understand, began. She guessed these were negotiations of some sort. After minutes of haggling the door was opened and the front rows of passengers were gestured to leave, stepping past the body, and trying to avoid the blood in the gangway Then there was more haggling and eventually Mildred's row was ordered to the exit, but instead of going forward Mildred went to the rear where the stewardess was sitting.

The right side of the girl's face was purple and swollen, her eye was bloodshot. "Are you all right, my dear?"

"I'll survive."

"Go on, get out. I'll stay here, you go and find that little boy you said you were responsible for."

"What goes on? The gunman looked at the two women suspiciously.

"She's got to go," said Mildred, "She has to look after that young boy, the one she told you about."

"Crew stay," he replied.

"No, she must go. I'll stay, that will do won't it?" Before he had time to reply she pushed the stewardess forward. "Go on, go now."

"O.K." The man made room for the girl to pass. Mildred sat down next to the other young stewardess. "Come on dear, things'll be all right. Don't cry now, that only makes them feel more manly than ever." She handed over a handkerchief.

After what seemed like hours of haggling, and the appearance of yet more armed troops on the runway, the hijackers allowed all the passengers to leave. The plane now contained only the five remaining crew, and Mildred. Negotiations seemed to have reached an impasse. Mildred didn't know the language, but she could sense that there was a finality about things. She recognised that things were not going forward. The authorities would not give in, and the hijackers wouldn't either.

"I think they've reached a stalemate. Someone will have to compromise."

"The Afghan authorities won't compromise with hijackers," said the trembling stewardess. "I don't know what will happen now."

A message came through the radio, which was relayed through the cabin, there was a final call through the loud hailer, all in a foreign tongue, and then the troops opened fire.

Mildred heard two isolated shots from the flight deck, as a hail of bullets smashed into the aircraft, one of which killed the gunman nearby. His automatic was firing wildly, even as he fell. One of the shots hit the young stewardess in the chest, another smashed Mildred's left leg, and then, just as suddenly, all was quiet. She looked up to find troops swarming over the plane. Two of the hijackers were dead and the third badly wounded, the pilot and co-pilot had been shot dead, and the navigator was unconscious from a blow on the head. Mildred was carried off the plane to hospital.

Back in England a steel plate was inserted to repair her damaged leg, and after four months she could walk normally, though it ached in wet weather. The young stewardess recovered physically, but never went on an aircraft again. The navigator was soon back on duty.

Mildred continued her membership of the W.I. "Oh, it's really very interesting," she said. "You can attend lectures and talks, you can go on theatre outings, even take trips abroad. There's more to it than just jam and Jerusalem."

WHEN DARKNESS FALLS

"Ironically, for the same sum that it takes to train this guide dog, cataract operations could be carried out in India to save 100 people's sight".(From a TVS documentary, 2003)

For Rajin Lal the world grew grey. A pale grey, then a dark opaque grey; and eventually black. It need not have stayed that way, but it did, and the reason his world remained black was because Rajin Lal didn't have a hundred and fifty rupees.

For Tom Wilson there was nothing gradual about it. A split second's loss of concentration, a tearing of metal and breaking of glass as two cars collided, and Tom was left blind. Dark glasses concealed the vacant stare, and slowly he began the painful process of finding his way around his darkened world. Tom was a courageous man; resourceful, tough, and not at all sorry for himself. He accepted that he had not been as alert as he should have been, and he was grateful that the other driver hadn't been hurt. He wouldn't want that on his conscience.

A few months after leaving hospital he began to study braille, and the use of instruments. They had laughed at him when he started work as an engineering inspector, but they soon found that he was as good as the rest. If the components didn't fit the gauges he found it as easily as his fellow workers, and his braille micrometer was no less accurate than his colleagues' more conventional ones. There were limitations of course, but he managed to live within them.

Ten months after his accident he applied for a guide dog.

Meanwhile, four thousand miles away, in his grey world, Rajin stumbled over the threshhold he hadn't quite seen. The little village hut in which he lived was in an agricultural area, and Rajin owned two small fields from which he eked a living. His two brothers owned similar fields, which had once belonged to his father. With eight such the family had prospered, but with two of the fields going for his sister's dowry and the remaining six being divided amongst the three boys when the old man died, there was scarcely enough to support their wives and families.

Two years after the onset of the cataract, darkness fell over Rajin's world. He could no longer see enough to till the fields and sow the seed. His eight year old son walked with him, guiding the ox as it pulled the heavy plough, and Rajin scattered the seed into the newly turned furrows. "Father," said the boy, "On the radio in the village hut I heard that there is an operation to make you see. Why don't you have this operation?"

"Because it's too expensive. The headman told me of this operation, and it costs a hundred and fifty rupees. We do not have a hundred and fifty rupees, and so I cannot have the operation. We can't afford it."

"But we can't afford for you to be blind either," said the boy.

"To be blind costs nothing, my son, but the operation costs more than we have. That is the simple truth of the matter. Sometimes perhaps, one has to be blind to see the truth more clearly."

"We could sell the ox, or one of the fields."

"And then we would starve. Is that what you want?"

The boy didn't answer, and they continued the sowing in silence.

In Nottingham Tom Wilson collected his dog at last. The training sessions were over. He and Lucky understood each other, and it was time for him to take the dog home. He walked down the street, his hand lightly on the harness, aware of the subtle movements which alerted him to go right or left; he felt wonderful. He decided to eat out; a small celebration of his new found freedom. He had a little difficulty finding the entrance door of the restaurant, but Lucky took him in, and led him to a seat. A waitress came with a menu. He had to ask her to read some of the main items, before he placed his order.

"Some wine sir, or a beer perhaps?"

"No thanks, just coffee, please. I'm sorry, but can you tell me how much it comes to." It always embarrassed him, not being able to read the prices, but he was not a rich man, and price did matter.

"That will be just ten pounds," she said. "I'll bring you a

111

bill when you're ready."

The radio in the background was tuned to some highbrow financial discussion, and as he finished his coffee, Tom learned the somewhat irrelevant information that fifteen Indian rupees were equivalent to one pound sterling. As he paid his bill he idly calculated that lunch had cost him a hundred and fifty rupees. Put like that it seemed a lot, but of course he knew it wasn't.

WHEN I SHALL DIE

When I shall die, please shed no tears of grief,
I shall be gone, my memory just a ghost.
So let me go, don't hold to might have beens,
Or half forgotten dreams, which time has lost.

For if my soul awakes to a new dawn
Of some, as yet, unrealised tomorrow,
Facing some new life's challenges again,
I won't have time to think of joy or sorrow
Which once, on this earth, may have meant so much,
But There, will be like sounds of distant bells.
I will need to live the Life that's Present,
And leave this Past where once I used to dwell.

Or else there may be nothing, no new day,
No resurrection, no rebirth of me,
And I'll be nothing. Tell me, would you waste
Your tears on Nothing? Foolish, don't you think
To shed such precious jewels on emptiness?

So cry no tears of grief when I am dead,
Just leave me be, go live your life instead.
Dance on my grave, and let remembrance go.
For I would rather have you smile than weep,
Even though I may not see, or ever know.

HALF A COW

"What you need is dhallia."

We were on a five hundred mile ride and had just bought some samosas. We wanted something which we could carry with us, to eat later, and this was the advice given by the bunnia. He sold only cooked food, but he told us where to buy the dhallia.

"It will keep well, and you can boil it into porridge, or have it with fruit or nuts, and even eat it dry if necessary."

This sounded exactly what we were looking for. When we bought some we found that it was oats, coarsely crushed, and reminded us of the porridge we had in school. It was cheap and light so it was easy to carry some in the panniers. We cycled on our way with one problem solved, and a valuable piece of information for our future rides. One of these rides took us to Sarjanwar.

The village is about two miles from the Sarju River, from which it gets its name. Four or five miles down river is the Sarju ferry, probably the busiest part of this small river. The ferryboat has a single deck on which everything is crammed. A makeshift barrier protects the grain and foodstuffs from the other cargo. We boarded the ferry, protecting our bikes from inquisitive cattle and goats, wanting to eat the dhallia in our panniers, or, in the case of the goats, the panniers themselves. Once across the ferry we left the road and took the dirt track to the village. A dozen mud huts were scattered round a bare earthen maidan on which some children were playing tip-cat.

As soon as we arrived the Headman greeted us warmly. I can't say why. We weren't expected and our appearance was dusty and unprepossessing. Even so, he greeted us as welcome guests, and invited us into his house.

"You must stay here," he said.

We realised that this would leave him and his family with nowhere to sleep.

"The weather is warm and dry," he remarked. "It will be no hardship for us to sleep out."

We wouldn't dream of it we said, pointing out that we had

114

the tent to sleep in, and assuring his that it was quite adequate. Eventually we persuaded this kindly man, truly one of nature's gentlemen, that we would feel uneasy if we were to put him out of his home.

We erected the tent and showed him how comfortable it was, telling him that we often used it for weeks at a time, and were quite happy in it.

In the morning his daughter, Surjeeta, came shyly to give us two bowls of dhallia. She was about twelve, with thin arms and legs, and eyes that looked too large for her face. Classic signs of undernourishment. Could they really afford to give us their dhallia we wondered, but it would have been churlish to refuse their hospitality.

Though usually bulgar wheat, dhallia could include any grain, oats, barley or rye, according to whatever grew easiest in the region. The grain was crushed, since this was cheaper than rolling, and though this made it coarser it also made it more universally available. Ubiquitous dhallia we called it.

Surjeeta's bowls contained a porridge of boiled dhallia, and she offered some milk with it. We ate the food, and later took the bowls back to the Headman with our thanks. It was then that we learned a little of the village. They did a bit of fishing, there were a few fields and one cow from which they got their milk.

It was a scrawny animal which none the less was well cared for by the villagers and repaid them with a daily supply of milk. Not the huge yields of proper dairy cattle, and not the thick creamy milk we associated with the breakfasts we had at home. No, this was watery stuff, but enough for each family to have about a pau. Pau means a quarter, and in this case it meant a quarter of a seer, which equates to about half a pint for the day.

The headman insisted we were the guests of the village, and we were treated accordingly. Each morning Surjeeta came with a bowl of dhallia, and some milk. We were acutely aware that this meant that for the duration of our stay each family had a little less than its pau of milk. We pointed out that we had dried milk with us. The Headman was insistent. He would not take no for an answer, neither would he allow us to pay for our keep. We were visitors of the village. That was all there was to it.

Two days after we arrived the Government Inspector came. He came in a Jeep bearing the insignia of the Govt. Health Dept, and he inspected the cow. He proclaimed that it was ill, and had to be destroyed. The Headman protested, but the Inspector had the mystique of his phials of liquid, the authority of his white coat, and the Government Insignia on his Jeep. With the weight of officialdom behind him, his word was law. He pointed out that the village would be compensated to half the value of the cow. The Headman argued that one does not get much milk from half a cow, a sentiment with which we were forced to agree.

To no avail. The cow was destroyed. Because of brucellosis I believe. At breakfast the following morning the Headman himself brought our bowls of dhallia, profuse in his apologies that there was no milk. We ate it dry with a few raisins. The rest of the raisins we gave to the villagers and left them our powdered milk. There was little else to do.

In the end, however, there was a happy outcome. The story we wrote, the pictures we took, were published. It was the first article we had ever sold. When payment arrived we rode back to the village, only to get involved in an argument. The headman refused to take the money because he said it didn't belong to the village. We were eventually able to persuade him that it was their story, and the pictures were of their cow, hence the money belonged to the villagers. In fact, we told him, it had been given for them. He could hardly call us liars, so reluctantly, he accepted the money.

One does not get much milk from half a cow, but together with the Government compensation, he could now buy another. Nearly five weeks after their cow had been destroyed the villagers of Sarjanwar once again had milk with their morning porridge.

BOILED RICE

Palampur was the poorest village we had ever come across. A dozen or so mud houses huddled round a village maidan in which there was a pump and one stunted tree. The railway station bearing the name was five miles away, and the line veered off, away from the village. The road was little more than a dirt track, and even that seemed to come from the village rather than go to it.

Few people had heard of Palampur, and those who had, wondered if we had lost our minds to want to go there. The truth was that it was an area prone to sandstorms. We had experienced fires and floods, landslides and earthquakes, but never a hurricane or a sandstorm, and we were anxious to see what it was like.

From the station we cycled the five miles to the village. When we got there the Headman was welcoming, and said we could stay in his little hut, being prepared to sleep out in the open. We assured him that we would be perfectly comfortable in our tent, and despite his protestations we pitched camp between the last house and the fields of sparse crops. For three days nothing happened, and though the Headman warned us that storms were likely, we decided to move on. It was while cycling away from the village that the wind began to strengthen.

We had barely gone a mile before the road was covered in inches of sand which was blowing in our faces. The sand stung, and as the wind grew stronger we realised that it would be foolish to battle our way into it. We lay the bikes down to form a makeshift windbreak and settled down behind it.

By this time the storm was getting into its stride, and we couldn't leave our barricade without the danger having our skin blasted off. There was nothing to do but stay in the comparative safety of our windbreak. There was no real danger if we stayed put, but to put our heads over the top of our panniers was to be sandblasted. It would take only a minute or so to take the skin off us, maybe a little longer, but we didn't really want to find out.

I had heard of sand dunes singing, and never quite understood what this meant. As the wind whipped the tops of the dunes and spread a fine spray of sharp cutting sand along the road, there was a humming sound, sometimes the note was higher, sometimes lower. I wouldn't call it singing, but I supposed that this might be what was meant by saying the sand dunes sang.

For three hours we lay behind our protective barrier, and then the storm passed over. It didn't stop, but just moved off. We got up, shook off three inches or so of sand, and returned to the village. There ought to be some pictures and stories there, and that, after all, was what we had come for.

Back at Palampur there was frantic activity. Now that the storm had passed all the villagers were out gathering crops. Most of the leafy plants had been mostly blasted away, and what remained of their edible leaves was being hastily gathered. I had supposed that the root crops would be safe, but the Headman assured me that even root crops wouldn't grow if everything above ground had been destroyed. After the leafy crops had been gathered in the root crops had to be salvaged before they rotted in the ground, even though they were only half grown. We took only a few pictures before we realised that we should join in the salvaging.

The following month India celebrated its Independence. The whole country was on a high. The whole country, that is, except Palampur.

In India, the staple foods are wheat or rice. Wheat is made into various types of flapjack, the cheapest of which is chappatties. Wheat and water, without fat or flavouring. Rice is similarly made into pillau or fried rice, or again, just boiled. Neither the wheat nor the rice are particularly tasty and any flavour has to come from whatever is eaten with them. This may be curry or dal or some other vegetable dish, but these, however, cost money. For the poor it can be an important consideration as to what one eats with the cheap staple food.

All the crops were ruined. After the sandstorm, while the country celebrated, the villagers struggled to survive. What does one eat with boiled rice? During the autumn of 1947 Palampur did not ask such silly questions.

REVELATION

A single leaf,
Wafted on the winds of a thousand years,
Floating on the stream of a million tears
Of joy, or grief,
Turned and fell from the topmost twig,
Danced and swayed with the wind's caress,
Then, out of Time, and out of Space,
Hung for a moment, motionless.

The valley lost in a distant mist,
The mountains lost in a purple haze,
And silky clouds went drifting by,
And I heard faintest rustlings,
And saw pine needles green and dark
Silhouetted thin and stark
Against an autumn sky.

And there within that hillside wood
Where all but Nature was subdued
I sat upon a grassy slope
Alone amid the solitude.

And you found me there, as I knew you would,
All of an instant, there you stood
Before me deep in the solitude,
A sweet angelic creature,
And I in that instant knew,
I was one with the heart of Nature,
One with the soul of you.

THE PORTRAIT

Bob Snaith was a wizened little man of indeterminate age. His thin, sharp features and shifty eyes had earned him the nick-name of Foxy, a name which suited his temperament as well as his looks, for he was cunning rather than clever. A petty thief, Foxy made a precarious living by preying off his fellow man, and he had survived thanks to one clever idea, but even that he had stolen from another of his shadowy underworld companions.

Foxy read the obituaries. He was not interested in those who had died, that was not his business, and sympathy or regret was not in his nature. His interest lay in the funerals. Funerals meant empty houses, and people taken up with grief. They were preoccupied, they made mistakes, and Foxy profited. Other people's errors were Foxy's opportunities.

There was little in the obituaries column, but the facing page caught his attention. "Death of local entrepreneur". He read on.

"Thaddeus Wainwright, owner of Wainwright's foundry, was found dead at his home at ten o'clock this morning. The 71 year old factory owner is believed to have died of a heart attack during the night.

Many will remember that Wainwright's Foundry was started forty years ago on the site of the old cotton mill. Thaddeus, and his late wife Dollie, would be there early every morning, he setting the sand moulds and she doing the office work. Because of their sheer enthusiasm and energy, everyone wished them well, this big man with the ready smile, and his small fragile looking wife. Many in the town have friends or relatives who later found work at the foundry once it began to prosper, and many of the displaced cotton workers were glad of Wainwright's success, for it gave them work as well.

Yet success did not spoil this young couple. Thaddeus never forgot that wealth had to be earned, he was always ready to take off his coat and get stuck in with his workers. A popular man, he could be tough when required, but none would ever say he had anything but a heart of gold. In fact, he was so popular that he was several times invited to stand for council, and it was even suggested that if elected he might become mayor. But no; this self-made man had no desire for the political arena. He always declined with his usual gruff sincerity. 'Nay, Dollie would never have wanted that. I work with my hands. She would have made a fine first lady would my Dollie, but she's gone now, and what would you want with a great big dolt like me'."

The article went on about the merits of this local boy who had made good, but there was much which did not appear in the paper, much which Foxy did not know.

It was Dollie who wanted the big house, The Gables, and after she died Thaddeus had lived there alone. "I grew up without servants," he said to his children. "If I could do without them as a lad, surely I can manage without them as a man. Besides, it's no job for one man to hold another's coat, or pull the boots off another's feet."

"Haunted?" he would laugh, "Yes, I reckon it could be at that, but I've seen nowt. Dollie always said the place had an air about it, like spirits were around, but I've not sensed it. Still, I never had her perception, but what would a ghost want with Dollie and me, I ask you. No, I guess the thingummybobs, poltergeists or whatever, have better things to do, especially since Dollie's been gone. Haunted, well maybe, but it don't bother me. It's Dollie's house, and that's what matters."

In Foxy's mean little soul there was no regret for this man's passing, only the thought that here was a chance of profit. Thaddeus had no servants at the Gables, it said so in the paper, and if there were no servants the place would be empty. Quickly he read on to find the day and the time of the funeral, and when he knew that, he began to make his plans.

He waited and watched as the cortege left the house. Then, sneaking round the back he forced open a store-room window and scrambled in. Long practice had taught him where to look, and he soon found the drawing room, dim with drawn curtains, in respect for the dead. The parlour, Dollie had called it, and over the mantelpiece was a portrait of Thaddeus. It was the same picture Foxy had seen in the paper, but this was in full colour. An oil painting, and a good one too. Even in the gloom it was vibrant with life. The mouth was firm but with the faintest hint of a smile, the thick mass of grey hair gave the head an almost leonine appearance, and the eyes seemed to look straight at him. They seemed to follow him round the room as he quickly packed the valuable things into a case. Not for Foxy the sentimental mementos of hard earned and fondly remembered holidays; he went for real value, for things that he could sell.

The parlour door had stuck when he entered. A firm push had opened it readily enough, but Foxy was careful, he left the door ajar. There was no point in slowing his getaway. Everything was going according to plan, it always did. Funerals ran to time, and people never came back early. This was the one clever piece of knowledge which Foxy had learned all those years ago. He had checked discreetly at the crematorium. He knew exactly how long he had, and experience had taught him just how much could be done in half an hour. By the time the mourners returned he would be miles away in his nondescript little car. That was what kept Foxy out of jail, everything about him was nondescript, no-one ever remembered him.

He gave no thought to the upset which would result when they found the room ransacked. He was a practical man whose imagination didn't run to such flights of emotional fancy; but even so he found the room uncomfortable, and he was sweating slightly. The heating was on, probably in readiness for the funeral party's return, but it wasn't that. He put it down to the staring eyes of the portrait which followed him wherever he went, and to the rumours about the house being haunted. He didn't believe in such things of course, but they added to the tension which always accompanied a job. It paid to be tense, he told himself, he mustn't become slack. He had mates who had become too sure of themselves, and now they were rotting in jail. Foxy didn't believe in taking chances, and, as a result, Foxy had never been caught.

Having taken all that was of value in the parlour he turned to find the bedrooms. Normally he would have gone there first, but men living alone didn't keep jewellery in the bedroom. A watch and a ring perhaps, but that was all.

As he turned to leave, he was startled by the chimes of a clock. Three o'clock! He surely hadn't been so long! He decided to forego the bedrooms. It was time he left.

The door which he had left ajar seemed to have swung to, and as he turned the knob he realised that it was stuck again. It opened into the room and he couldn't push as he had done before. He had to pull on the knob, but pull as he might he could not open the door. He tried the window, hoping no-one would see the tell-tale movement of the curtains, but the window was fitted with security bolts and he had no idea where the key might be. He looked for something with which to break the glass, but all he could find was a heavy brass paper weight. "Wainwright's Foundry". The words were cast into the face. Foxy smashed it against the window. It simply bounced back, jolting his arm. He realised that the glass wasn't glass at all, it was unbreakable Makrolon. No amount of smashing paperweights at it was going to do any good, it would need a hammer. He went back to the door.

He was still tugging at the knob when the funeral party returned. The suitcase, full of silver and fine china figures, told its own story. There was no point in denial. As they led him away Foxy took one last glance at the portrait. The eyes looked straight at him, and the strong, firm mouth seemed to have just the hint of a slightly cynical smile.

MOTHER AND CHILD

Vaak crept forward silently. He could sense the presence of strangers near the dense undergrowth. Four or five hunters were looking in the woods for game to catch. They were native to the area, long limbed and slender, built for the chase rather than for foraging. Short and powerfully built, he was not afraid, but caution was an inbuilt part of his nature, besides, there was Imna to think of. She was due to have the child any day now, and she must be protected at all costs. In any case he wouldn't want to tangle with four of them.

The creeping cold had driven them south, the ice sheets covering the northern lands in which they had grown up, relentlessly forcing the tribe to abandon its habitual habitat. Imna was heavy with child and could not keep up the rapid pace. He had pulled and carried her where he could, but at last they had lost touch with the tail enders and been left on their own. That was when he had decided to enter this dense wood and find some sort of a shelter until she gave birth and could travel again.

As the tribe had moved south so they found other people occupying the land. Whether they had always lived here, or whether they too had been forced south by the change in climate Vaak didn't know, besides, he wasn't given to deep thought about hypothetical questions, it was problem enough to survive. Game was scarce, and the leaves and berries which were his main diet were hard to come by. The vegetation in this southern land was unfamiliar to him, and it was difficult to know what was safe to eat. He tasted everything first before he fed Imna, she must be nurtured and cared for, so that their child would be born healthy and grow up strong.

He gripped the thick piece of wood which he carried as a club, it was the only weapon he had, but the new people he had sometimes seen from a distance seemed to have other weapons, long slender poles with pointed ends which they could throw or jab at people without getting too close. Vaak would have liked such a weapon but though he had found poles a-plenty, he had no way of sharpening the ends to a point, and a thin pole without a point was less useful than his heavy stick with its knobbly end. He had lost all his tools on the journey south. Not that his tribe made many tools, they found sharp edged flints for scraping, or rounded ones for hammering, but as far as he knew few had ever made these things.

He kept as still and silent as he could. Food was scarce and any band of strangers was competition for resources, and therefore a threat. He had no wish to involve himself in any battles, especially with people who may well be better armed than he was. The four or five hunters moved slowly away, and Vaak breathed out through his open mouth to keep it soundless. Until they had gone he daren't seek the leaves and the white fungus on which they had been subsisting. When it was safe, he gathered what he could and took it to the shelter. He was hungry, very hungry, but he gave it first to Imna.

Words were difficult for him, and he couldn't tell her how much she meant to him, but he thought she knew. He was sure she felt the same about him.

She accepted the fungus gratefully, but was careful to leave at least half for him. After she had eaten the fungus she started on the leaves. They were bitter, but not unpleasantly so, and being hungry made them palatable. She knew that they would be safe to eat, despite their bitter taste. She had complete trust in Vaak. He had taken care of her since they had left their birthplace, all through the long exodus to this strange land, and he would continue to look after her as long as it was necessary. She knew that without any doubt.

She too had difficulty with words, but she placed her hand against his cheek in a gesture of tenderness, and he smiled quietly.

Suddenly a spasm of pain gripped her. She moaned and doubled up. Vaak, alarmed at her discomfort, took hold of her, but she gestured to him that it was the baby. The spasm went, and then, in a minute or so, it came again. She moaned quietly as the pain came and subsided, and between the spasms Vaak held her gently making soft soothing noises.

This must have gone on for about an hour, and then, the

baby was born. It gave a healthy cry, and Imna bit through the cord. Where had she learned that? She hadn't, it was instinct, and it was instinct too, which made her put the infant to her breast. Even though there was no milk as yet the infant sucked strongly. Gradually the milk began to flow. She gave a contented smile and after a while, held out the child to Vaak.

He took it with trepidation, meanwhile gazing at Imna with puzzlement and wonder. When they were still with the tribe he had learned that women had babies, but he had never been present at such an event, and now here he was with his own child, their child. He looked at Imna with adoration. In all the world there had never been such a child, and in all the world there had never been such a woman as Imna. As he handed back the baby he wished he could tell her how much she meant to him.

Exhausted she lay back with the child on her bosom. It was nearing dusk, and there was not much time to go foraging. Vaak decided to call it a day. He lay down beside Imna and put one arm over her and the child. They fell into a deep and peaceful sleep.

It was a fantastic find. A complete family group. The dig had thrown up little of interest till now, but this was incredible. Three skeletons, almost intact, in a shallow rock depression, beneath layers of soil, deposited by thousands of years. No tools, no artefacts, no sign of a struggle. The last wasn't surprising, the head of the spear was still embedded in the woman's chest. All soft tissue had, of course, long since gone, but three complete skeletons, and in a particularly poignant posture. It was the find of a lifetime. The archaeologists tried to piece it together.

Potassium-argon dating put the fossilised bones at 360 thousand years. The short bowed legs and facial features caused some argument. Neanderthal? No, too large a brain case for that argued one, but certainly not Homo sapiens, the limbs were not long enough and straight enough for that, and the jaw too heavy. The man would have been about five foot four inches tall and the woman five inches shorter, say four eleven. Homo sapiens were taller than this, and in addition, there were no weapons. Who were these people? Controversy reigned.

In the end the consensus was that they were either Homo ergaster or Home erectus, but it was never agreed which. What the experts did agree on was that they were not Homo sapiens. They were unlikely to have had the ability to make sophisticated tools, nor to have developed the power of speech, nor the mental capacity for love and affection.

No, not homo sapiens, they decided, certainly not at all like humans.

PEACE AND QUIET

We put the house on the market. 'Charming four bedroom family home in quiet village, favourably priced for quick sale.'

The old vicarage at Nether Compton was indeed a charming old place, and many of our friends were surprised that we should wish to move from it. Just down the road was the church of St. Nicholas, and behind the church was the graveyard, and an ancient Saxon barrow.

"Well," said Janice, when we viewed it, "At least the neighbours will be quiet!"

The church was now handled by the Vicar from Compton Manor, and the Nether Compton vicarage had been put on the market. It needed a bit of work to modernise it, but we had taken that into account in the price we paid. All in all it was a satisfactory transaction, everyone involved being happy with the outcome.

We moved in, and for the first few weeks had builders coming and going, but eventually they finished. Peace at last.

It was good to go to bed without negotiating the obstacle course of tools along the stairs, to have a bath without first cleaning out the grit left by plasterers and carpenters, and to eat a meal which didn't taste of cement or emulsion.

Sunday was the least peaceful day, because of the church bells, but we didn't mind. The St. Nicholas bells were particularly melodious, and rang out with an air of joyfulness which was quite refreshing after the week's work in the city. At least, so it was to start with.

As the weeks went by, and the summer approached, the bells took on a harsher note. I suppose it was the expansion of the metal, but there was no longer the same joyousness in the sound, in fact to my ears it took on a melancholy, and as the days grew warmer, I felt the sound become oppressive, almost menacing.

"Don't be silly," said my wife. "How can church bells be menacing?"

How indeed? It was silly. In any event I'm practically

tone deaf. I told myself that even if the sound had changed, my ears weren't sensitive enough to have picked it up.

I was just about to dismiss the whole thing as imagination when I noticed the dog's behaviour. The stray had wandered in one wet afternoon. We fed it some scraps, and after that it wouldn't go. Since we couldn't find its owner it took up residence in the utility room. We allowed it to come and go as it wished, believing that one day it would disappear as mysteriously as it had come, but three months later it was still there.

Usually it went walkabout on Sunday, but this Sunday the door was closed. The bells started their clangour, and the dog immediately rushed to the old settee and tried to hide itself under it. Failing to get under, he cowered behind it and whimpered pathetically until the bells stopped for a while. When it started again, with the tolling of a single bell, the dog again showed signs of fear and distress.

"What's up boy?" I reached out to stroke him, but he shrank away from me, towards the door. As soon as I opened it, he rushed out.

"There's something odd, "I said. "Even old Bonzo doesn't like the bells."

"Nonsense, it's just the pitch, probably hurts his ears. You're imagining things. It's a lovely old church. It's a pity that the congregation is too small for it to have its own vicar." My wife is an eminently practical woman, not easily upset by what she calls my imaginings. For her the peal of the bells was part of the charm of the village, and though not a churchgoer herself, she still felt that every village should have its own church. "Something essentially English about it, if you know what I mean," and you couldn't argue her out of that.

Not that I wanted to. I would have been more comfortable to have argued myself into her pragmatism than have her worrying like me. Even so, I couldn't get it out of my head, and the dog hadn't helped. Why had he been so upset, and where had he run off to?

June the twenty first dawned dull and grey. "Summer solstice," I thought, "longest day of the year, and here we are with typical English weather." I felt unusually edgy, but my musing was interrupted by a knock on the door.

I had seen the woman occasionally. She lived in one of the small cottages on the outskirts of the village. Close up she seemed more markedly gipsy than I had noticed. "Yes?"

"Have you seen a goat?" she asked. "Black and white goat, with horns, and a wicked look in his eye."

"No,"I replied. "If I do see him I'll let you know. What's your phone number?"

"That won't be no good, we got no phone, see. If you see him you catch him if you can, otherwise it'll be too late."

"Too late? For what?"

"Just too late, that's all." She seemed flustered, as though she'd already said more than she ought.

"Right, if I see him I'll try to catch him. Then I'll bring him back to you."

"No, not to me, he's not mine. He's ... he's not mine."

"Then what do I do with him?"

"I don't rightly know, but catch him, and don't let him go till tomorrow." She turned away and practically ran out of the gate before I could ask any more.

The day was oppressively warm and muggy, and there was thunder in the air. I found myself looking out of the window. I didn't see any signs of a goat, but if there was a storm it would presumably seek some shelter.

As the day dragged by my head began to ache. I wanted to go to bed, but somehow it seemed too light to sleep. Ten o'clock, half past, eleven struck and still it wasn't fully dark. It must have been about quarter to twelve when I was startled to hear the church bells. Who on earth was ringing them at this time of night? I went downstairs to peer out, and it was then that I heard the chanting. Weird chanting, coming from the direction of the graveyard. I looked that way and my breath caught in my throat.

There was a group, all dressed in winding cloths, coming down the barrow and dancing among the gravestones. Ghosts? Surely not. Ghosts don't really exist, and it's too much of a cliche for them to be dancing round the gravestones. No, it must be the villagers, up to some strange ritual of their own. But at the front of the line, walking on two legs, and leading them in the dance, was a black and white goat. Except that it wasn't really a goat. As the clouds parted and the moon shone through, I could see it more clearly. More like a satyr.

It faced me, and I could see, even from that distance, how it beckoned me to join them in the dance. I found myself wanting to go.

Janice joined me, took one look at the scene outside and screamed. "Janice," I yelled, "grab my hand, don't let go of me, they're trying to lure me to them."

She gripped me then, and kept hold of me. Something was pulling me towards the window. Janice was hanging on to my arm with all her strength, but she was losing the battle. I was being drawn closer and closer to the open window, and I knew that once there I would be pulled away. The dancers were weaving in and out among the gravestones, still led by the goat, but its eyes were fixed in my direction and I could feel that inexorable pull. The storm seemed all around, the wind howled through the room. I wound my arm around the table leg and held on for dear life. Suddenly Janice let go.

"Stop," I screamed, but too late. She ran.

I was being dragged, and the heavy old-fashioned refectory table was being dragged with me. I heard an unearthly chuckle, and I saw the face of the satyr. It was triumphant. I couldn;t resist much longer. I tightened my grip, but the pull on me increased. It was only a matter of time. My arm was already tiring, my grip weakening. I braced my feet against the wall, determined not to give in. The wind increased, and I could hear the clanging discordant pealing of the bells.

Then Janice rushed past me. "No!" I cried as she headed for the window. "Janice, no!"

For just a moment she was at the open window, and then she was through, blown by the storm. I let go my grip and ran to help her, only to see her rising to her feet, braced against the wind, and as I joined her the throng surrounded us, dancing around us, hemming us in. The weird chanting rose and fell in unearthly rhythm, and as the throng circled I could see the Satyr between us and the house.. No way back. I put my arm around Janice to support her against the blast which was threatening to knock her down. She pushed something in my hand. It was the crucifix which used to hang above our bed.

The Satyr approached, with a fearful leer. I felt lost against the ancient force which was engulfing us. I took the heavy crucifix and wielded it like a club, but he just laughed, and kept coming.

"Not like that," shouted Janice, and taking my hand in hers she held up the cross before us. Immediately the Satyr stopped.

"Go!" I yelled. "Begone, you devil, go back you dead. In the name of the Father, go!"

There was a terrible scream as the Satyr looked at the cross, and then a shuffling sound as the figures in their winding robes faded from sight. Left alone, the Satyr stared at us with a mixture of hate and fear, and then it turned and ran off into the night.

I put my arms around my weeping wife. "It's all right now, it's gone. Let's go home."

The wind died down, but I didn't let go of the crucifix until we were safely inside, with doors and windows locked.

We were awake for the rest of the night, not daring to sleep. When morning broke I looked out over the garden, and beyond it, to the graveyard.. There were no signs of the storm, none at all. It might never have happened. The dog had returned, and up on the barrow a black and white goat was peacefully browsing.

'The Old Vicarage, Nether Compton. Charming four bedroom family home in quiet village, favourably priced for quick sale.'

WHAT'S IN A NAME?

Lovely Walters was a sweet girl, but the credit was hers, not her parents'. They had stacked the cards against her by naming her Lovely.

Beauty is in the eye of the beholder, and in the eyes of the fifteen year old boys, Lovely was regarded as plain. Not ugly, by any means, but unprepossessing. Given her sweet nature, this would not have mattered at all, except that her name drew immediate attention to the fact that, in terms of physical beauty, she fell short of her mother's expectations.

When parents think of naming their offspring they generally choose names which they like themselves. It is, however, important that they do not at the same time inflict on the children a burden to bear through their school days, and possibly longer.

Mr. and Mrs. Barber presumably did not foresee that Alison would be faced with a contraction of her name, and consequent jokes from her playmates. Ali, in fact, had a trying time of it until she reached her teens, when her class finally outgrew the story of the forty thieves. Similarly Mr. and Mrs. Case need not to have named their son Justin, unless of course, they intended to hedge their bets!

Colleen Batty was reasonably satisfied that her parents had done her no wrong, but her sister Madeleine was upset when her name was shortened to Maddy. Maddy Batty was an outcome which her parents had not expected, and Maddy did not appreciate. The Welsh, somehow, seem to have solved the problem of the diminutive, especially in the case of boys. Bob Roberts, Ted Edwards, and Bill Williams all sound rather better than their unshortened and repetitious originals.

Most names are perfectly unremarkable unless we find them in some particular context. There is nothing at all wrong with the name Curry, until that is, he planned to marry Miss Rice. The wedding announcement of Curry and Rice inevitably raised a smile, but at least they had the satisfaction of knowing that they did go well together!

I knew of a girl called Iona Boot. This was inocuous enough until she was introduced to a colleague of mine. "Iona Boot, meet Ivor Slipper!"

These are matters of pure chance, and noone can be blamed, assuming indeed that any blame should ever be attached, but there are cases where one is bound to feel that parents should have been more careful. My father had a schoolmate called Felix Aloysius Smith. He became the best fighter in the school! It is also just as well that the all-in wrestler, Big Daddy, was big enough and fierce enough to hold off any would be mickey takers, for his christened name was Shirley! And when Mr. and Mrs. Pipe named their son Duane it was surely an unnecessary complication in his young life. Duane Pipe is unlikely to please him even when his school days are far behind.

Our second son had a narrow escape. We decided to call him Kim. This has subsequently become almost exclusively a female name, and I have no doubt that he is pleased we forgot it at the last minute. We remembered it started with a K, but couldn't think of it when the Registrar was there. Thus he became Kevin, and not Kim. He regards this as a lucky escape!

Cann should not be teemed with Gerald, however much the Canns may like the name. Gerry Cann, Gerry Builder and such, will do poor Gerald no favours.

Miss Garden should not perhaps be called Rose, and if one's surname is Flower, names such as Violet and Primrose are maybe best avoided. There is no maybe about Miss Worth. She felt decidedly undervalued when called Penny.

At our school, there was a childish joke that Janet May, but Susan Wood. Childish indeed, until a teenage pregnancy showed that Susan did! Janet, I am glad to say, remained problematic. Childish too, because nothing can be done about the names, and there is nothing wrong with either, except to the ears of unkind, puerile schoolboys. However, parents should remember that schoolboys are unkind and puerile, and wherever possible should choose with care.

Indeed, to you your child may be a rose, but some other name may serve as well, or possibly even better!

WOODY

When I went to feed the goats Woody was lying down. He didn't get up even for his food, and showed no interest in either his cereal or his hay.

I stooped down to stroke his head, and noticed that there was blood above his eye. "What's the matter, old boy?"

He looked at me dolefully. There is very little expression on a goat's face, but there can be a look in the eye, or something about the tilt of the head, which conveys how they are feeling. Woody wasn't feeling right, that much was evident.

"Come on, get up and eat something." He tried, but he fell down again and bumped his face against the manger. It was clear how he had cut his eye. More alarming was the fact that he couldn't get up. It is disturbing when a pet won't get up, it is even worse when they want to, and can't.

I put straw all round, and a sack over him to keep him warm. Then we phoned the vet. There was nothing obvious to find, and he gave Woody an injection of antibiotics along with something to encourage his appetite.

By evening he still hadn't eaten. I tried, but he didn't seem to want any food. I used a syringe to give him some water. His brown eyes kept following me as I got some feed for Jack, the other goat, and when I took Jack in for the night Woody tried to get up once more. All he succeeded in doing was to bump his face again.

Next morning we called the vet again. The advice was to put him down. A blood sample taken the previous day had not given the vet any clues, but Woody had not eaten for twenty four hours and had drunk only when water was syringed into his mouth. All day, and through the night, he had been unable to get up. From new injuries it was apparent that he had tried.

The following afternoon the decision was made. I sat with his head on my lap while he was injected with barbiturate. It seemed to take an age to have any effect. When there was no apparent effect the vet gave him another injection.

"Come on Woody, go to sleep. I kept stroking his face.

Lying there, with the side of his face on my lap, one eye looked up at me, and I felt it was reproachful. I got the distinct impression that he didn't want to go.

"Are you sure we're doing the right thing?"

"We can't leave him like he is,was the reply. I could agree with him there, but would time effect a cure? The vet thought not. "How old is he?"

He was sixteen. Goats live about fifteen years, so perhaps it was time for him. I bowed to the vet's greater wisdom. In any case, there was no going back now, he had already had two massive doses of barbiturate.

All I could do was to stroke his face and talk to him quietly, hoping I had made the right decision.

How much, I wonder, do animals understand what we try to do? I feel sure that Woody knew I was killing him. What I'm not sure was whether he was so ill that he was ready to die, or whether he wanted to struggle on. All I had to go on was the expression, imagined or real, in his eye, and the fact that he was not responding to the injections as we expected.

It must have been about twenty minutes, though it felt longer, that we sat there, the vet and I, with Woody's head resting on my lap. The stethoscope still indicated a steady heartbeat. "He should have gone by now," said the vet.

"I don't think he wants to go," I said. "I still think we might be making a mistake."

"No. He can't get up, he can't stand, and he won't eat. There is nothing else to do. It would be cruel to leave him."

And, of course, there were the barbiturates already in his system.

"I'll have to give him some more. His veins and arteries are so collapsed that I may not have got it into his blood stream properly. I'll inject straight into his heart It will be a more certain way to get it into his system."

The large needle looked horrible. I expressed my doubts, but fortunately, Woody didn't seem to feel it. "He can't feel anything," said the vet. "I wouldn't do it if I thought he might."

Five minutes later Woody was dead. We had had him

since he was four months old.

We buried him in the paddock.

There was something ignominious about covering him with the sacking, and then putting concrete slabs on top of him to protect him from any scavengers. It would have been even worse if some animal had tried to dig him up.

We made the mistake of not letting Jack see Woody's body. I believe that had we done so he would have known he was dead, and would have accepted it. Instead, he was inconsolable. For a fortnight he did nothing but bleat and we finally had to get another goat from a sanctuary to keep him company. After a shaky start they settled down. The sanctuary goat, Stormy, was not Woody, and Jack kept this in mind for several weeks, but he did stop showing so much distress, and they eventually became friends.

Meanwhile, I am left with my uncertainties. Was I right to have Woody put down? I shall probably never know. One does one's best, with the facts available. The fact I would have liked to have had was Woody's opinion. It is something I still wish I could have had. One does one's best, but is that enough? I tell myself that it has to be, but I have my doubts, I really do

LINES TO A HOSTEL ROOM

I turn the key, and there you are,
The shattered dream of something far,
Of home, of home across the sea,
Where all my hopes and fancies are;
Of all the things that used to be
On last year's tattered calendar.

Living, vaguely discontent,
I think of times that I have spent,
Of pensive hours when we would lie
By that old tree, grotesquely bent,
Which twists its branches to the sky
Like some outlandish monument.

Beneath those gnarled and twisted boughs
How oft the old eternal vow's
Been pledged, how oft a maiden's breast
Pillowed soft comfort to a brow
Grown furrowed in some sweet unrest;
How many loves, forgotten now?

Some day, perhaps, once more I'll stand
In that so far, so distant, land,
With that one most special She
Neath those same branches, hand in hand.
But there you are, I turn the key,
You do not, cannot, understand.

THE ELIZABETHAN COTTAGE

We live in a changing world, yet nostalgia has perhaps never been so popular. The other day we were going to Brighton, and somewhere along the A27, we passed a Restaurant, The Elizabethan Cottage. There are many cottages dating from the reign of Elizabeth, though one can't help wondering whether they are still the original cottages or not. How much have they been repaired, and with what? The answer may well be similar to the virtues of hand knitted socks. If one replaces the feet when they need it, and the tops occasionally, they will last for a very long time.

So it is with Elizabethan cottages. New thatch is to be expected, but over the years there has probably been the odd wall reconstructed, and a few well chosen alterations carried out. Is the original cottage still visible, still recognisable? Or is the structure standing before us so restored that it cannot really claim to be Elizabethan? I would not know. Particularly would I not know about the Elizabethan Cottage Restaurant, for we flashed by in my daughter's car, and did not stop to savour the Restaurant's no doubt excellent cuisine

I wish we had, for it may have satisfied my curiosity as to what the owners may have done with the original cottage, to prepare it nostalgically for the twenty-first century. It was at the very end of the sixteenth century that Good Queen Bess granted the charter for the East India Company. Now, four hundred years later, it seems that the Elizabethan Cottage is still going strong. What, you may wonder, is the connection between the two? Just this, that the Cottage, has, as its full name, The Elizabethan Cottage Tandoori Restaurant.

I wonder whether Queen Bess would have approved? I fancy she may have done, for she had embraced Raleigh's potatoes, and his tobacco, and rumour has it, Raleigh himself. She was from all accounts an adventurous sort, and may well have fancied the culinary flavours of Tandoori cooking, though whether she would have appreciated the reversal of British emigration by having the Indians coming here, bringing their spicy food and foreign ways of preparing it, is rather more doubtful. Except, of course, that it may not have been quite so foreign in her time. Contrary to what I always believed, the sixteenth century Indians did not curry everything. They had a much more mundane diet. It was not until the seventeenth century that the chilli was introduced from Mexico, and hot curry came into being.

Elizabeth may therefore have gone into the Cottage, and partaken of a meal which she might have quite enjoyed, and which may not have been so far removed from what she was used to. The Indian owners could have greeted her as the Mother of the Empire, and would no doubt have given her the meal free of charge. But no, such fanciful imaginings are not correct, and have no basis in fact. For there was then no Empire, and the Indians would still have been subject to the Moguls, and Elizabeth was not seen as a mother figure, not even by the British, let alone the Indians.

But what strange musings went on in my head when I saw that sign as we whizzed by. The Elizabethan Cottage Tandoori Restaurant! It conjures up the most bizarre of images, and I can only hope that the locals do not feel historically deprived by the smell of spicy food in what ought to be a listed building. I would hope, instead, that they feel enriched by this added dimension to four hundred years of architectural heritage.

The history of most nations is full of foreign incursions, and Britain is no exception. Elizabeth was a Tudor. There were Stuarts, and Hanoverians after her, and Normans and Saxons and Romans before. At least the present Queen need have no fear that the occupiers of the Elizabethan Cottage are planning to occupy her throne as well as her cottage. I guess they will be content to continue plying their trade, and hopefully making enough money to keep them out of trouble. In this way they will not give the immigrant community a bad name. And, after all, a small change of diet now and then can scarcely do anyone much harm!

HINDU KUSH

Have you ever camped up in the Hindu Kush
With the temperature twenty below?
Where the mountains reach for the wintry sky,
With icy fingers of snow

Above the peaks there's a cold dead moon
That shines so awfully clear,
And the quiet is an almost tangible thing
That seems to strain the ear,
And half awake in your sleeping bag
With a shock you suddenly hear
The hungry howl of a mountain wolf
That chills your blood with fear.

And the answering cry of the starving pack
Sets you wondering if they can scent
The sweat of fear, the smell of food,
That is you, in the flimsy tent.

And you tell yourself that they won't come in
For the tent might be a snare,
And you tell yourself that they won't come in
As you offer up a prayer.
You remind yourself of the things you've heard,
How wolves won't come near the embers
And you wonder if the camp fire's out,
And you struggle to remember
Was the fire still going, was the ash still red?
You'll be safe in a tent they said
But what if they're wrong you think with dread;
You should throw a stick on the embers.

It means opening up the flap of the tent,
It means venturing out in the snow,
It means being seen if the wolves are there,
But you must go out or you'll never know.

So you crawl out of the little tent,
And yards away there's a wolf.
The hairs rise up on the back of your neck
As your eyes meet his 'cross a hungry gulf.
So you stare at each other, forever it seems,
Some unspoken message goes out, and back,
Then the spell is broken, a throaty growl
As the wolf goes off to join his pack.

Throw a stick on the embers, go back in the tent,
Spend a wakeful night in the frozen hush,
And swear to yourself that never again
Will you camp in the Hindu Kush.

PEACE

"Peace!" cried the dolphin, but his voice was drowned in the noise. War was unknown to the race, and legend had it that millions of years ago they had returned to the water rather than join the constant strife and turmoil which overtook the land.

Not that the oceans were without their perils, but these were individual, not global. He was large enough, and strong enough to ward off the predatory shark, and the clasping tentacles of the giant squid. They left him alone, as they had left his ancestors alone, long ago, in those far off days of the return to the sea.

In the racial memory were long ages of peaceful evolution. An intelligent race, they lived in harmony with the ocean, adapting so perfectly that they had no need for technology.

Through a system of logic unknown to man, something akin to meditation and insight, they found out about their origins, of the Great Whale who had created all, and to whom all things returned. Yet they knew it for a symbol; no more than an attempt to bring that great unknown Creator one small step closer to their comprehension.

By thought and discussion they had found the key to this and other problems: the air which they still needed, and the space beyond the air. They knew of the cycle of the stars and the birth of the galaxies, but had no wish to visit them. And they knew of the beauty of Earth.

Then man had brought the noise. He had subdued the animals, and taken over the habitable areas of the land; and he had sailed upon the water. This had not affected them, but in the last hundred years he had embarked upon the oceans with mechanical ships, the noise of which penetrated the quiet depths, disturbing their thoughts and drowning out their discussions.

They called and were not heard. They called, and for reply they got the thud thud thud of the engines and the turbulence of the propellers, or else they were caught in the tangle of the nets. On a personal level they saw these things as individual tragedies, but on a racial level it stopped their evolution. Intelligence, far older than Man's, had still not grasped the elusive concepts of Truth, and among these constant interruptions, the finding, the bonding, the mating, fell to a level which endangered the survival of the race.

They wondered what to do. Man would have waged war, but war was alien to their nature. Unable to communicate over the vast distances of the ocean, they congregated, by some instinctive consent, near the Sargasso sea. There, among the thousands gathered with minds concentrated on one single problem, a strange thing happened. The tiny electrical currents, set up by their thoughts, were amplified by the numbers thinking in unison, and ships crossing the area found that their instruments did not work. Anything electromagnetic went out of alignment, compasses pointed in wrong directions, computers gave unpredictable results, even satellite observations could not be properly relied upon. Vessels were lost without trace, and ships began to avoid the area.

The elders of the race were aware of the losses, but it took time for them to determine the cause. When they did, a careful decision was taken. They could not wage war. It was against their belief, and against their nature. Who was to know where the future of the planet lay? They already knew enough to know that whatever road evolution may take, it would be from one of the warm blooded species that the final outcome would grow. That may be from the mammals of the land, or the whales, or the dolphins, or the seals, or perhaps it may stem from the birds, who swam their way among the clouds. Evolution could come from any of these, and they could not battle against these creatures, because if they did, they might be killing the future of the planet itself.

But they could think! They set up a rota, and grouping together, turn and turn about, they thought. The early experiments, in the region of the Sargasso sea, were haphazard affairs. Aircraft as well as ships, went down, and a legend was born, the tale of the Bermuda triangle. It caused their race a deal of sadness, but these were incidental casualties, and they knew that the general trend of evolution was not endangered. Gradually

144

they were able to perfect their techniques, gradually the control grew better and the range grew wider; and gradually Man, without discovering why, found the seas untenable.

And Man, though an infant in philosophical matters, was a technological genius. Unable to find a solution to the problem, he found an alternative. He took to the air.

When the last great tankers ran aground, when the last throbbing engines were stilled, then the sonic tones of discussion could once again be heard. "Peace!" cried the dolphin, and so far did it carry through the water, that it was minutes before the reply came back. "Peace!" echoed the whale from the Arctic, and "Peace!" shouted the porpoise as he rode the tropic waves.

PALLA

The fishermen on the Indus fish for palla. It is a river fish, known to biologists as hilsa ilisha, and it seems to have more bones than a herring.   When I was in India I didn't know the scientific name, and the local name of palla seemed quite adequate.

The fishermen on the Indus have no boats, they are too poor to have boats, so they fish for palla by they swimming out into the river with a net and save their catch on a long spike until they swim back to the bank. All of this must seem terribly simple, and so it should, for the palla fisherman is a simple man, but there are complications to the apparent simplicity.

For a start the Indus is tidal for a fair distance from the estuary. This causes some tricky currents which makes swimming difficult. Add to this the fact that there are crocodiles in the river. Swimming, and more particularly fishing, is not made easier by these marauding reptiles. Then there are the thorn trees which are occasionally uprooted by the currents and float down the river. Being thorns, rather than wood, they tend to be half submerged. They can be easily seen from above, but to a swimmer they are practically invisible. You may wonder why this matters. It matters because if the swimmer gets caught among the thorns he will begin to bleed. When the blood gets carried in the water the crocs will smell it, and come in to investigate. But they will find little, because long before the crocodiles the turtles will home in on the unfortunate swimmer and nibble him to bits.

There is some controversy about how well turtles can distinguish colour, and their sensitivity to smell. On the Indus it is firmly believed that the turtles can smell, or perhaps taste, very dilute concentrations of blood in the water, and the fishermen are more wary of turtles more than they are of crocodiles. Fresh water turtles are omnivorous, and though they have no proper teeth they have sharp bony ridges in their mouths. A few dozen turtles snapping at a man will very soon reduce him to a skeleton. Before this happens, however, the crocodiles arrive to complete the carnage.

It is against this background that the palla fishermen tie gourds round their waist to keep them afloat, and swim out with a long forked stick. Reaching the open river away from the bank they float downstream. A net stretched across the fork catches the fish and a long spike stores them. When the fisherman reaches the end of his particular stretch of river he swims to the bank, walks back to where he started, deposits his catch, and swims out to repeat the whole process again.

It is an inefficient and time consuming way to earn a living, but I repeat, the fisherman do not have the money to buy boats. Poverty causes them to risk their lives in this constant struggle to surive. Most of them do, but not all.

To augment their income they will also cook the fish for you, but only round about sunset, after the fishing time is over. The filleted fish is cooked on a griddle, almost dry, with only the oil which comes from the fish itself. There may be a little river water to prevent it burning, but this soon dries off, and various spices are added. It is not a conventional curry, but I can vouch for the fact that it is delicious. It is also very satisfying to pay them some money for a lot less risk than is involved in catching the fish.

One particular man who almost didn't survive still fished, but also got money from tourists to whom he would show a row of three crocodile teeth embedded in his skull. His story was that he had been caught by the croc but had managed to get free. Whether the story was true, and whether the teeth were really embedded I don't know, but they were certainly there, apparently stuck in his head. At least it gave him an additional source of income. Unfortunately there weren't enough tourists at that time for him to get much money out of it, but who knows, there may be many more by now. And who knows, by now the Government may have realised that the palla fishermen do need to have boats, if only for the sake of safety and because of common decency.

But I left the newly formed state of Pakistan nearly sixty years ago. The Indus has had huge dams built across it for irrigation, and I doubt if there are many crocodiles or turtles in these reservoirs. The fishermen are safer than they were. The palla is still plentiful, and regarded as a delicacy, which has led to fish farming. No longer are they caught by the use of gourds and nets on forked sticks. Put it down to progress, but in terms of survival, the palla fisherman could well find that modern business interests may ultimately be no safer for him than the crocodiles and turtles.

THE HOLIDAY

My name is being Ram Das Gupta, and I am working as a clerk on the East Indian Railway. Today, however, I am not working as a clerk, because today is my holiday. For the holiday I am on the train going to Dehra Doon, because I want to see the games. I am taking with me my binoculars, and a camera with a long lens, what is called telephoto, and makes the games much closer. I am very interested in watching the games, and near Dehra Doon there are many big games, especially the leopard, the antelope and the wild boar.

I am having the compartment to myself, but just before the train leaves there comes into the seat opposite me a soldier. He is having a gun and a long knife, what is called I think a bayonet, and he is drinking whiskey. His eyes they are red, and I am deciding that he is slightly drunk.

The train starts and he drinks more whiskey, straight from the bottle without benefit of glass.

"Hello Babuji," he says, "are you going far?"

"To Dehra Doon, Sahib, I am going to see the big games".

He drinks more whiskey and looks at me with a red eye. "That's where I'm going. We'll go together. Here, have a drink."

"Thank you, Sahib, but I am not one for drink."

"Suit yourself, more for me." He takes more whiskey, and begins to sharpen the big knife.

After a long silence, and more drink, he says to me "Babuji, what is that?"

"It is my lota, Sahib, my drinking vessel."

"I don't like it. Throw it out."

"But Sahib," I am protesting.

He looks at me with a red eye, and sharpens the big

knife. Quietly I am throwing it out.

"Have a drink," he says again, handing me the whiskey. There is no glass and he has drunk from the neck of the bottle. I do not like drink, and there is also the matter of caste, but he is looking at me with a red eye and sharpening the big knife. Quietly I am taking a sip. It is burning my throat, and I am thinking that Krishna will perhaps forgive me, for he is a wise god, and knows that all men cannot be heroes.

After another silence he says, "Babuji, what is that?"

"It is my turban Sahib, to keep my head from the sun."

"There is no sun inside the train. Throw it out."

"But Sahib, there will be sun in Dehra Doon."

He looks at me with a red eye and sharpens the big knife. Quietly I am throwing it out.

The train she is stopping! I am putting my head out of the window. I am shouting "Guard! Guard!"

The guard he is walking towards me. I am shouting again, with urgency, "Guard, Guard." The guard he is running.

He is looking at me with a red eye and sharpening the big knife. Quietly I am saying, "Guard, what is time please?"

At Dehra Doon we are leaving the train, and the soldier is insisting that we share a tonga to the hotel. It is my misfortune that we are both at the same hotel, even greater, that we are in rooms which are next to each other.

In the morning I am rising early to go to the Doon forest and watch the games. But though I am early I see the Sergeant already at breakfast. He calls me over to his table and insists that we go together to the Forest. "I have hired a Shikari," he says, "who really knows the Forest, so we'll have the best views of the animals. I hope to shoot some."

"I am not one for shooting Sahib, I wish only to take photographs, and observe."

"Well you observe, I'll shoot, You'll see more than you will on your own."

I am not happy about going with him, but he is having his gun, and his eyes are still very red. I am not wishing to offend.

The Shikari arrives and we go off to the Doon forest, and deep among the trees we climb into a machan. "Here Babuji, have a drink."

"No, really Sahib, I am not one for drink."

"Oh go on, loosen you up a bit." He leans over to be giving me the bottle. He is losing his balance and with a shout he is falling from the machan. It is sixteen feet to the ground. He is breaking his leg.

The shikari and I lift him onto a make shift stretcher and take him out of the forest, where we are finding a tonga to take us to the hospital. The doctor is saying that he will have to stay for twelve days.

Meanwhile, the Shikari has been paid for the next fortnight, so he will be able to show me the best places for views of the games. I am buying a lot more film, and he is leading me back into the Forest.

I am giving a quiet prayer of thanks to Krishna, who is a wise god, and is no doubt arranging things in this way so that I shall have a fine holiday, with many good views of the games. I must be admitting that I am a little sorry for the Sergeant, but only a little!

PATT DESERT

They woke with the first light of dawn. She cooked a big bowl of porridge, consisting of the coarsely crushed oats called dhallia, while he packed the tent and filled the water bottles from the stream. It was nearly three hundred miles to go around the desert and they had decided to head straight for Jacobabad.

"Have we any more containers for water?" Apart from the water bottles on the handlebars they had no water carriers, but he filled the billy cans and laid them flat in the base of the panniers. That gave them three pints in their bottles and another two in the cans.

Jacobabad was approximately south east, and seventy-four miles by their calculations. The clay desert was flat and smooth, and with the sun just above the horizon the surface gleamed like glass. It was baked by the sun and felt as hard as concrete.

"It'll be just like riding on a road," she said. "We'll be there by tonight."

"All the same, drink as much as you can before we start. We don't want to get thirsty and use our water before we need to."

They drank their fill from the stream and set off towards the sunrise. The sun shone almost directly in their eyes and they were thankful for their Polaroids, which stopped the worst of the glare. There were no discernible landmarks and they steered by compass, but they had covered less than a mile when they discovered that they would not be able to ride in a straight line after all. As they rode farther into the desert the clay was baked dry and was crazed with cracks. Many were two inches or more in width. They had to ride with care, for if a wheel fell into a crack it would be buckled beyond repair. They twisted and turned, crossing each crack at a safe angle. To the seven vultures circling above them their progress must have looked erratic in the extreme, but the vultures could afford to wait. Animals which wandered out on the desert invariably died of thirst; they weakened and staggered and moved erratically, just as the two figures below were doing. The vultures circled patiently, waiting for a meal.

As the sun rose higher it shone less directly in their eyes. Their attention was concentrated on the ground immediately in front of them, alert for the ever dangerous cracks, well aware how disastrous it would be to be left afoot. The light grew less direct and was easier for their eyes, but the higher the sun rose the hotter it became, and the more it was reflected from the pale straw coloured clay. After two hours they felt as if their whole world was filled with that small changing area of clay which lay just in front of their wheels.

They stopped for a drink and a rest. The girl removed her sunglasses and already her eyes were showing signs of reddening. The boy, with his darker colouring, was not so much affected, but even so, his eyes were stinging. Without their glasses the world was a shimmering, burning haze of glare, and after a quick dab with a handkerchief they were glad to don the Polaroids again.

"We'll drink the water in the billy cans first." It meant unpacking the panniers down to the base, and when they did, they found that a lot of the water had spilled with the movement of the bikes. There was a little over a pint left, and they shared it between them.

"The clothes are wet through," she said, but in fact they were merely damp, and the air was so hot and dry that fifteen minutes later, when they were ready to move on, everything had completely dried out.

According to their map there were three rivers between Gondava and Jacobabad, but they had crossed the Patt often enough by rail. Their present route took them nowhere near the railway, but they knew full well that there were no rivers. Perhaps in spring, when the snow melted in the hills, a hundred miles away, some trickle of water may get as far as this, though even that they doubted. Certainly in July there were no rivers, and the rainfall in the Patt was less than half an inch a year.

"How much water do we have?"

"Just what's in the water bottles," he replied, "about three pints."

"And how far have we come?"

He looked at the milometer on the fork of his bike. "Twenty-two miles."

"We can't have! Here, look at the map, there's the first river, see. We haven't passed that yet."

"Don't forget, we haven't been going in a straight line." He took the map from her hands. "I figure we're about here."

"That's only fifteen miles or so. At that reckoning the seventy miles across will be more like a hundred."

"Yes, unless the ground improves and we can hold a straighter course. We could go back to Gondava if you like."

"And then go three hundred miles round the edge of the desert? No, let's go straight across to Jacobabad. Even twisting and turning, it can't be all that bad," she said. "I reckon we'd best keep moving. I thought it would be smooth and flat and we'd be across in no time at all."

"So did I. I never expected all these cracks in the ground, I've never noticed them from the train. We'll have to be careful with the water."

She gave a little laugh. "I was expecting to be careful for the seventy miles. For a hundred I'll be positively miserly! How do the Hurs ever manage to live out here?"

"They don't. Nobody lives out here."

The vultures had settled in a group some fifteen yards away, but flew up as soon as they started to ride again. "They're expecting us for dinner I think," she said.

"I'll decline the invitation!"

"That's terribly ungracious of you!"

Six miles later the jokes ran out as they passed the first skeleton. It lay beside the dry valley, which was marked on their map as a river. It may have been a goat, or an antelope. White and clean on the clay, it was a grim reminder of the reality of the desert. The vultures had already swooped down on the bones and quickly found them worthless. They resumed their slow circling above the two riders.

"What on earth is it doing here, miles from anywhere?"

"I expect something scared it and it ran till it was exhausted," said the boy. "By then it was probably lost and died looking for water."

"Poor thing! It can't have been here all that long. The bones soon fall apart," she explained. "This is almost a full skeleton."

They could not ride across the dry river bed. There were too many stones and boulders, which forced them to dismount and push their bikes, sometimes even carrying them across the obstacles. "Surely the river's not this wide, even in spring," she said.

"If there's a river at all it'll be just in that little

channel over there. The rest must be some remnant of the past, when perhaps there was a real river."

"There are two more rivers shown on the map, I wonder if there'll be any water in either of them."

"I shouldn't count on it. They'll probably be dry like this one."

They carried the bikes up the steep, cliff-like edge, and were able to ride on. The sun was high above them, the rays burning on their backs. Their shirts were wet with sweat, and they could feel their shorts sticking to them against the saddles.

"I'm absolutely sweltering," she said. "I'll take off my shirt. There's no-one about to see me."

"Don't do that, the sun will burn you raw. In fact I think we should tie our hankies round our necks."

"God, no! Who wants a scarf in this heat!"

"Not a scarf! We should keep the sun off the back of our necks. I've heard that's the worst place for sunstroke, the base of the skull."

They never wore hats, but she obediently folded her hanky in a triangle and tied it loosely round her neck. "I don't know for sure," he explained. "It's just something I've heard."

"That skeleton proves there's a real danger. It won't get any less real by us disagreeing about details."

"Not scared are you?"

"No, but there is some risk. It would be stupid not to recognise it, that's all. If I do get scared you'll have to hold my hand. That never fails."

"I can't live up to ideas like that!" he exclaimed.

"You don't have to. I'm never scared when you hold my hand, that's just a fact. You don't have to live up to anything."

By afternoon they felt as though they were in an

oven. The sun beat down from above and reflected back from the clay. Their shirts were no longer wet. As soon as the khaki drill absorbed the sweat the sun dried it off. Only the seats of their shorts felt sweaty, and there was a slight rim of dampness where their sunglasses touched the skin. They took frequent sips of water, but could not afford a good long drink. The water in the aluminium bottles was warm and flat and did little to quench the feeling of thirst, but they both knew that the feeling was unimportant. In the end it was the actual amount of water that would decide how they fared. The handlebar grips were sticky with the heat. She moved her hands to the middle, and found the metal too hot to hold. "What do you think the temperature is?"

"It goes up to a hundred and thirty in the shade."

"What shade? There isn't any, and if there were, the heat would simply bounce up from below us. I feel as though I'm being slowly baked. How are we doing for distance?"

"Hard to tell with all the turning and twisting. When we get about five miles beyond the second river we'll be half way across. We can't be far from there now."

"Let's hope it's more of a river than the first one! I could just do with a bath."

"Bath! I'd settle for a good long drink!"

Thirst was not yet a problem, but he could see that it could easily become one. Progress was not nearly as good as they had expected, and one day's water would have to last two, maybe three, times as long. Instead of going from dawn to dusk they would have to spend all night in the desert. In the dark they could go no further towards Jacobabad. It would be wasted time, yet hour by hour they could, and would, grow thirstier. How much of the following day they would need he could not tell. "Yes," he thought, "I'd settle for a drink, or better still, a jerrican of water."

The heat was causing unexpected problems. They had experienced heat before, but never so extreme, and never with so limited a supply of water. Six to eight pints a day, they knew, was recommended in such conditions. They had carried less than two pints each, and had drunk a pint before they started. Three pints each would see them through the day, but would it see them through the night, and the following day as well? They had never before worried about how much water they drank or how much sweat they lost, but now the hot dry air seemed to draw the moisture out of them at an alarming rate.

Their eyes were red-rimmed and sore, and the girl's were beginning to look puffy. He spared a dab of water to bathe them with a moist hanky. They passed two more skeletons, one of a cow and the other of a dog or jackal, though they could not imagine how or why these creatures should have wandered so far into the desert.

It was late in the afternoon when they reached the second river. As the boy expected, it was dry. He tried not to show his worry, but he was downhearted as he pushed his bike across the river bed. The girl, ever sensitive to his feelings, realised his disappointment and gave his hand a squeeze. "Don't worry. As long as we're together there's nothing we can't do. I'm OK, really I am."

"Not scared?"

She gave him one of her impish grins and shook her head, and then, incredibly, she began to sing. "One more river, that's the river of Jordan."

"One more river, there's one more river to cross." He joined in, and they rode on with spirits high again.

They did not know it, but when the sun went down they were less than a mile from the third and final river. It was cooler but they dared not ride in the dark. The danger of buckling a wheel became almost a certainty if they rode through the night, and for the bikes to become unusable would not just be serious, it would be fatal. Reluctantly they stopped. Their milometers read seventy-three miles, but as a straight line on the map they had covered less than fifty. The boy's eyes were red and stinging, but the girl's were puffed and looked really sore. Again he spared a little water to moisten her hanky and place it over her eyes. "We'd better eat something. I'm afraid there's only dhallia, and no water to cook it."

"So we eat it dry," she said. "I'll get it."

"You stay where you are, and keep those eyes covered!"

Dry uncooked dhallia was an unappetising meal. Dry mouths and sore throats did nothing to improve it, but dutifully they chewed each mouthful sixty-four times before they swallowed. They needed to keep up their strength.

"Get some sleep. You need to rest those eyes."

"Aren't you coming?"

"No. See them?" He gestured towards the vultures, which had settled in a rough circle around them. "If we both go to sleep they'll start pecking at us, and I believe they start on the eyes."

"Ugh! They give me the creeps, horrid looking things! You sure you don't need company?"

"If we both stay up neither of us will have any rest. You go to sleep. I'll wake you when I get tired."

"You're already tired, and your eyes are sore."

"Not as bad as yours. Go to sleep, you need to rest. There's still tomorrow to deal with."

They did not bother with the tent. Fully clothed she slipped into her sleeping bag and pulled the top over her head as protection against the vultures. With no moisture and no dust there was nothing to scatter the light. When the sun set the air grew cold and the darkness was intense. They had thought of walking by night, when it was cool, but it was too dark for even that to be safe. The only light was from the stars. The birds looked like denser black patches against a black background. His eyes felt as though they were out on stalks as he strained to peer through the darkness. Minutes dragged into hours. The vultures did not seem to sleep. Perhaps they did, but there was no way of knowing, and he could take no chances. He had hoped that they would fly back to their nesting place, but they were on the scent of food and it made them more persistent. The stillness of the sleeping girl, and of the boy sitting near her, made them bolder. They hopped a little closer.

It was the sound rather than the sight of the movement which caught his attention. He stood up and walked in a circle. The nearer birds retreated slightly, and he sat down again by the girl. As time went by his eyelids drooped more and more, and he began to doze. Each time his head fell forward it jerked, and woke him again, and he walked around to keep himself awake. He longed for sleep but was waiting for the moon to rise. He knew that the girl's sore eyes would see little or nothing in the faint glow of the stars. It seemed longer, but by his watch it was less than three hours later that the moon came up over the horizon. The narrow sliver shed little enough light, but it was a dozen times brighter than the starlight. Gently he woke the girl and reminded her to keep her pistol handy. Then he crawled into his sleeping bag, and by the time she had yawned, and stretched, and shaken herself awake, he was already sound asleep.

The girl did not like the vultures. To her they personified the threat of the desert. The big powerful birds settled in a circle, so that two or three were always behind her, out of sight. She realised that by now they must be getting hungry, and though they were basically scavengers, she knew that they did, on occasion, attack their prey. She felt very much alone. In the vast emptiness of the desert she could sense only the hostility of the ugly birds. Imagination ran riot and she found herself getting apprehensive. She was tired and weak, her eyes were sore, and her throat was so dry that it hurt. She felt very defenceless and vulnerable and she wished that the boy was not so deeply asleep. It made him seem so far, yet she knew that he had to rest. As he had said, there was still tomorrow to be faced. Somehow she fought off her fears for the next two hours, and then, teetering on the ragged edge of her own imaginings, she woke the boy.

"You all right?" he asked.

She nodded, but later, from her sleeping bag, she said

quietly, "Will you hold my hand?"

The night dragged on. It was a beautiful desert night, the stars were big and bright against a velvety sky, and the thin crescent of the moon crept slowly across towards the west. He tried to appreciate the beauty, but could not. All he wanted was for the dawn to come so that they could ride out of this desolate, waterless clay. The night was wasting time, and this galled him. He wanted to do something positive to get the girl to safety. The comfortable weight of the pistol in his hand overcame any fear of the vultures, but their presence annoyed him. He wished they would go away.

His fear was of the desert itself. They had often been out in the desert of northern Sind, where the nomadic Hur roamed the sands. It was desert, but there were some small streams and occasional water holes, and the nights were almost mystical in their beauty. This was different. This was killer desert. The clay formed an impervious layer so no water came up from the subsoil. There were no springs and no waterholes. Rainfall was less than half an inch a year, and that came as dew not rain. Even the vultures must be thirsty by now, and that could make them bolder than usual. He was not afraid of the birds, but he did not underestimate the danger if they did attack. He was more worried about the girl, whose lighter colouring did not protect her so well from the sun. He had seen her wince when she lay down, and he guessed that her back was sore from the sun's continuous burning. He had not asked, because even if she was being cooked alive there was nothing he could do to help. At least his silence left her pride intact. He was forced to rouse her when he could no longer stay awake, but when she woke him again, dawn was in the sky.

They started as soon as it was light enough to see. The more miles they could cover before the heat became intense the better it would be. Their procedure was the same as before. They chewed dry dhallia for nourishment and drank sips of water when it seemed absolutely necessary, but for all their care and caution, by half past ten they had swallowed the last of their water. "How far to go now?" she asked.

"I figure about twenty miles in a straight line, say about

161

thirty the way we're weaving around."

"Will we make it?"

"Of course we'll make it. People don't die of thirst that quickly!" He had no idea how quickly people died of thirst, but he had no intention of saying anything that might dishearten her.

"If we don't..." she began.

"Don't be silly, we'll make it all right."

"If we don't," she repeated, "I want you to know something. You saved my life at Kanpur; I would have died without you. Anything after that has been like an unexpected gift. I want you to know that the extra time has been wonderful, so you mustn't worry about me."

"Don't talk like that. We'll be OK. You mustn't give up."

"I'm not giving up! I just wanted you to know, that's all. Here, have some chocolate."

It was practically liquid. They tore the silver paper in half and sucked the chocolate off the wrapping. It ran down his chin. "You look funny," she laughed, and then winced as the skin of her lip suddenly split.

By the afternoon water was the only thing he could think of. Dryness was a tangible taste in his mouth, and he felt burning hot. "I think I've got fever."

"So have I, but it's not fever. We're not sweating enough to keep our bodies cool. I should have expected it"

"Will it get worse?"

"I guess so," she said. "If we can't sweat our temperature will go up."

It was something he had not anticipated, an added complication in an already serious situation. "Will we get delirious?"

"I don't know. If our temperature keeps rising I guess we might. It's not like a disease though, so maybe we won't. I really don't know."

"Well, just in case, we'll fix our course. It's forty degrees south of east. No matter what, even if we become delirious we must stick to that." With his knife he scratched a mark on the compass. "There, that's our direction. If one of us goes a bit ga-ga

162

the other will just have to lead the way."

The vultures were still with them, circling low. They must be very thirsty by now, and the boy hoped that thirst and hunger would not spur them into an attack. Apart from keeping it in mind he took no steps to do anything about the birds. He needed all his energy to get to Jacobabad. Time enough to do something if they did attack, though what exactly he had no idea. Fortunately they must be feeling as weak and tired as he was himself. As for the girl, behind her glasses her eyes were so inflamed that he was not sure how clearly she could see. There was a small dark patch on the right shoulder of her shirt which looked like blood, but when he asked if she was all right she simply nodded. They tried not to talk much because it hurt their throats. They had just one object, to push the pedals round until they reached Jacobabad.

His eyes smarted every time he blinked, and his forehead and cheeks were burning hot. He guessed he was running quite a temperature. The girl, if anything, was worse. Her golden tanned skin was raw and peeling where the sun had caught it, particularly on her thighs and the tip of her little nose. The split lip glistened red but oozed no blood, for which he was thankful. Even a drop or two was more than she could afford.

She caught him looking at her and made a little 'O' with her thumb and forefinger to signal that she was all right. She even managed a bit of a smile. "She's got more guts than I have," he thought. He was doing his best to keep it from her, but he was really worried that they might not make it to the town. He had no accurate idea how far they had yet to go. With all the changes in direction they had made the readings on the milometers gave little indication of their true position. He prayed that they had not drifted away from their proper course. Meanwhile, they pedalled doggedly. The clay immediately in front of their wheels was the centre of interest. "Avoid the cracks, avoid the cracks." It repeated in his brain like some sort of catechism. The unchanging focus made his eyes glaze over, so that at times he found himself looking at the ground without really seeing it, at other times the sharp shadows of the cracks suddenly blurred and went out of

163

focus.

About three yards behind, the girl obediently followed in his tracks. She asked no questions and made no complaints. If he guided them wrong he knew that she would still make no complaint. He did not even know if she could still see the cracks he was so carefully guiding them across. More and more frequently he got spots before his eyes, until at last he had to stop. The whole area of clay seemed a criss-cross of cracks and crevices. For a few moments he could not tell which were real and which were merely images in his eyes. She stopped too, standing astride the crossbar of her bike. She looked as though she was asleep on her feet. When he took off her glasses he saw how badly her eyes were inflamed. They were closed, but she slowly opened them and looked at him as though awakening from a trance, and then she gave a little smile. "I'm OK. Just tired, that's all."

He took a hanky from his pocket and began to suck it. At first he could barely feel it in his mouth, but gradually a slow flow of saliva started, and he could taste the salt of perspiration on the fabric. It took nearly half a minute to dampen one corner, which he placed on her eyelid. When the hanky dried he repeated the process with her other eye. She made no comment but simply squeezed his hand in thanks and gestured that they should move on.

He took the compass, and peered out in the direction they were to take. The heat haze shimmered like uneven glass, but there, out on the horizon, he thought he saw something. He reached for the binoculars and looked again. It was bigger, but no clearer. If that was Jacobabad, it could only be about twelve miles away. That was roughly the distance of the horizon on the flat desert, but it may have been a mirage. There was a well known mirage on the Patt and they had both seen it many times from the train, but that had been nearly forty miles from where they should be now. He prayed that they were not completely lost. If they were forty miles from where he thought they were, they would have no chance at all. Until he could see it more clearly, however, he said nothing. It would be too cruel to raise her hopes and then to dash them again.

The image of the town shimmered on the horizon, sometimes there, and sometimes as vague as a dream. He kept pedalling. Slowly, wearily, the hazy shapes grew clearer. Two more miles convinced him, and he stopped. "Look, there's Jacobabad. Only about ten miles to go."

She looked where he was pointing. "I can't tell. It's too hazy. It doesn't matter, we'll soon be there. Let's just keep going."

Her voice was hoarse and he could see that it hurt her throat to talk. He felt as bad, so he said no more but set off in the direction of the town. So too did the vultures. They would scavenge their fill and then head for home. But he was in no state to speculate, he was just glad to see them go.

It was the longest ten miles of his life. The constant repetition of crack after crack passing under the wheels, his concern for the girl, who was now riding so slowly that he wondered how she kept her balance, and the continuous burning of the sun which dried out all the moisture from their skin, so drained him of emotion that he could hardly even feel relief at the sight of the town. He looked round at the girl. It was as though she was a machine. On her face there was neither hope nor fear, just a blank acceptance that somehow her tired muscles had to push the pedals.

It was a little after four in the afternoon when they reached the town. At last his dulled emotions came to life and he felt a sense of thankful relief as their wheels left the clay of the desert and touched the concrete surface of the road. There were no public taps, water was far too precious, here on the edge of the desert, and the reservoir was fenced. He headed straight for the Railway rest house, and without even waiting to check in, they entered one of the suites. The boy filled a glass with water and handed it to her, while he cupped his hand directly under the tap. He knew he should drink slowly, but as soon as the water touched his lips it seemed to go down his throat of its own accord. He was quite incapable of preventing it. The girl was the same. The tumblerful of water had been swallowed in one single draught.

"OK. now?" He just asked when they both suddenly retched and hung over the basin, acrid water spilling from their mouths. When they stopped heaving they were able to drink more slowly. This time they deliberately kept themselves half empty, and the water stayed down.

"You lie down and rest, I'll get booked in." When he returned he found the bedroom empty and the girl lying in a bath of tepid water.

"This is lovely, having enough water to soak in. No more deserts for me!"

"I'll have one as soon as you finish."

"I'll be here for hours! If you want to soak you'll have to join me."

He sat at the other end of the old fashioned six foot bath and slid slowly into the water, savouring the luxury as it lapped around his neck. Her feet were near his chest. He took hold of one and gave it a little shake. "Well, we made it!"

"I knew you'd take care of me." She wiggled her toes in his hand. "But next time, let's go somewhere greener, somewhere full of grass and trees."

They lay in the bath for nearly an hour. Two nights earlier he had been uneasily longing to make love to her. Now the sight of her sun-scorched body roused him to concern rather than desire. "Your thighs look sore."

"They are, but there's something hurting my back. I can't see what it is." She turned on her stomach and he could see a raw red patch on her shoulder. He sat up to take a closer look and found that the skin had been rubbed away, and the flesh had been oozing blood.

"You've skinned yourself."

"Is that it? I thought maybe the sun had blistered it."

"It probably did, and then your shirt rubbed the skin off. It looks bad, you'd better put some ointment on it."

"Let's just lie here for now," she said, "the water's soothing it a bit. I'll put something on it later. How far did we come?"

According to their milometers their winding route had

covered a hundred and twenty-eight miles. Later, when they enquired, they were to find that on that July day in 1947 the temperature in Jacobabad had been 128 Fahrenheit. In Sibi, on the other side of the Patt, it had been 127. Out on the desert it would have been three or four degrees more, up to 132 Fahrenheit.

"In the shade of course!" quipped the girl. "Why do they always say in the shade?"

"Because that's the air temperature. In direct sunlight it can be twenty or thirty degrees hotter."

"I'll vouch for that!" she said as she gingerly applied some ointment to her smarting skin.

BAG LADY

Life, in its way, she thought, had not been bad;
She'd married, had a home, fulfilled her role.
But Cardinal polish on the step
And blacking on the grate,
Each took its toll.

Roughened hands, back bent by constant toil,
Still young in years when old age came her way,
Worn out by Monday's washing, Friday's wage,
The skimp and scrape of every passing day,

When widowed by TB, she struggled on
To raise her sickly, undernourished boy,
He was the only legacy she had,
The only thing she found worth while in life,
But even that she could not long enjoy.

The cemetery was full, there was no room
For paupers, so she sold all she possessed,
With head held high, she bought a tiny plot
Of hallowed ground, where he was laid to rest.

Her world now held within two carrier bags,
She kneels beside his unpretentious stone,
Out of place among the family vaults
In the posh part of the graveyard,
Where he lies among a wealthier class of bone.

THE FINAL BIRTHDAY

Man's allotted span is apparently three score years and ten. This should be slightly alarming since my next birthday will be my seventy-seventh. There are, of course, exceptions. Adam lived 930 years, Seth 912, and Methuselah 969, but there were others too. Unfortunately, these are all mentioned in Genesis, whereas I am of this millennium, a gentile, and therefore, not a follower of ancient Judaic writings.

I am left with the allotted span as an expectation, and any deviations as purely incidental. Fortunately this doesn't worry me.

Most people profess to believe in an afterlife which is an improvement on this one. Why then the reluctance to experience it? It would be farcical if one saw it in a play.

St. Peter stands beckoning from the pearly gates. "This is a much better place that the one you are in now. Come in and enjoy it."

"No fear, do you think I'm daft? I'm staying right where I am!"

"Oh come on in! It's much nicer, I assure you."

"Forget it mate, I like it where I am."

"But this is much better. Don't you believe me?"

"'Course I believe you, but I like it here."

"Then why are you always complaining?"

"Well, that's just human nature, isn't it."

"But you've got to come, sooner or later."

"Then make it later. I'm in no hurry." And so the conversation might go on, for the rest of our lives, until there is no longer any option.

Nurses and doctors say that many people who die do not fear it at the time. The fear seems to come only when it is contemplated in cold blood. I wonder why this should be? Either we don't really believe all the myths we so glibly put out, or there is some attachment that we can't bear to part with.

For many of us this attachment will be our loved ones. In it's purest form, we don't want our wives or husbands to have to manage without us. Less pure perhaps is that we don't want to

169

have to manage without them. Both are valid reasons for not wanting to go.

To face a new existence without the support of the partner with whom one may have lived most of one's life could be a terrifying thought. To see that partner go into the unknown without our love and support could be worrying and heartbreaking too, but either way it makes a nonsense of our so-called faith.

The new existence is better. We can't know that for a fact, but it is an article of faith. We throw aside all the promises of religion if we don't believe it.

I'm not suggesting that we should kill ourselves. That would be to throw in God's face the gift of life which he has given us. But nor should we fear death. That is to throw in his face the promises he has made. It doesn't much matter which of the formal religions you follow, you have been promised salvation if you live a reasonable life. In Judaism, Christianity, and Islam, the belief is in one life, and the judgement will be made on it. Other religions believe there may be several transitional stages, but either way, we humans tend to reject the idea that we have been so awful that we deserve to be sent to everlasting damnation.

Hitler thought that he was purifying Germany and making life better for the German people. He didn't see himself as doing what he did for no reason. Judas Iscariot was not trying to betray Jesus, he simply wanted to bring things to a head, so that the Messiah would declare himself and bring his kingdom into being. When you and I have acted in some thoroughly unprincipled way, we too, will find some rationalisation for why we did it. None of us will burn in hell without making out some sort of case for our defence!

Speaking for myself, I have been promised that whatever form it takes, the next life will be full of joy and happiness. Of course, I could be mistaken, yet I have no doubt whatsoever of the honesty of that promise. The arguments of leaving loved ones behind still apply, and what I have is a belief, not an absolute certainty, but it's a belief in which I have no room for doubt. For this reason I have no desire to be remembered when I go. It would only make people sad. I shall be too busy living my new life to want people to mourn my death! In the current phraseology, they can celebrate my life if they wish, but no, don't mourn my death.

I don't believe in a god who intervenes. This seems to border on arrogance, for where then is the strength to face the adversities of life? My answer is that we have within us some part of the creator, or, if you prefer, that our spirits are made of the substance of god. And that creator, too mighty to understand, too complex to grasp, is yet also within us, in all his infinitude. We need no miracles, for the set-up is such that we can find our own. Seek and ye shall find, knock and it shall be opened to you. Our spirits may be confined within our physical limitations, but Spirit consists of the substance of god, and the substance of god cannot be limited.

According to modern theory our universe has either ten or twenty six dimensions. I don't understand the mathematics, and I can't even conceive of ten dimensions, let alone twenty six, but maybe they contain the secrets which I cannot grasp. The truth, perhaps, lies in those other dimensions. Science, like religion, seeks the truth, but some do not see the truth in science, and believe it to lie in the scriptures, of any religion. Yet the scriptures are vague and open to interpretation. They, like science, can give rise to different conclusions from the same evidence. One can believe the scriptures, but that, of itself, does not bring revelation, and if you are lucky enough to be granted revelation, you wouldn't need the scriptures.

Three score years and ten, or fifteen, or more, it makes no difference. It is the start of the next stage of the journey, the next great adventure. For my relatives' sake my practical affairs will need to be in order, and for my own sake, my philosophy will also need to be in order. I'm glad to say that it already is.

SCIENCE

Look up and see the Milky Way, where stars wink mysterious. What are they? With wonder we can see their various hues, some tinged with red, or yellow, green, or blue. God made it all, we're told, in seven days, but I believe a longer time has passed, and while religion urges us to praise and magnify the Deity whose love created us from nothing, let us pray that science will enable us to see the real wonder of the universe.

Far from negating the creator's role, I find that science forces me to think of all the real magic of the skies, how subatomic particles can join themselves in galaxies and more, and things we cannot see with eyes, but must accept by reason, and by thought alone.

Compared with the creation which is shown by microscope, or telescope, or particle accelerator giving faint traces in cloud chambers, compared with that, the God, who made the world in seven days, was playing with children's building blocks. We do him a disservice if we think he can't create a more effective universe than that.

Science, far from opposing religion, enriches it, by hinting at the true extent of what is really there. Not just a man, but cells forming the man, by carrying out the pattern of the genes, and genes in turn carrying within themselves the history of all life, from monocellular amoeba to us, who we are told are made in his own image.

It doesn't matter what we may believe. The truth remains the truth no matter what. If God exists, or indeed if he does not, our beliefs will have no power to change the facts. Atheists do not cause God to cease, nor theologians bring him into being.

So, whatever made this cosmic speck of dust which is my world, I know it's far more wonderful than stories told by priests, or fairy tales of jealous gods exacting sacrifice. Yet, if there's no creator, no-one there, then that's the fact, and my beliefs are wrong. It doesn't alter anything outside, but it makes a difference here, inside my soul.

CARRIAGE

My early years were lived on the railway, in particular, the North Western Railway of India. It covered Sind, the Punjab, Baluchistan and various other smaller sections like the track up to Simla. Most of this area now falls within Pakistan, but I have never lived in Pakistan. When I was there it was India, and in 1947, just before the partition, Dad decided to move from what was to become an Islamic state to the south which was mainly Hindu, but remained secular. It also remained democratic, which Pakistan did not.

Much of my travelling was done First Class. This was because Dad got more free rail passes than we could possibly use. The rest was done in even more luxury. Because of his position Dad had his own carriage, which he could attach to any train he wished, and go anywhere on the North Western Railway. Naturally this was limited to the work situation. During school holidays it was on these trips that I liked to accompany him, travelling extensively on the NWR.

Most railway officers were expected to spend at least one week a month on line. I don't mean the computer term, this was a long while back, BC, before computers. On line meant travelling around seeing that everything was going according to plan. Dad's responsibility was the control of movements on the railway, so he frequently went to some station or other to see that the rules were followed, both for safety, and economic reasons. Occasionally there were crises such as floods or landslides and again he would make sure that all the emergency procedures were properly applied, as well as arranging for relief trains to take in supplies, or to evacuate stricken areas as necessary. During these periods he went to the area and lived in the carriage.

It was set up like a caravan. A full length 'bogie' carriage, it had the servant's quarters at one end. There was then the kitchen, from which a corridor led past the heating and air conditioning units, the toilet and shower room and opened into the central living area. This was a lounge where the bunks could be adapted for sitting or sleeping, and were equally comfortable for either use. Beyond the lounge there was the observation room, which had two bunks, the lower one acting as a window seat going right across the carriage. A large curved window stretched the full width of the compartment. One could sit on the seat and look out at a panoramic view of all the area one had just passed through. Since the carriage was always placed at the rear of the train this view was never obstructed. This also ensured that it could always be coupled or uncoupled at any station along the way, without interfering with the rest of the train.

A chaprassi, a railway servant, was there to look after Dad. He cooked, cleaned the carriage and generally took care of all the mundane chores. In a really serious situation, such as the movement of refugees during the partition, Dad might occupy the carriage for as much as a month at a time. This, was exceptional but, was no hardship, the accommodation was excellent, and Dad's chaprassi was a whizz. He was a Pathan called Sukki. He took his job seriously, and Dad never went short of anything when he was on line. Sukki worked behind the scenes, but I once saw him in action.

"Station Master, ji, what sort of station is this that you run?"

"What do you mean, what's wrong with my station?".

"There is my Sahib in the heat of the sun, with the dust everywhere, and I can get no cold beer to refresh him.

What am I to tell him?"

In due course a dozen bottles of ice cold lager would arrive. Later Dad would enquire of the Station Master how much he owed him, and invariably the answer was "Oh nothing Sahib, it was a hot day and I thought you might enjoy some cold beer."

"Sorry Station Master, but I insist."

"Oh Sahib, just a small token of respect!"

It took a deal of persuasion to pay for the goods, and Dad was not always successful in doing this. It was no good pointing out that it wasn't hot in the carriage because of the air conditioning. It was no good pointing out that he was quite capable of paying for meals from the refreshment room. "A small token of respect" was the start of protracted argument. For Dad to win the argument he first had to counteract the insidious groundwork done by Sukki. It wasn't always easy.

In really remote stations, where there were no refreshment rooms, it might even be necessary for Sukki to go and buy some ingredients to cook a meal. I dare say that even that he managed to fiddle somehow or other. Despite this, his loyalty to my father was beyond any doubt, and with the partition, when we left to go south of the border to India, Sukki wept to see us go. As a Muslim he, of course, stayed in Pakistan, and Dad advised him to do so, but he was very upset.

When we left the NWR, now renamed the Pakistan Railway, the carriage was left behind. Dad was tranferred to the Oudh and Rohikund Railway, centred in Gorakhpur. The carriage was, of course, replaced, but the OR was a metre gauge railway, so though the new carriage was slightly longer it was narrower. Dad found it quite comfortable. I never travelled in it, but to me it never seemed quite as good as the one on the NWR. The Oudh and Rohikund Railway never seemed quite as good as the NWR either. Was I, even at that age, getting set in my ways?

Maybe, but rail travel has never since been the luxurious mode of transport to which I had become accustomed. Tinted windows for the glare, heaters for the cold, air conditioning for the heat, and a chaprassi to attend to ones wants. Fare paying passengers don't get that sort of service.

To be honest I don't think British Rail could compete, but to be equally honest, neither am I sure that the Indian Railways still supply that sort of thing.

"I'LL LOOK AFTER YOU"

Jimmy had died three years ago. The wounds were not as raw, the dreadful nights less dreadful, the loss was getting easier to bear. Susan had been over her depression for two years now, but controlling the depression hadn't controlled the grief. Jimmy stayed in her thoughts.

His birth had been difficult, and there would be no more children. This made him doubly precious, but when he was six, Jimmy died. Meningitis; but, whatever the cause, he was gone.

Susan cried herself to sleep for months. Henry tried to console her, but there was no consolation. She was made to be a mother and was denied her natural function. The depression returned, culminating in the slashing of her wrists. Hospitalisation followed, and when she was discharged, she came home to find Maria. The housekeeper was necessary because Susan was in hospital, but she seemed closer to Henry than Susan had expected. At first Susan didn't care, depression making her indifferent, but gradually, as she got better, she became angry.

Henry wouldn't even pay her the courtesy of taking her seriously. "You've been ill, dear, you know the doctor said you may feel paranoid. Of course there's nothing going on, what nonsense! Maria is a good housekeeper. Just look around, she's kept everything spotless while you've been away, and now she's going to look after you."

"I don't want her looking after me, I want her out."

"Now, darling, you don't mean that. It's just the depression. Go lie down in your room, and she'll bring you up a nice warm drink to make you sleep."

Maria brought a cup of malted milk. She hated it. "Please Mrs. Anders, it will help you sleep. I'll sit here till you doze off."

The drink tasted horrible. Ever since childhood she had disliked malted milk, when her mother had given it to her because she was supposed to have a weak constitution. It hadn't helped then, and it didn't help now.

Maria drew up a chair beside her. Susan didn't feel

177

sleepy, just a little sick. After a while, "Mrs. Anders," Maria said softly. She didn't answer, feigning sleep, and through half shut lids she watched the woman rise and remove the cup. At the door Maria put her finger to her mouth and whispered, "She's asleep now. It'll be hours before she wakes."

She heard Henry ask, "What did you give her?"

"What we agreed. She'll be out till morning. She'll feel better for a good night's sleep, but that'll only be temporary!"

"Then we'll turn in. Might as well have an early night." A slight chuckle accompanied his words.

Susan struggled to stay awake. She felt awful, and her stomach ached, but eventually she fell asleep, dreaming of Jimmy.

"Hello Jimmy, it's so nice to see you. I don't like Maria, and I don't like your Daddy either. He seems to be so different now."

"It's all right Mummy, I'll look after you."

"Oh darling, you're just my little boy, I should be looking after you."

"You can't Mummy, but I can look after you. I can, you'll see, really I can!"

In the next room there was a sudden crash. The large mirror with the heavy frame had fallen off its hook. Henry and Maria jumped from the bed, startled, gazing at the pillow which was covered with broken glass. Henry had a cut on his forehead where the corner of the frame had hit him, but otherwise there were no injuries.

Maria was trembling. "It's all right, Maria, it's just the mirror. I always said it was too heavy for that hook. I'll see to it in the morning. For now we'll find somewhere else. Too much glass around here."

He peered round the door to see Susan still sound asleep, and silently followed Maria to her own room, where they spent the rest of the night.

In the morning Susan was still sleeping soundly when Maria came in with some breakfast. "Good morning Mrs. Anders, did you sleep well?"

Henry followed her in. "How was your night? The

178

mirror fell down. Didn't it wake you?"

Susan tried to clear her head. "No, I must have slept through it. Dreamt of Jimmy. What's this about the mirror?"

"It fell off it's hook. Always thought it was too heavy for that hook, but the hook's all right, so I don't know why it fell."

Susan shrugged, only half awake. "Jimmy, I suppose," she said.

"Yes, dear. You said you dreamt of him. Was it a nice dream?"

Susan nodded sleepily, and Maria had to shake her to wake for her breakfast.

That afternoon Maria came rushing to Henry in a panic. "Someone's thrown everything round my room. Henry, what's going on? I'm scared."

They hurried to her room. All her belongings were strewn about, nothing broken, but nothing undisturbed either. "Burglars," asserted Henry. "Check if anything's missing."

A quick check confirmed that nothing seemed to have been stolen. "They must have been interrupted," said Henry. "We'd better tell the police."

The police sergeant and the constable looked round carefully. "Were any doors or windows open?"

"Only the kitchen door. That was on the latch, everywhere else was locked."

"Well," said the Sergeant. "There's no sign of any break in, so that must be where they got in."

"But I was in the kitchen nearly all day, and I lock the door when I'm not in this part of the house." Maria's voice was shrill.

"It only takes a moment for an opportunist, Miss."

"But they'd have to get out again. I'd have seen them."

"And did you see anyone, Miss? Or hear anything?"

"No. That's why I'm frightened."

The two policemen went away, promising to check on any local incidents which may be connected. Nothing had been taken, no-one had been hurt. It wouldn't be given a high priority, Henry could see that.

179

He put his arms around her. "Now stop worrying. They'll keep an eye on the place, and we'll keep the doors locked more carefully. I'm here, I won't let anything happen to you."

When Susan was told about the attempted burglary, she wondered how they'd got in, but was too fuddled to think straight. The security system had been installed only a year ago. She was sure she'd seen the red light blinking when she had staggered to the bathroom. She couldn't forget her dream. What did Jimmy mean, he'd look after her? Did she need looking after? Why did she feel so confused?

She knew she'd been ill, and she was on medication, but that was in the hands of the doctor. He was looking after her, why should Jimmy want to do the same? And that spicy soup Maria had given her for lunch. For some reason it had spilled over the tray. The bowl had simply fallen from her hand. Maria had been very sympathetic, and cleaned up the spillage, but Susan felt the undercurrent of frustration. Henry too, had quite obviously been upset.

"Is there any more soup, Maria?"

When told there wasn't he said, "Well, Susan has to eat something. Will you prepare something for her, please." The tone was impatient, yet Susan couldn't help feeling that the impatience was with her, not Maria.

After the herb-tasting scrambled eggs which Maria prepared, she dozed. She thought she heard voices on the landing. "I think she spilt it purposely. Maybe she suspects."

"I doubt it." Henry's voice. "Probably just an accident. You were there, what happened?"

"The bowl just seemed to come off the tray. She seemed as surprised as I was, but it could have been deliberate. There was no reason for it to fall."

The voices faded as they went downstairs. What did they think she might suspect? Had the doctor prescribed some medication which he didn't want her to know about? Yes, that must be it, she'd ask Henry this evening.

But when the evening meal was brought there was no time to ask questions. Henry and Maria sat on either side of the

180

bed and insisted that she swallow down the broth. Henry even went so far as to spoon it into her mouth himself.

It tasted vile, and she gagged. Henry took hold of her tightly, and Maria started to feed her. But then a strange thing happened. Maria seemed unable to control the spoon. It turned and moved towards her mouth. She cried out in terror, and as her mouth opened the spoonful of hot broth poured down her throat.

Her hands covered her face as she cried out. "It burns. Henry, help me!"

Suddenly realising that Maria was in trouble, Henry tried to dash the bowl to the floor. It wouldn't fall, the broth wouldn't spill, and then the spoon came towards him.

He ran from the room and down the stairs. He wrenched at the front door but it wouldn't open. The spoon kept following him, and behind it the bowl of steaming broth. He sank to the floor, whimpering, as the remnants of Susan's lunch came relentlessly towards him. His last thought was the fear of that thick boiling soup scalding his eyes.

They found him dead. The post mortem confirmed it was a heart attack, brought on by stress. Of course, his wife had been ill for some years now. It must have taken its toll on him. There was a lot of sympathy for the dead man.

Maria was distraught. Her hysterical claims of spoons and bowls chasing Henry down the stairs were put down to the trauma of seeing him dead. She was kept in hospital for treatment, and as soon as she was discharged she returned to Malta, refusing to go near the house again.

After the funeral Susan made a good recovery. All her problems seemed behind her now, but in times of stress she could still hear Jimmy saying, "I'll look after you, Mummy."

MINOR MATTERS

God moves in mysterious ways, and of course he knows everything. It is none the less reasonable to expect that great earth shattering events will be granted more divine attention than the simple minutae of our everyday lives. This at least is what I assume.

When my grandfather decided to give up Catholicism and become a Protestant it was a very minor matter in the grand scheme of things, and as such it was delegated to God's earthly minions to deal with. The relevant minions were the leaders of the Roman Catholic church in Barcelona, who responded to his heretical attitude by forbidding him to attend Mass, or to take communion, in the Catholic Cathedral. Since this was exactly what he had already decided to do I doubt if he found it any particular hardship. If God had dealt with the matter himself I dare say he would have come up with a more appropriate solution, but, as I say, it was a very minor matter.

Probably of more immediate import was his disinheritance from the family. They were reasonably well off, with their own ships involved in trading for spices in the east, so his change of faith meant renouncing more than just the Catholic fathers, and the holy communion in the Cathedral. It led to him leaving the family, travelling on one of the family ships, and eventually finishing up in India. Being familiar with sextants and other instruments of navigation he could work out his position, so he became involved with the surveying of the country. One of the areas he surveyed was the tribal territory occupied by the Naga Indians. History tells us that at that time the Nagas were still headhunters, though there is some doubt whether they were still cannibals as well. This is perhaps where he may have come to God's notice, for he survived unscathed, and considering the perils of the situation, it is not unreasonable to suppose that some divine intervention might have occurred. It did not, however, divert him from his stance as a Protestant.

On the scale of world events, his marriage to an Irish lass

was another minor matter, though it raises the question of whether she was a Catholic or a Protestant. This I don't know, but their four children were all Protestant, which leads one to believe that either she was not a Catholic, or else that his renunciation of that faith was a serious and determined one.

Anyway, she died, and seven years later so did he, leaving the four children orphaned in a land without any welfare provision. Again, in a very minor way, the children were perhaps, brought to God's attention, for they made out all right in spite of the handicap of being orphans. The youngest of them was my father.

In the first world war he fought in East Africa, where he was mentioned in despatches. He also nearly died of blackwater fever. Ironically he was treated by a German doctor, and his life was saved. This seems to indicate at least some slight interest on the part of his creator.

When he returned home he rose to a fairly good postion in the Railway, and was quite a devout fellow, always worshipping God, but although officially an Anglican he did not follow any particular faith. If he felt the need to pray, to "talk to God" as he called it, he would do so in any holy place which happened to be handy, whether it was a church, a temple, or a mosque. In fact he believed that if God was our father we needed no intermediaries to approach him. The appointed representatives, God's religious minions, be they chaplains, fathers, mullahs or priests were merely middlemen who might get in the way, and were in any case, irrelevant to the important issues. God showed no signs of either agreeing or disagreeing with this idea, but I know that Dad gained considerable comfort from his chats with his maker.

Later it seemed that God may have forgotten our existence altogether, for, as far as formal religion was concerned, we were left severely alone. God's minions went about their business of saving souls, each in his own particular way, but they didn't try to save ours. The reason was fairly simple. As Anglo-Indians the various Indian religions did not expect us to share their particular beliefs and made no special efforts to gather us into their fold. With our Spanish surname it was not surprising that the Anglican padre thought we were Catholics, so he ignored us. Meanwhile the Catholic father was well aware that we were not Catholics, so he also ignored us. As far as salvation went, it seems we were on our own!

In my own case, the only people who ever discussed religion with me were yogis, and then only if I broached the subject. When I was seventeen, questioning any and everything, I had some interesting conversations with yogis, and whatever they told me always seemed to make sense. I thank them for some remarkable, though unusual, ideas.

My father died at the age of sixty-four. I hope God did not entirely ignore the event, and recalled some of the chats which Dad had had with him, whether in churches, mosques or temples. If he did recall, then I daresay he would have taken Dad under his wing. I hope so, for from the age of nine Dad had existed as an orphan without either a maternal or a paternal figure to act as a parental role model. I would not wish his after life to be similarly deprived.

For myself, at this late stage of my life, I was persuaded by my wife, Jacqui, to accompany her on an Alpha course, which is a sort of Bible discussion programme. Many will know what it is. For those who don't, I think it would be unfair of me to give my rather unorthodox view of things. I would say simply that those who are curious should go and find out for themselves.

Alpha has made some impact on Jacqui, but very little on me. I find it interesting but by no means convincing. If it has had any effect, it is to reinforce the beliefs I already hold, but these are based on rationality rather than any scriptural texts. Alpha is no exception to the general rule that evangelists, of any religion, tend to assume that their beliefs are the right ones, and other beliefs are wrong. Until now, at least, I have been unable to accept this. I hope I shall continue not to accept a view so narrow as to reject the truth of every creed except my own, but then, who knows? God, after all, moves in mysterious ways.

VOICES

"I tell you there are voices coming out the wall."

Dr. Jones tried hard not to let his scepticism show. "When does this happen?" he enquired mildly.

"Anytime. In the night mostly, but not necessarily. In the day too, oh I don't know, it can happen any time."

"And what do they say, these voices?"

"They don't say anything, just mumbling, and sometimes laughter. Not childish laughter, quite grown up sounding, and the mumbling is never clear enough to make out the words."

This was ridiculous. The doctor had a waiting room full, and here was this fool taking up his time with tales of non-existent voices coming out of the walls of his house. He tried to hide his impatience.

"Well, Mr Carstairs, I'll give you something to calm you down. If you feel calmer and more in control you may find that the voices go away."

"You don't believe me, do you? Imagination. Stress. Give me a few tranquillisers. Well, why don't you come and hear for yourself. You'll soon see I'm not mad or making it up. There are voices coming out the wall I tell you." His voice was growing angry, and the corner of his mouth began to twitch. "You can keep your ruddy pills. If you don't even believe me, how do you think you'll be able to help."

"Now calm down Mr Carstairs. Of course you're hearing something, but it's not voices in the wall. Walls don't talk. The sounds are in your head, and we have to find out what's causing them, but first we need to settle your nerves. When you feel calmer we'll be able to do some proper investigations, but we can't do much while you're all jittery like this."

"You'd be jittery if your walls were talking to you," muttered Carstairs angrily, reluctantly gathering up the prescription from the doctor's desk.

God! The man really was at the end of his tether. The doctor felt bad about his impatience, "Take those for a few days and then come and see me again in a week. By then you should feel better and we'll sort this out. "

He sighed as the door closed behind the departing man. "Paranoid," he thought as he pushed the buzzer for the next patient to be shown in.

The week passed, eight, nine days, before he remembered the man who was supposed to come back. He buzzed for the receptionist. "Jane, Mr Cartairs was supposed to come in. Get me his address and I'll call in when I do my rounds. I think it might be as well to see why he hasn't come back." Who knows, he mused, a little calmness and rational thought may have cleared up the mystery.

The house was in a terrace of old Victorian dwellings, once very desirable no doubt, but now run down and in need of a makeover. He knocked on the door of number thirteen. There was no answer. He tried again. Still no answer. He was just about to leave when the door of the next house opened and a middle-aged woman came out.

"Don't know if he's in," she said, "haven't seen him for some days. Hasn't taken his milk in either, I've put at least three bottles in my fridge for when he turns up."

"Thank you. I'm Doctor Jones, if you do see him please let him know that I called."

The woman nodded, and picking up her shopping bag she walked away. The Doctor turned to leave, but as he did so caught a glimpse of something through the bay window. Straining to peer through the net curtains he thought he saw something lying on the floor. He looked again. Yes, there was someone there. It might not be Carstairs but there was definitely someone lying there. He rapped sharply on the window. There was no response. He tried again, then pulled out his mobile phone. "Ambulance please, to number thirteen Curzon Terrace." He briefly gave the details of the situation. "I'm his GP, but I'm getting no response and I can't get in."

The ambulance arrived, followed very shortly by a police car. The constable looked through the window, quickly assessed that there was no easy access to the back of the terrace, then broke a pane in the door and forced an entry. Jones hurried in and checked the patient's pulse. The paramedics deferred to the doctor but took over when he said, "I think he's dead, try to resuscitate him I guess, though I think we're too late."

The paramedic took a look. "Much too late, I'm afraid. Heart attack I think. What's your opinion, doc?"

"Yes, I agree, but the look of him puzzles me. He looks as though he was scared to death, as though he literally died of fright. I've never seen it before, but it's possible I suppose."

As the ambulance men did their work and the vehicle drove away the doctor and the policeman talked briefly. "Shall I say he died of fright?" asked the constable, as he made a few notes.

"No, I think it was a heart attack. May have been caused by fright, but it was his heart. They'll check it out at the hospital, but I think they'll agree."

The policeman nodded and finished writing. As he snapped his notebook shut both men were startled to hear the sound of smug, satisfied laughter. It seemed to be coming from the walls of the room.

THE OTHERWHERE

I looked out of the mirror at my real self. There he was, engrossed in his everyday life. He was getting ready to go to work, straightening his tie, combing his hair. He checked that his laces were properly tied, the hankie in his top pocket neatly folded, and then he was off. As he left the front of the mirror I was free. No longer did I have to copy his mannerisms, I was free till he returned and stood before me again.

Having moved out from the back of the mirror I wondered where I should go. The world was mine to wander in, this other world, where I felt unconstrained by time and space. I decided to visit her again. She was real, like my other self, but she was an angel. Oh, not a real angel, an 'earth angel', someone who lives on earth, but is an angel to someone else. I knocked on the door of her apartment.

"Hello," she said, "this is a nice surprise, I didn't expect to see you. Come in."

"Hi! I was just passing so I decided to see if you were home."

"Come on in. Have you time for a coffee?"

"Yes, I'm in no hurry."

"I thought, maybe, as you were just passing ..."

"No, I've got all day as it happens. Coffee would be nice."

She put the kettle on. We sat down together and chatted about this and that, until the water boiled, and she made coffee. Half milk, the way I like it.

"This coffee's lovely, thanks. What are you doing today?"

"I was going shopping, but it's not important. I can easily go another day."

"Why don't I come with you?"

"To the shops? You'll be bored."

"No I won't." By the time we'd drunk the coffee it was agreed. We got in her car and drove into town. She wanted a new dress, and she was right, it wasn't very interesting, but it was a chance to be with her and that was what mattered.

We'd known each other about four months. She knew that I loved her, and I think she felt the same, but there were problems I had to work out before we could be together.

In the department store we went to the third floor, 'ladies fashions', and she started selecting dresses. "What do think of this?" It was the fifth one she'd tried.

"It looks good," I said, so she went into the fitting room again. When she drew back the curtain and stepped out she looked stunning. I looked at her, open mouthed. I hadn't realised she was so lovely. The dress didn't look as though it was off the peg, it fitted her like a second skin, showing off every curve of her body.

"It looks great," I said.

"Yes, I like it. I don't need to look any more, this'll do nicely. It's in the sale as well, so it's a bargain."

When she'd paid and we left the store she said "Well, that didn't take long. What shall we do with the rest of the day?"

"Let's go along the sea front," I said, reaching for her hand. She allowed me to take it, and left it in mine as we walked along. Then we went down to the beach and sat on the sand. We didn't need to talk, just sitting there quietly was enough. When I pressed her hand affectionately she returned the pressure with a little smile.

"Come on, I'll buy you lunch. My way of saying thank you for your support."

"What support?"

"It's not much fun accompanying a woman when she's buying clothes, but you never complained at all."

She bought me lunch. That was always a problem. I only had reflection money, wrong way round, and it didn't look right when I handed it over. I wanted to buy her nice things, but I couldn't. My real self could have bought her nice things, expensive things, as she deserved. My real self! I remembered.

"I must be back by five thirty," I said, "I have to meet someone."

"There's lots of time yet, anyway you're free today, you said so."

"Only till five thirty, I'm afraid."

"Then let's go back to my place."

She drove back and went through to the bedroom. "Pour yourself a drink," she called, "won't be long."

She came out wearing the new dress, and gave a little twirl. It looked even smoother and slinkier than in the shop, and then I realised why. No pantie line! No bra line either!

My interest was obvious. With a little laugh she beckoned me towards her, and going into the bedroom, she removed the dress. I was right about the underwear!

Well, one thing led to another, and it was past six o'clock when I left. I hurried, but I was too late. My real self had come home. Things had been all right, until he washed his face and looked in the mirror, and I wasn't there!

Something bad happened. I don't understand it, but I'd broken the rules, and it damaged him. My theory is that when he couldn't find his reflection in any of the mirrors he thought he must be a ghost. Of course that's just my guess. Anyway he had a massive stroke, and now he's in intensive care. They don't expect him to recover, but even if he does, the trauma's affected his brain. He's convinced he must be dead because he couldn't find his reflection.

Meanwhile, I have a problem too. If he dies he won't need a reflection, so where does that leave me? I love her, but I'm not real. We can't have an enduring relationship unless I can stay in front of the mirror, and that's never been done. I had to tell her.

She listened quietly, with tears in her eyes. "And there's no way you can join me on this side?"

"Not that I know of," I said, "Not permanently. I'm stuck in the Otherwhere, and I don't know what will happen if he dies. Dead men don't need reflections."

190

She became very quiet. After a long while she sniffed away her tears and said "Come with me. I have an idea. It may not work, but anything's worth trying."

Back in her apartment she took me once more to the bedroom. Standing in front of the full length mirror she held me very close, and kissed me very gently. Then she gave me a little push towards her reflection.

"Go now," she said. "Go back to the Otherwhere. Be happy."

There was a sob in her voice as she added, "It'll be all right. You'll find she's just like me!"

NIGHTMARE

The night was dark and stormy,
The wind was moaning wild,
Trees were shaking, waves were breaking,
And I was alone and frightened,
Me, like a frightened child.

Dark clouds looked down at me,
Dark faces in the sky,
And white foam looked up at me
From out the watery grey.

Then the clouds broke and a misty moon
Peeped through the angry sky,
For suddenly I thought of you
So many miles away.
I willed to think that you could be
Upon that stormy isle with me;
And then I laughed and dreamed of you
So many miles away.

The night was dark and stormy,
The wind was moaning wild,
Trees were shaking, waves were breaking,
But I was no longer frightened
There on that stormy isle.

For nothing else was real,
And nothing else was true,
But the white brilliance of the moon
And my bright dream of you.

IT MUST HAVE BEEN HOT!

The first photographic exhibition I visited was in 1945, when I was fifteen.   Not surprisingly, it was almost all monochrome pictures, and to this day, I prefer black and white photography to colour.

The picture, hanging centrally on one wall, confused me. It was of a flat landscape, with what appeared to be a shimmering reflection coming off the ground, and a cloudless sky, bright near the horizon and darkening slightly as it went closer overhead.   In the distance there were some whitewashed buildings, but not big enough to form a centre of interest. It seemed a monotonous and uninteresting subject.   As I stood in front of it, wondering why it had ever been taken, two adults drew up behind me.   One said to the other, "Gosh, it must have been hot when that was taken!"

That was when I realised what the photographer was trying to do, and I could see how well he had succeeded. Yes, it must have been hot.   The picture conveyed that without any doubt.   My only excuse for not seeing it sooner was that I was young and inexperienced.

I was just taking up photography as a hobby.   I bought myself a reasonable camera, and, eventually, took some halfway reasonable pictures. I also began to form my opinions about what constitutes art.   Many will not agree with me, but for what it's worth, I think that art is what goes on in one's head. The business of conveying the image in tangible form, is craft. I am not talking only of photography, but of any graphic art, and possibly of all art.

Let me give an example. I have a sharp, clear photo of a very pretty cottage.   It's a pleasant picture, and has even won commendations at club exhibitions, but it isn't art.

It is sharp and clear.   I was using a Leica with a top quality lens. It should have been sharp. That is a reflection of the skill of the maker, but sharpness isn't art.

It is well exposed.   The Leica is fitted with a very expensive exposure meter. There is little excuse for it to be other than properly exposed. Ernst Leitz would be upset if I were so

193

uncaring about the quality which had been lovingly built into the equipment! But that isn't art.

The picture is quite appealing. It is a very attractive cottage, but I neither designed it nor built it. A pretty picture, which accurately shows a pretty cottage, is a straight forward record, but not art!

How then, do I define art? I said it goes on in the head. The artist should reveal something to the viewer. He should say something about the subject which is not immediately obvious. In this respect I would repeat the advice of my English teacher at school, "If you have nothing to say, say nothing."

If we find things interesting, we may wish to show other people what we have seen. The holiday snapshot falls into this category. So, too, does the news photo. When do these cease to be mere records and become art? I believe it is when they convey more than the viewer normally expects. The picture of a starving woman carrying the body of an undernourished child may be more than a mere record. It can show hunger, desperation, despair. These are not visual objects captured by the chemistry of silver halides on plastic film. They are in the mind, and if they can be conveyed from the mind of the photographer to the mind of the viewer, then I would say the picture qualifies as art. If it has nothing to say, it is merely craft.

I have nothing against craft. It is a perfectly legitimate use for any medium, but it's not art. Photos aren't allowed in courtrooms. We are given sketches of the people instead. These are records. They aren't intended to be art. It might even be damaging for them to be so. If a sketch were to reveal the accused as an utter villain, with a cruel and malicious nature, it might prejudice opinion. The sketch is intended to show his features, not his character.

This leads to an interesting comparison between photography and other graphic arts. If we say that a photograph is a good likeness, we usually mean that it reveals the subject's character. This means that the expression in the photo must be in keeping with our impression of the person. The same goes for painting, or a sculpture, but these can show a composite of several

194

expressions rather than a single typical one. This composite expression may never actually exist in reality, but it may be more 'true' than the single expression caught by the photograph. In either case, if the image doesn't convey some indication of the person's character, I would question whether it is art. Yet character is not a visual thing, so the non-visual needs to be shown visually.

Even without people, pictures can convey mood. One cannot paint or photograph mood, yet one expects a good picture to convey it. Art demands more of the medium than is normally expected.

Photography, painting and sculpture can all achieve their own versions of accuracy. In the case of the starving woman, however, photography wins. A painting of a starving woman may, indeed, be art, and so can a statue, but I doubt that they will move anyone to action. A photo, particularly a black and white photo, carries an air of realism, which can stir people's emotions, and give rise to responses like Live Aid. Somehow, despite the cinema, we still seem to react as though the camera doesn't lie. We know it does, but yet we believe it!

I happen to prefer photography to painting, but I take no sides as to their artistic merits. They may both be merely craft, and generally they are, yet painting and photography can also be raised to the level of art. Of the two, I think it is the painter who is more upset to be called a mere craftsman, whereas the photographer is somewhat surprised if he is called an artist.

I make no claims to be either. I am neither artistic nor a competent craftsman. Sometimes I get wonderful ideas in my head, but I cannot express them as I would wish. Of my writing, or my photography, nobody has made any comment which could be construed as being even vaguely equivalent to, "Gosh, but it must have been hot!"

SEEPAGE AND EVAPORATION

In the drier parts of India much of the population depends on wells. Water seeps in from the surrounding ground and care is taken that too much of it doesn't evaporate away. It is a very real concern, and lives may be at stake if such care is not taken. Seepage and evaporation, however, are not usually applicable to people, though my father did apply such a usage to the Anglo-Indian Community. But let us start at the beginning.

The European is superior to the Native. This is God's law, and as such is not open to debate. I am referring, of course, to the European God. From this premise it requires only basic arithmetic to see that the Anglo-Indian, being part European, cannot be as good as the white man, but is obviously better than the native.

The Muslim believes that we are infidels. There is but one God, and Allah is his name. Islam is not impressed by these claims of superiority. The Hindus have various gods, most of whom have several arms and legs. They rest secure behind this multiplicity of limbs and are similarly unimpressed by the European belief in God given superiority. Of the natives of India, only the Anglo-Indian believes in the European God, thus acting subservient to the English and feeling superior to the Indian. Among a supposedly educated minority this is a peculiar anomaly.

Furthermore it has been said that in India there is no colour prejudice because everyone is brown, but that it is better to be a light brown rather than a dark brown! I cannot vouch for the accuracy of this statement, but Hindu and Muslim alike were Aryan invaders, and Aryan preferences may remain to this day. One of these preferences is for a light complexion, and both Hindu and Muslim women try not to mar their beauty by getting too sun tanned. This, however, is a preference, not a prejudice, and it doesn't apply to the men, although they may find their women more attractive if they have a light skin.

The Anglo-Indian is said to have no such prejudices. A-I's come in all shades, very often in the same family. My maternal

Grandma was from the south of India and may well have been of Dravidian stock. The Dravidians were early inhabitants and were a very dark people. She married an Englishman and their children ranged from my Aunt Lily, white skinned with brown hair, to my Aunt Addie, almost black and with black hair. An obvious outcome of Mendel's Law I suppose.

Add to these variations the social climate of the time, when Anglo-Indians were paid preferential salaries, and the English were supposedly superior. Some Indians who spoke sufficiently good English claimed to be A-I's to get more money. Mr. Ram Din became Ramsden, and Mr. Hether Ali became Heatherley, but these were exceptions. Most Indians were far too proud of their heritage to change their names and claim any ancestry but their own.

Very much more common were instances of white Anglo-Indians claiming to be British. This brought no financial benefit but they believed it gave them some additional social standing. My father detested this hypocrisy and was quite mischievous when dealing with it. A fellow officer named Rose retired and said he was "going home" to England. Dad agreed to have a wagon put at his disposal to transship his belongings. Because he was a colleague, Dad arranged for all documentation to be forwarded directly to his office for his personal attention.

All went according to plan. Mr. and Mrs. Rose boarded their ship and their furniture and Indian memorabilia were duly loaded into the hold, but all Railway records were with Dad. Since the shipment was organised by the North Western Railway the shipping line also could not trace the goods to somebody called Rose.

"Cannot find any record of belongings. Very worried," said the cable when the family was already on the high seas.

My father replied, "I gather the wagon was duly sent to your home in Saharanpur where it awaits unloading at your convenience."

With no official records available the Roses were well on their way to England before they were assured that their possessions were safe and all was in order!

This was not a very kind prank, and I dare say Rose regretted claiming to be anything but the Anglo-Indian which he really was. Kind or not, it was the sort of reaction this type of hypocrisy roused in Dad. While not causing any real or material harm, he was sometimes quite evil in the way he dealt with it.

His picture of racial hierarchy did not include words like "better and worse" or "above and below". To him, differences may exist, but they were based on merit, not race, wealth, or social class.

None the less the examples I have quoted show how the Anglo-Indian community gained a few Indians who shouldn't have been there, and lost a few A-I's who weren't really Europeans. Dad's fluid metaphor was not intended as a comment on social worth. "The community," he said "suffered seepage from below and evaporation from above." I suppose it was a fair enough description.

THE SCAN

As she entered the scanner she could feel that they were right. There was something affecting her brain, but what? The faint drone of the machine, and the subdued light which surrounded her, were all conducive to making her feel drowsy, but Susan felt wide awake, fear gnawing at her as she thought of what they may find.

The procedure finished, she dressed again and prepared to see the surgeon.

"I've seen the preliminary read-outs," he said, "but of course I'll need time to see the full analysis before I can make a proper assessment."

"And is it a tumour? I'd rather know."

"At this stage I don't know. I'd rather wait till I'm more certain of the findings. Let's wait for the full assessment. I don't want to alarm you unnecessarily, or give you false hope, when either could be unjustified. Bear with us, it'll only be a day or two. These days tumours can be operated on, so even the worst scenario may not be so bad."

He rose and held out his hand.

"Thank you, doctor," she said as she shook it, and hurriedly left before tears embarrassed her.

It was five days before the phone rang. Mr. Phillips, the surgeon, would like to see Ms. Manning. Could she call in to the surgery at 11 o'clock the following day? "Could she?" thought Susan, "She'd have to, wouldn't she?"

Bad news. She could see it in his face as she sat opposite him the following morning. "It is a tumour," he said, "but a very unusual one. I took the liberty of sending all the results to a colleague in New York, and he agrees with my conclusions."

"So soon?" queried Susan.

"Oh, we used a computer link, E-mail, including scanner pictures, biopsies, past medical history, the lot. He's the world's leading authority on this sort of thing, and we had a long talk about you. Anyway, the bottom line is that the sooner you can come in, the sooner we can operate and get you right again."

It all happened in a matter of days. The speed worried Susan, because she realised that to be admitted so quickly meant that her case must be regarded as serious.

As the anaesthetic took effect she was surprised that she could still see all that was going on. See was perhaps the wrong word, she was aware of it, but in a strange way, not through her eyes but through the monitoring equipment. She should sense the steady beat of her heart, the slowing of her breathing, and the penetration of instruments into her head. She could feel the panic rising in her too. The bone was trepanned and a small probe inserted. The image from the camera was quite clear to Susan even without the screen on which the surgeon was concentrating. Tiny instruments cut away the infected tissue in her brain, the pulse monitor began to falter, and then she died.

Attempts were made to revive her, injections of adrenalin, electrical jolts to the heart, but to no avail. The electrodes were removed, and only then did Susan really grasp the fact of her death. She screamed in frustration and fear, but the screams wouldn't come. Slowly she grew calmer, explored the strange silent world in which she found herself, and tried to make sense of her situation.

As she thought about herself, her new self, she realised that she wasn't in the world with which she was familiar, for one thing there was no sound, for another she couldn't feel anything. Yet there was a lot going on. Electrical impulses passed by her, sometimes even through her, and as she paid more attention to them she realised that they all made a sort of sense.

"Think," she told herself, "think of what this could be. All these messages. Where would one find so many messages?"

Suddenly, like a blinding revelation, it came to her. The Internet! She was, had been, a top computer expert. She thought she knew where she was. Her brain scan had been passed through to New York by E-mail, so her mental 'map', so to speak, had been put on the internet. When her brain died, this copy had taken over and carried on existing in this electronic matrix. Susan now had no fears any more. She was in her own environment, on the inside of the work she had always loved.

200

"Wow!" she thought, "This is incredible! This is my world, where I can fit in as I never could from the outside." She had always been a bit of a loner. Attractive enough, but her keen brain and passion for computing had meant that few men interested her. She was only interested in the brightest men, and they were either married with families, or married to their research. There was Harry, of course, but their careers had kept them busy, and somehow there hadn't been time She regretted that now.

She wandered round the matrix, trying to find her way about this strange and wonderful place. The knowledge of the world was here for the taking, every encyclopedia open to her questing mind, everything ever put on the internet, hers to explore. "Susan," she said to herself, "you've come to heaven!"

Just for the hell of it, she made her way through the web to find the City's computer where she was registered. It was like a maze, and she had to retrace her steps many, many times. It was days before she found the Registrar's records, and read that at fourteen fifty-two on the fifth of July 2003, Susan Manning had died.

"Died? Like hell, I died! I'm very much alive." She explored the matrix, up and down the intersections, trying to find Harry's computer. It was a hopeless task, there were billions of possible routes. She became agitated, and it took all her self control to remain calm.

"Stop it! Use your brain! All Internet messages go through the same satellite servers. Look for him there."

When she did at last find him, she left a message. "Hi! 1452, 5/7/2003. Do you understand? Love you, Susan."

It wasn't till the morning that he saw the message among his E-mail. He pondered for hours, trying to make sense of it. She waited in her electronic world, ready for him to key in his response.

"I don't fully understand. You died, but you're still somewhere, so you didn't really die. Where are you, and how can I find you? I need to find you. Harry."

No sooner had he finished than the screen filled with

words. She explained what had happened, that a copy of her mind was on the World Wide Web, and she told him that she could read any message he left for her on his computer. She omitted to tell him that she could also read anything else he put there. "Leave the man some privacy," she thought.

"I love you," came his reply. "Tell me how to find you."

She told him what she knew, adding a few details which she wouldn't have known if she was still on an earthly plane.

A few days later, paying out a fair amount of his savings, Harry had a detailed brain scan, and E-mailed the results to his home computer. Now his scan, too, had entered the Web.

"Hey, it worked! I wasn't sure it would, but we're together! I don't think you'll be aware of it in the real world, but you're here, and don't forget, to me this is the real world. It's nice to have your company, even if you don't know it!"

Harry read the message and smiled. He was prepared to wait. She was worth it.

THE PAINTED BOARD

It had cost only a few pounds at a house clearance sale. Looking at the painting I had a feeling of deja vu, yet the scene was not one I had ever encountered before. There was a lake, backed by a steep mountainside, and houseboats moored along the banks. People in eastern garb were in long gondola-like boats, and there were lilies, masses of water lilies, covering at least a third of the water.

It was a charming scene, yet something in it gave me a feeling of unease. There was, underneath the painted water, a faint image of ... I paused in my thoughts, an image of what? I looked more closely. No, there was nothing there. The water was beautifully painted, shiny ripples reflecting the green slopes of the mountain, and picking up the broken outlines of boats. Calm and peaceful, but as I looked away, I saw again that doubtful glimpse of something below the surface.

I took the picture off the wall and studied it more closely, moving to the window where the light was better. The detail was exquisite. The tones and outlines were clearly the work of a real artist, but there was no signature, nothing to say who that artist may be. I turned it over to see if there was any indication on the back of the frame.

The wooden back was painted a dark brown, and stuck in one corner was a faded paper label, partly peeling away. The ink had all but disappeared, but with the aid of a magnifying glass I was able to make out the words 'Dal Lake, Kashmir, 189..'. The last figure of the date was missing.

Lower down there were two small areas where the brown paint had worn away. One showed a hint of skin tones, and in the other was what looked like part of a painted eye, seemingly peering through the opening. I was surprised that there should be another picture behind the one on the front. If it was nearly as skilfully crafted as the first one, it was indeed a find. I was quite excited as I carefully began to remove the obscuring paint.

After a few minutes I stopped. I might too easily damage it. I decided to take it to a professional restorer, and have the job done properly. It would cost a bit but it was intriguing enough to be worth it. Besides, if the picture on the back was half as good as that on the front, it was probably a good investment.

I took it back to its place on the wall. As I looked at it again I could see more surely that vague something under the water, but the more intently I looked, the more elusive it seemed to become. It was odd and unnerving.

After a thoughtful lunch I decided I must sort this out. I wrapped the painting in brown paper and drove to a well known dealer. Showing him the painted back, and the eye which was partially revealed, I asked for the rest of the dark brown paint to be removed, to reveal the picture underneath. He scraped away a tiny flake from one edge of the backing and took it into his workshop. A few minutes later he returned and said, "Yes, as I thought, it's ordinary house paint of the period, the sort of thing people would use to paint wood. Fortunately the solvents those days weren't as complex as some of our modern chemicals. Come back, say in two weeks, and I'll have it cleaned up for you."

A fortnight later I was able to see the painting. It showed a young woman, about eighteen years old, with long shining hair, and heavily made up eyes, outlined in kohl. The black edging made the eyes look bigger than ever, and the rosebud mouth curved with just the hint of a smile. The delicate oval face, with its perfectly proportioned features, gave the impression of unbelievable beauty and innocence.

Who was she? From her clothes I guessed she would be a harem girl, a concubine, or perhaps even one of the wives of a Rajah, but I didn't know enough to be sure.

I returned the painting to its hook, this time with the scene against the wall and the portrait looking out. I gazed in fascination. She was exquisite! What a pity that the pictures were on two sides of the same board. Both were worth looking at, yet only one could show at any time.

It was weeks before I decided to turn the picture over again. As I did so I saw the image in the water. It was now quite distinct. The girl, in her luxurious sari, was floating below the surface. She was drowned. Her long hair billowed out around her head, one hand was clenched tightly enough for her nails to draw blood from her palm, her beautiful face was contorted with the effort to breathe.

After the first shock I felt a profound sadness. That this was a true picture of events I didn't doubt for a moment. It didn't need reasons or confirmation, I just knew. This lovely young girl had been drowned, and not by accident either. For some reason she had been killed, executed perhaps, though such was her look of purity and innocence that I couldn't imagine her being guilty of anything. I turned the picture round again. It was too painful, seeing that image floating there in limbo, neither rising to the top, nor sinking to the bottom. It was hard to explain, but I knew that the image had been imprinted on her mind in her last minutes, in those out-of-body moments, just before death, when she was both spectator and participant.

Research. Month after month I delved through the archives of the British Museum's reading room, I approached the Indian High Commission, the India Office, the Pakistan Archives. It took ten months to unravel the story.

Her name was Roshni Gulab, 'Bright Rose'. She had been taken by the Rajah as a concubine, but she was in love. Rather than betray that love she had thrown herself into the lake and drowned. Her artist lover had secretly painted her portrait on the back of another painting, but it had fallen into the hands of her Master. When hung in the palace, however, the eyes had always seemed sad, so it was kept with the lake scene facing out. But her grief still showed, and her image was still seen drowning in the water. The only remedy seemed to be to destroy the portrait, but it was too beautiful for the Rajah to do that, so her picture was covered over with dark brown paint.

With eyes obscured she could not look out, and the image faded from the lake. Almost a century later, when the paint began to peel, she could see again, and the image returned, faintly at first, until I had the obscuring paint removed.

I stood in front of the picture. I lit a candle on either side and tried to tell her that I understood, that I knew how her artist lover must have felt, how she must have felt, but it was all a long time ago. I tried to explain that no man could see her picture and not want to possess her, so I asked her to forgive the Rajah, and be at peace. I prayed, to God, and to Allah whom she had worshipped.

The picture still hangs in my living room, but now there is no sadness in the eyes. Every so often I turn it round. The lake scene is calm and serene, and nothing floats beneath the surface. The Bright Rose has forsaken her sorrow and is at peace.

THE OLDEST MAN IN TOWN

"Good evening. Welcome to the Willie Forrester Show. This is Willie Forrester, and today we are in the town of Dry Gulch, California. In the days of the California gold rush, this was a bustling mining centre, but now Dry Gulch is just a sleepy little backwater in the Not-so-wild West. With me I have Mr. Thomas Starkey, popularly known as Old Tom, reputed to be the oldest man in town. Hello, Mr. Starkey."

"Howdy"

"They tell me you're the oldest man in town."

"Yeah. Since my brother died."

"Oh, your brother died, I am sorry."

"Yeah, so was he."

"Yes, of course. Well, tell me, Mr Starkey, exactly how old are you?"

"…………"

"Mr. Starkey?"

"Wal, I can't say exactly, not to the day."

"No, not to the day, of course not, but how old do you reckon?"

"I don't have to reckon, I know. I'm ninety seven."

"Ninety seven? Well that's a good age, isn't it?"

"Yeah, but so was ninety six, and ninety five afore that"

"And when were you ninety seven?"

"On my birthday."

"Yes, of course on your birthday, but when was that?"

"When my brother died."

"Your brother died on your birthday! That was sad."

"Yeah."

"And how old was your brother when he died?"

"Ninety seven"

"No, no, Mr Starkey, you were ninety seven on your birthday. How old was your brother?"

"I told yer, ninety seven"

"But if you were ninety seven he must have been older."

"Nope"

"So it was your brother who was ninety seven?"

"Yeah"

"And how old were you"

"I keeps tellin' yer, Ninety seven!"

"You were the same age?"

"Yeah"

"Ah, I see, you were twins!"

"Yeah"

"And he was the older twin?"

"Yeah"

"You didn't say!"

"Yer didn't ask."

"And the big mausoleum with the Starkey name on it, is that where he's buried?"

"Yeah"

"A family tomb?"

"Nope"

"But it does bear the Starkey name?"

"Yeah, that was his name."

"And how did he come to be buried in such a fine mausoleum?"

"I guess it's 'cause he died."

"Yes, that goes without saying, but why such a fine tomb?"

"He was a fine fella."

"I see. So now you're the oldest man in town."

"Yeah"

"And are there any other Starkeys?"

"Nope"

"You had no children?"

"Had a son. He died."

"And Mrs. Starkey?"

"There warn't no Mrs Starkey."

"The boy's mother?"

"She warn't Mrs Starkey, she was the Preacher's wife."

"You had a son by the Preacher's wife!"

"Yeah"

"And how did the Preacher react to that?"

"Preacher was pleased."

"Why would he be pleased?"

"Wal, he thought the boy was his."

"I see. And the boy died you say."

"He warn't a boy by then, he was forty two."

"Even so he was still quite young."

"I guess so"

"What happened to him?"

"He up and died."

"Yes, but why?"

"Preacher didn't come from a long lived family."

"But he wasn't from the Preacher's family."

"That's true, but he didn't know that! So he up and died."

"I see, so your son died young. What caused his death?"

"I guess it was religion."

"Can you explain that?"

"Wal, his Ma was Preacher's wife. Because of her religion she felt guilty, yer see, so she never did tell Preacher, or the boy, about me. Boy thought he was Preacher's son, and like I said, Preacher's family allus died young. So I guess it was religion as killed him."

"A sad story. And to what do you attribute your great age?"

"It's because I was born a fair while back."

"And were you born here in Dry Gulch?"

"Yeah"

"And you've lived here all your life."

"Not all of it, not yet"

"No, not yet, not yet a while I hope. But you must have seen a lot of changes"

"Yeah"

"What sort of changes, Mr Starkey?"

"Just changes, things are different."

"Yes, but how are they different? In what way?"

"They ain't the same, that's how they're different. they're just different"

"Can you describe some of these changes?"

"Nope, I can't rightly say I can describe 'em, they're just not the same."

"Well folks, we're out of time. Mr Starkey, thank you for an interesting interview. That was Mr Tom Starkey, the oldest person in Dry Gulch."

"Not the oldest person, the oldest man, my cousin Mary's a mite older. She was ...."

"Thank you, thank you Mr Starkey. This is goodbye from the Willie Forrester Show in Dry Gulch, California. Goodbye."

"Like I was sayin', my cousin Mary, she was.. ......"

"This is goodbye from the Willie Forrester show.   Cut!"

A MARK UPON THE VIRGIN SNOW

Like a mark upon the virgin snow
Of a yet untrodden field,
I feel again a sudden ache
In a wound I thought had healed.
But Time perhaps does not heal all,
Perhaps all memories do not fall
Into the depths beyond recall,
To be forever sealed
Against the idly wandering thought,
Haphazard straying through times I knew,
To stop.
               To suddenly stop short.
At one far, longing, thought of you.

FOOTPRINTS

Footsteps, quiet upon the forest floor, rustling leaves beneath your gentle tread, with steps so soft they don't imprint the moss, but swirling leaves will show me where you passed.

Sun shines summer-bright, and like your smile, it lights the shadows on the sloping banks, it dapples grass where I can trace your path by gentle whisperings among the trees. The breeze is like your voice which calls to me. I follow, up the path, around the turn, and catch a distant glimpse, perhaps of you, but when I reach the spot, I find you gone.

The butterfly on silent wings, sheds bright colour in the forest glade, as once you shed a brightness in my life, but that was long ago. The butterfly goes off, and leaves no mark, and of course, there are no footprints on the ground.

I look around for signs of you, but indelible, your footprints are only in my mind.

THE PERIPHERAL MAN

The Railway Running Room at Multan is said to be haunted.

I first saw him out of the corner of my eye. When I turned to look directly at him he was gone.

He was a grey man. Whether this was real or just the result of peripheral vision I didn't know. Things on the edges of our vision are usually seen in shades of grey, but his greyness went deeper than this, as well as being physical it was a greyness of mind, and of spirit.

For days I tried to look at him properly, but always without success. In the end I gave up in frustration. "Get out! Get out of my space. I don't know who you are, and you obviously won't let me see you properly, so just go. Why hang around?"

"Because I must talk to you."

"Well, here I am, so talk. No good saying you must, and then doing nothing about it. Talk!"

This is what he told me.

The Railway Running Room is haunted. There have been several apparitions seen at different times, but the most common sighting is of a young woman sitting at a dressing table, combing her hair. Her name is Mrs. Marchant. She was married to a Railway Auditor in 1918, just after the war finished, and occasionally she went 'on line' with him, living in his special carriage, while he travelled round doing his regular inspections. When they came to a large junction like Multan they would make use of the wider facilities offered by the Running Room. This set of apartments was provided for the use of train running staff, drivers, guards and conductors, when they were away from home. It was run by a franchise holder who cleaned and cooked. There was a charge for these services, most of which went on paying for the franchise, but even so, due to the generous subsidies given by the Railway, Running Room franchises were quite profitable, and much sought after.

In 1921, when the Marchants had been married three

years, they stopped at Multan. It was a busy station, an important junction, and the inspection would take several days. Emily Marchant spent much of her time at the Railway Club. Ladies played whist or bezique some evenings, but the place was generally deserted in the day, and she whiled away her time at the billiard tables. There was little fun in knocking the balls about on her own, but even that was better than moping about in the heat, with nothing to do.

It was there that she met Jack Pearce.

"Hello, who're you? I heard the noise and wondered who it could be at this time of day."

"I'm Emily Marchant. My husband's the Deputy Auditor."

"Bill Marchant? Yes, of course. He'll be a while auditing a busy place like Multan."

"I know. He told me it'll take about two weeks to get done here."

"Even longer I should think. And meanwhile, you're perfecting your billiards?"

She laughed. "Hardly, but it's something to do. Too hot in the Running Room, and even hotter in the carriage. Have to do something to pass the time, stave off the boredom."

"Why not come to the Reservoir? It's cooler there. We could do some fishing. Give Bill a freshly caught dinner. That'll surprise him!"

It was cool under the trees which lined the edge of the reservoir. Jack brought along a rod and taught her how to bait the hook and throw out the line. His arm was around her as he stood behind her, guiding the throw. "Easy now, watch the float. Pull when it goes under."

Again his arms encircled her as he helped her hold the rod. "Pull!"

She felt the line pull away.

"Easy, let him run a while, now stop him. Gently. Good. Now reel him in. Slowly. Not too fast." She could feel his arms through her flimsy cotton dress, the press of his chest against her back, occasional touches of his forearm on her breasts.

214

"Give him his head a while, then take up the slack as he approaches. There, now lift him out the water."

His arm tightened slightly as unhooked the fish. Then as she turned, he bowed and said, "Madam, your fish!"

"Oh, that was great! Thank you!" In her excitement her arms went round his neck and she kissed him, then drew away, embarrassed.

Back at the Running Room she ordered the cook to prepare the fish for dinner. "There'll be enough for three. Why don't you join us, Jack?"

"You sure Bill won't mind?"

"Of course not, why should he?"

Bill did mind. He was a fiercely possessive man, and he minded very much, but tried not to show it. Emily sensed his disapproval, but it made her all the more determined to enjoy her stay. The heat, the thin dresses clinging to her body, the boredom, and her own warm nature; it wasn't really planned, it just happened. It could have been prevented, but because she was bored, it wasn't. By the third afternoon she and Jack were lovers.

The Railway colony was far too small a community for secrets. Inevitably Bill found out, and in a jealous rage he killed them both. He offered no defence at his trial, and was sent to the gallows.

I tried to look at the grey man. Was he Bill Marchant or Jack Pearce, or somebody else? I couldn't tell.

Meanwhile, Emily sits at the dressing table, and combs her hair. Is she getting ready for Bill to return for the evening? Or is she preparing to meet Jack for the afternoon? Whichever it is, she'll be disappointed, for both Bill and Jack are long since gone.

She waits alone in the Railway Running Room at Multan …. which is said to be haunted.

THE LODGER

"I don't like him. He has a shifty look."

"Oh, I don't think that's quite fair, Mother, we know hardly anything about him."

"He's been here a month!"

"Yes, out all day and in his room most of the evening. You only see him at dinner."

"Well," the lips were pursed, giving her that disapproving expression which Margaret had come to dislike so much, "I'm a good judge, as well you know. You mark my words, there's something not right there. You keep away from him."

Margaret gave a harsh little laugh. "Keep away from him! For God's sake Mother, he's our lodger. How can I keep away from him when we are living in the same house, eating at the same table! Besides, I'm thirty-six years old, not some starry-eyed teenager."

"All the same, just you mind." The woman in the wheelchair moved her heavy bulk to one side. Since the accident, sixteen years ago, she had found comfort in her food and had grown larger and larger with the passing years, and as she grew fatter, so it seemed to her daughter, she grew more querulous too.

"I'll just serve the dinner. Is there anything you need first?"

The woman shook her head, and went back to her reading.

She was still reading when Margaret called up the stairs. "Robert. Dinner!"

"Don't be so familiar. He's not a friend, call him Mr. Smith. Smith! that's never his real name, and why shouldn't he use his own name if he's on the level."

"How do we know it isn't his name? Now shush,

he's coming down. Just remember we need the money!"

A tall, well-built man in his forties came into the room. "Good evening Mrs. Willoughby, how are you this evening?"

She looked up at him as he bent forward and enquired solicitously about her day. "Bored," she said ungraciously, "There's never anything to do, and Margaret's out all day. No-one cares about an old woman like me."

"I do have to work, Mother," but the only response was a sniff of disapproval. A quick glance passed between the daughter and the man. He gave a slight smile and the smallest hint of a shrug.

Margaret released the brake and pushed the chair towards the table. "Let me do that." He reached forward to take the handles.

"She can manage!" Mrs Willoughby's voice was sharp, almost hostile, and he drew back.

Dinner was quiet, tense. "Any luck Robert?" Margaret tried to bring some normality into the meal.

"No, there's not a lot of work about for retired army officers I'm afraid. It's a youth culture now. Over the hill as far as they're concerned."

"You're not over the hill!" There was a touch of warmth in Margaret's voice. "You're still in your prime at forty. And you're very fit," she added, ignoring the glare of disapproval from her mother.

"Forty-five," he corrected. "Lucky enough to have stayed fit, I grant you, but they don't care about that. Date of birth? And as soon as I tell them, that's it."

"Well I'm sure something will turn up. Don't give up hope."

"Why should he do that?" Mrs. Willoughby's tone did nothing to ease the atmosphere. The meal relapsed into silence, which continued through coffee. Margaret rose to clear away the dishes.

"Do you want the television on, Mother?"

"Nothing worth seeing." The reply was grunted. "Rubbish, that's all there is. Don't know what we pay our licence for! I'll read my book."

"Do you want to watch anything, Robert?"

"Perhaps not. Not if Mrs. Willoughby wants to read."

"You watch if you like. But keep the sound down, it's all trash anyway." She picked up her book and dismissed the topic.

Margaret switched on the set and went to the kitchen to do the dishes. Above the sound of the water she could hear the television; the voices, and the background music. Then, as she began the quieter chore of drying up, she could identify the words of the play. "He's in a wheel chair now. There's no danger, he can't walk. Take him to the cliff top and just let him go over the edge. There won't be a damn thing he can do about it."

"Yeah, and it'll be taken for an accident. No reason for anyone to harm him, no motive, see. Just a tragic accident, that's what it'll be."

She put the last plate in the cupboard and returned to the lounge. As she walked in the door Robert looked at her, and her cheeks went scarlet. He knew, or at any rate he guessed!

That night there was a quiet knock on her door. Tiptoeing across the carpet she opened it carefully. It was him. She had known it would be. Without saying a word his arms went around her and his lips came down on her mouth. Silently they moved to the bed and all her years of pent up longing for a man were released in a flood of sexuality.

Lying beside him in the aftermath of passion she was somehow not surprised when he said quietly, "I'll help you get rid of her. That's what you want isn't it? I saw it in your eyes when you walked in the door."

"It was only the words of the play. I've never thought of such a thing, really I haven't."

"But you have now, and you won't forget it. The idea will haunt you, picking at your mind until either you go mad, or you do something about it."

"There's nothing I can do about it, you know that. Anyway, I'm sure I don't want to, even if I could."

"Oh yes, you want to; and I'll help you. I was in the SAS. I know more ways of getting rid of people than you could ever imagine."

"But why would you do that?"

"For a home like this." His gesture indicated the room. "And for this." His arms drew her close to him once more.

Her passion was tempered with a sudden thrill of fear as she realised that he was deadly serious.

THE PUPPET
(A Short Story in 100 words)

The puppet hated me. After the show, when I put him back in his box, fury would blaze from his ceramic eyes. So, last night, I sat him on the shelf instead.

I wakened with a start, and turned to switch on the bedside lamp. Something struck the pillow behind me, and there, embedded where my head had been, was a sharp pair of scissors. They were clutched tightly in the puppet's hand.

This morning I threw him on the fire, but God help me, as he burned, I swear I heard him scream

IMPRESSIONS

It was a pleasant autumn day. The sun shone on my face, and the leaves were rustling in a gentle breeze. Dead leaves, falling from the trees, to carpet the ground in the park. I could feel them, thick and soft beneath my feet as I walked towards my favourite bench.

It stood in one corner of the park, not far from the edge of the small lake. I liked it because it was usually deserted and I could sit down, peaceful and quiet. There were ducks on the lake, and they quacked as I threw down the bread which I always brought with me on these excursions. If I held out my hand, with pieces of bread on my palm, the bolder ducks came up and took it from me. They chattered at each other, vying for the bread, but despite the noise they made, and the speed with which they took the food, I was never pecked by any of them. They were always too gentle for that.

There was a smell of flowers. Autumn flowers. I couldn't recognise them, but they smelt like jasmine. Does one get jasmine in the autumn? I don't know, but it was a well remembered smell, reminding me of the cottage I lived in as a child.

My thoughts turned to nostalgia. All so long ago, that cottage, and the little boy who grew up to be me. I recalled the long back garden, where I used to play, and mother calling me in for jam and bread at eleven. Always looking out for me was Mum, frightened in case I hurt myself. I could never understand that. This was my own familiar world, and I was quite at home in it. Yet she was always saying "Take care, don't go near the roses or you'll be scratched by the thorns." I was very seldom scratched, even though I often held the roses close to my nose to savour the smell of them. Dad was a keen gardener and grew some special roses, the old fashioned sort, which had a lovely scent, but didn't bloom for very long.

It was autumn now, and roses were all past blooming. Yes, it was autumn now, time had fled and youth was past regretting. The old cottage had eventually been pulled down,

221

along with all its neighbours, the gardens all stripped bare, and a new housing development took their place. An ugly development. Shoes clicked on stone pavements, the sound of children everywhere, echoing back from plain brick walls. I am sensitive to sounds, and when there's no vegetation to break up the starkness I can hear the echoes. They bounce back from all directions, confusing in their conflict.

It was an ugly development, and the echoes were not the echoes of childish laughter, but of squabbling kids, and nagging mothers, and the sweet smell of roses never came into those harsh streets, concrete and barren. Instead there was the smell of newness, a gritty sort of newness, from newly laid roads, and the recent building which had been going on. One could almost taste the powdery cement, and feel the dust of plaster on one's skin.

Yet the names were pretty. Petunia Drive, Primrose Walk, Daffodil Close. The names had to make up for the reality, a reality of concrete and skateboards, laced with the smell of car fumes and engine oil.

A spot of rain on my face drew me out of my reminiscing. Why worry? It was all a long time ago. Mum and Dad have long since gone. I'm glad that they never had to see the cottages bulldozed flat and the new estate go up. In some ways I'm glad that I didn't either. I pick up my white stick and make my way home. I can't see the ugly sights, and my memories aren't dependent on my eyes.

THE LOCAL GOVERNMENT OFFICER

He joined the local government staff
With three A level certificates,
And quickly rose within the ranks
Doing everything in triplicate.

But then alas, he fell in love
With a bright young thing who wanted more
From life than forms in triplicate,
And thought the Council was a bore.

He wooed her, and wooed her, and wooed her again,
His hand and his heart he offered her,
But she said
    she'd rather be dead
       than wed
To a Local Government Officer!

She said that his work was an empty charade,
She viewed his ambitions with scorn and contempt,
She wanted a man who had 'get up and go'
And true to her principles, got up and went.

His well paid job he then resigned,
His Union card he handed in,
He fell into a slow decline,
Relying on whiskey and on gin,
And some have thought
    when cash was short
       he'd even resort
To paraffin.

As he prepared for bed one night
He glanced upon the mirrored scene,
Reflecting him, as now he was,
A ghost of what he once had been;
And suddenly he realised
To what low depths he'd chanced to fall,
And in a fit of deep despair
Resolved that he would end it all.

He sat upon his lonely bed,
Her photograph he fondly kissed,
He raised a pistol to his head,
He three times fired, and three times missed!

Shaken by this strange respite
He sat and pondered for a while.
And then he wrote a farewell note -
Then wrote two copies, for the file.

But as he went to post the notes,
Blinded by the tears he'd wept,
He tripped on a kerb, still unrepaired,
And fell in the gutter, still unswept.
A broken bottle, not picked up,
Gashed his neck, he lay and bled,
By morning light a sorry sight,
The poor man was clearly dead.

The coroner's verdict you can guess
Was based upon the farewell note -
'The officer in his distress
Had cut his throat…
                    his throat….
                              his throat'.

THE MUSTARD SEED

The vehicle came to a sudden halt. All around was desert, shimmering with haze, heat cloaking them like a shroud.

"Damn, double damn." Mohindra Gopal, the driver, was not amused. If he couldn't get it going they would have to walk. He turned to his three passengers.

"I'll see what is wrong. If we can go we will go...."

"And if we can't?" inquired the big red-haired man.

"Then we walk."

The driver was perhaps the only one who realised the import of what he was saying. Forty miles of steady walking was not an impossible task, not if one's life depended on it, but when the temperature went up to 120 Fahrenheit, or more, in the shade, and there was no shade, it might be different.

"We'd better get down to it then." As Kelly lifted the bonnet a blast of hot air struck them, noticeable even above the heat of the desert. The engine was streaked with oil, and there was an ominous hissing of steam. He reached for the radiator.

"No, Sahib, it is too hot." Taking a dirty rag the driver gave the cap a partial turn, and steam hissed out. After a while he removed the cap. "It looks dry. When it cools we will put in water and continue."

While waiting for the engine to cool, he checked the oil. The sump was empty. Lying on the hot sand the young man looked up at the crankcase. With dismay he noticed the crack, and the dripping oil. He beckoned the red-haired passenger away from the car.

"It is no use. There is a crack and the oil has gone. We will have to walk."

"Are you mad? How can the ladies walk in this heat, it must be over a hundred and twenty, and how far is it?"

"About forty miles."

"They can't walk forty miles, it's ridiculous."

"The car will get very hot. To stay is to get heat stroke. It would be safer to walk."

The big man was in no mood to listen. "They can't walk. That's all there is to it. You'd better fix the car."

"I cannot fix the car, Sahib, it is impossible."

A hand gripped his shoulder, "Get the bloody tools!"

Kelly was never the brightest of men, and now, stuck in the desert with the wife and daughter of his business partner, he found himself unable to think straight. Mohindra Gopal quietly went to the boot, rubbing his bruised shoulder, and brought out a comprehensive tool kit. There was nothing in it which could help, he knew that, but Kelly insisted. Let him see for himself. Once he was satisfied, they could start walking.

It didn't take long to realise that there was nothing they could do. "Avril, there's a problem. The car's kaput. We'll have to walk."

Avril Foster looked out at the desert with a frown. She knew something was wrong, she had felt the judder, heard the clanking, but surely the driver would fix it.

"Walk? We can't walk. It's too hot. We'll wait till it cools down."

"Memsahib," cut in Gopal, "the longer we wait the more thirsty we will be. It is safer that we start right away. It is only about twenty-five miles, about eight hours walking."

"You said forty miles," said Kelly.

Gopal raised his eyes upwards, and walked away. Kelly ran after him. "Make up your bloody mind, twenty or forty?"

"Please, Sahib, do not disturb the ladies more than necessary. It is forty two miles I think, but I tell them less, so they won't worry."

"Oh I see. Yes, of course, good idea."

The four set off. Avril Foster carried a parasol as though out for a gentle stroll in the park. Jennifer showed more sense than her stepmother. She donned a wide brimmed hat, and carried a container of water. Kelly and Gopal took the rest of the water and led the two women along the faintly discernible road. It didn't differ much from the rest. Sand drifted with the wind, and the road was visible only until covered again by the desert.

By midday they had travelled eight miles. Avril

226

complained about the heat. She complained about the glare. She complained about the dryness. She used nearly all the water in Jennifer's container.

Kelly kept his counsel, but the more she irritated him, the more he directed his anger against Gopal. "Why didn't you check the car before we started? You had no business to take passengers in an unsafe vehicle."

"The vehicle was not unsafe, Sahib. It was the detour, when you insisted that we see the ruins. We hit a rock on that rough track. It must have cracked the casing."

"Don't make bloody excuses. If the track wasn't all right you shouldn't have gone."

"I told you we should not go, Sahib, but you were determined."

"Oh, you natives never accept responsibility do you? So now it's my fault I suppose."

"Please Sahib, let us not argue. Keep our strength for walking, not for fighting."

Jennifer came up beside the two men, and they fell silent. After a while Kelly dropped back to walk with Avril, and Jennifer spoke quietly to Gopal. "It's not your fault, I know that, but tell me truly, how far is it to Bikampur."

"I told you."

"I'm not a fool, Mr. Gopal. How far is it really?"

"About forty miles from where we stopped. I think about thirty two from here."

"Thank you. Will the water last?"

"If we don't waste it. Your mother should not wash her face. We should only use water for drinking."

They walked on in silence. "How hot will it be?" she asked after a while.

"Over a hundred and twenty."

"Mr. Gopal, I told you I'm not a fool. That's in the shade, but there isn't any shade. How much in the sun?"

"Up to one-forty, one-forty-five."

She made no reply but trudged on. It was hard going, with feet sinking in the sand, and with the occasional outcrop of

227

rock jutting unevenly above the surface.

After ten miles Gopal called a halt. "I think a little rest. We will stop for ten minutes."

"We're not bloody stopping in this," said Kelly. "We'll be dehydrated if we don't get out of here."

"The ladies need to rest. Only for a while, then we start again."

"Come on Avril, I'm not risking you with this idiot. We're going on."

"Please Sahib, a short rest...."

Kelly picked up the water and moved away. "Come along Jennifer."

"No. I'm doing as Mr. Gopal says. He knows the country and I think it's best to follow his advice. Besides, we need him to guide us."

"Guide us! We wouldn't be in this mess if it weren't for him."

"We wouldn't be in this mess if you and Mother had listened to him in the first place. He said we shouldn't make that detour."

"Oh, suit yourself! You're over eighteen, as you never cease to tell us. Your stepmother and I are going anyway." Taking Avril's arm he pulled her away and strode down the road.

"We should stay with them," said Gopal, "they could get lost."

"He deserves to be lost. The man's a fool. How Daddy chose him as a partner I can't imagine."

"Still, we should stay with them." They followed the pair, making no effort to catch up, but keeping them in sight.

"We'll be all right, won't we Mr. Gopal?" Her throat was dry and sore. The sun blazed down, reflecting back from the sand, hurting her eyes It was like being in an oven, even the wind was just a hot blast which didn't help to cool her.

"Have faith Miss Jennifer. It takes three, four days to die of thirst." Less in this heat he thought, but he mustn't dishearten her. "We've only been a few hours, and we still have water left."

"Not much," muttered Jennifer. "Mother kept swilling

the sweat off her face!"

Near nightfall Gopal called out. "Stop Sahib. Stop for the night or we'll surely get lost. We'll go on in the morning."

"To hell with that! We're going on now. I'm not bloody well dying of thirst out here."

The driver shrugged resignedly and continued trudging behind them, Jennifer by his side.

The orange streaks left the horizon, and the temperature dropped quickly. After only a few minutes of twilight the darkness was complete. Stars showed brilliant in the clear air, but gave little light. It was a new moon, so there'd be no light from that either.

"I can hardly see them," said Jennifer.

"I know. We must stay close to them, but I can't see the way. I don't know where he thinks he's going."

"That fool will get us all lost," she replied, then called out. "Mother, please stop. We can't see where we're going. We must wait for daylight."

"Patrick knows what he's doing," was the reply, half carried away on the wind.

Jennifer started forward to remonstrate with her, but caught her foot on a rocky outcrop and fell headlong to the ground. Gopal went to her, but she didn't respond to his questions. He could barely see her, but lowered his cheek to her mouth. At least she was still breathing!

"Kelly Sahib, come quickly. Miss Jennifer has fallen!" There was no reply. He set off quickly in the direction he had last seen them. "Kelly Sahib," he called again, but his words were lost in the wind. He returned, but couldn't find Jennifer in the dark. After twenty minutes of searching his foot kicked her inert form, and made him stumble. She gave a little moan, which brought him some relief. At least she was still alive, though he couldn't see her condition. He sat down beside her, knees drawn up for warmth, and waited for the dawn. Finally he fell asleep.

In the pale light of morning Jennifer opened her eyes and sat up unsteadily. Her ankle hurt and her forehead was swollen. She shivered with cold, despite the cotton shirt thrown over her.

Near by the young man was asleep on the sand, his bare chest rising and falling slowly. She shook him gently, and held out his shirt.

"Thank you." She hesitated, "thank you, Mohindra." It seemed odd to use the taxi driver's first name.

"Forgive me, Miss Jennifer, I did not mean to be forward or familiar, but I was unable to wake you, and the desert gets cold at night."

"Just as cold for you, you must be perished! Please put it on."

"We must seek your Mother and Kelly Sahib. It would not do for them to lose direction. The desert can be dangerous."

"We'll find them, but first we must find the water. I had it when I tripped last night." They soon found the canister. The fall had cracked it, and the water was gone.

Gopal became quietly decisive. "We go on. We cannot help them, the best thing is to reach Bikampur and send assistance. It is the wiser course, Miss Jennifer."

"I know you're right, but to leave them...."

"Even if we found them we could do nothing. We have no water, they probably have none either. It is better for everyone for us to send help, a helicopter will soon locate them. Besides, we could go looking, and they might already have got there."

"You think so?" She seized on the faint hope.

"Have faith, Miss Jennifer. Trust me, they will be found. Now save your ankle, put your weight on me."

They struggled for hours towards the town, still out of sight over the horizon. "How far?" she asked.

" It's flat, the horizon must be about twelve miles. When we get that near we should see the town."

"I'm so thirsty. I'm sorry about the water."

"No matter," he said. "People don't die so easily. How is the bump on your head?"

"A bit sore, but I'm all right. I do have faith, you know. Only a little, but at least as much as a mustard seed I hope!"

He looked at her, uncomprehending. "Private joke!" she said, taking his hand. " Come on, let's get to town and start the search. Thank you for looking after me!"

"I wish to." He squeezed her hand. "Look!"

Through sore eyes, and a shimmering haze which made the scene shift and quiver, she made out the tops of buildings. "Bikampur," she said. "Only twelve miles to go!"

ABANDON SHIP!

It was worth thirty pounds of anyone's money. Unfortunately we couldn't find anyone who felt the same. Twenty pounds? Ten? Apparently not. We decided to give it to our son, but he didn't want it enough to collect it, and we were finding it too awkward to lift it onto the roof rack, which was the main reason we no longer used it.

It had given us a lot of fun, but now obviously it had to go. It was of no use to us, and it cluttered up the place. A ten foot sandwich-construction plastic dinghy is not something one can readily put in a corner and ignore.

"I know," said my wife, "we'll bury it in the lawn and make a feature of it!"

It was a novel suggestion and I didn't take it seriously, but when I returned from work the following day she had dug a big hole in the garden. The next day she had made the hole even bigger. The undulating lawn had a lot of sticky clay spoiling its previously pristine appearance. Muddy footprints passed from hole to summer house, from summer house to garden shed, and then back to the hole. Even the flower beds had not escaped some damage.

The place looked a mess! Considering her love for her garden, this was serious stuff. The hole would have to be at least three times as deep to bury the boat and I didn't see how we were to achieve this without mechanical help. For all I knew, by that depth we may have hit the water table.

"No," she said, "it's deep enough. Now help me get it in."

We manhandled the dinghy into the opening. It didn't quite fit. We manhandled it out again, and continued to dig. On the third try it fitted in the hole with a modicum of space around it. This we proceeded to pack with some of the earth which had been dug out. My wife is the artistic one of the family. I am the technical one. It was my idea to use a spirit level. The boat was decidedly squint. We manhandled it out of the hole, made some adjustments, and manhandled it in again. It was still wrong, but by packing earth selectively we were able to level it up.

By this time we were both pretty tired. It is as well, for if we had proceeded any further I am sure the soil would have sunk and ruined all our work so far. Another week at work intervened, and by the time we got back to the project of "Abandon ship!" the earth had settled quite nicely. A few more adjustments with the spirit level and my wife pronounced herself satisfied.

At this juncture the boat was half in and half out of the lawn, with soil heaped all round it. This was carefully banked up against the edges of the boat forming a sort of border ready for planting. On one side we built a low wall on which to sit, and placed a few slabs in front of it.

As a garden feature it was unique. It looked exactly like a boat, half stuck in a lawn, half hidden by a wall. We had already used concrete slabs in front of the wall, so we used some more to disguise the shape of the boat. We overhung slabs across the corners of the stern so that it looked semicircular, and we covered the bow with a curve of slabs so that it also looked semicircular. We now had an oval looking boat half stuck in our lawn, packed in soil, and surrounded with concrete slabs.

"Great!" said the artistic one of the family. She then planted the bank of soil with a specimen drooping Japanese acer and numerous smaller plants, heathers, primulas, and a small variegated euonymous.

Meanwhile, I, as the technical one put the bung in the bottom of the boat and filled it with water, praying that all would be well and the water would stay in. It did!

All that now remained was to put in some pond plants and let things settle down. Some fish were later introduced. The koi carp were not impressed with this unprepossessing home and I'm afraid they didn't survive. Some minnows which we brought from a nearby stream lasted longer, but even they didn't survive very long. Perhaps they found it altogether too plush! The less exotic shubunkin and goldfish, however, seemed to like it well enough. The pond "balanced", the oxygenating plants kept the water clear, the water snails cleaned away any dirt, the waterlilies looked good when they flowered, and eventually we had the greatest accolade of all - the fish bred!

So if you have a dinghy which you don't want, and you can't sell, don't abandon it, bury it! It could make a great garden pond.

THE SALE

Debbie was worried. For some time now the practice had been going downhill. Dr. Fothergill was looking worn and haggard, bags under his tired eyes. How she wished she could solve his problems, but Dr. Fothergill, Tim, was an independent man, determined to face up to anything that life could throw at him. How she wished he would let her help!

The surgery was in what had been a poor part of town. Tim's father, Doctor Sam, had had a full list of National Health patients, the practice had thrived, but then came the redevelopment. The old tenements had been torn down, and new executive homes built on the land, bought up by the well-to-do retired, or up and coming yuppies. They all had private health insurance, either personally or through their companies; and they got their medical care from more up market surgeries. The old National Health patients left as their homes were demolished, and fewer and fewer of the newcomers registered with Dr. Sam Fothergill and his son.

Debbie was the practice nurse when old Dr. Sam had retired, but as patient numbers dwindled she became telephonist, receptionist, practice manager, and general dog's body. She worried about it, but not for herself. She would do anything for Doctor Tim, anything at all, but even she couldn't force people through the door.

One Saturday morning she was going through the books, and she saw how bad were the practice finances. Something had to be done, but what? she asked herself.

"Must end Bank Holiday Monday". The caption stared up at her. MFI were having a 'more than 50% sale.' Land of Leather were selling off sofas at less than half price, Furniture Village and DFS were offering huge reductions and nothing to pay for a year, That was it, thought Debbie, we'll have a sale.

"Tim," she called, "Tim! I've got it! We'll have a sale. That should bring them through the door."

"How can we have a sale?" said Tim. "Why would they be interested in cut price treatment when they don't even come for free treatment under the National Health? No Debbie I can't see how this idea will solve anything."

"No," she cried, "we won't sell them treatment, we'll sell them diseases. You know what these rich snobs are like, if they developed some high faluting ailment they would brag about it at the dinner table. The rarer the better. Lhasa fever for instance, that should be good for a few months of 'Where did you get that?' and 'I thought that was only found in Tibet, you haven't been to Tibet lately, have you?' Oh go on Tim, you could clean up with a few good diseases."

"I'm a doctor, I can't go giving people diseases, I'm supposed to cure them, not make them ill."

"They're doing it all the time in hospitals. Not intentionally I grant you, but making people ill all the same. MRSA and the like. In any case you don't have to give them anything you can't cure. Just give them a feeling of one-upmanship, make them feel good!"

Tim was reluctant, but Debbie was persistent. She was determined to save Tim from his own high principled folly. She won her battle when Mrs Fortescue-Smythe wandered into the morning surgery. There was nothing wrong with Mrs Smythe, except for an excess of time and money. It was inverted snobbery made her use the National Health, and she called in every so often, mainly to pass the time.

"Ah, Mrs Fortescue-Smythe," smiled Debbie, "how are you today? Oh dear, I see you have a bit of a sniffle."

"Have I? Must be catching a cold," said the patient.

"Oh no, Mrs Smythe, not a cold. This sounds like coryza, acute I would say. You must let the doctor sort out some medication for you."

"Coryza? Is that bad?"

"Not life threatening," Debbie assured her, "but it's quite incurable. At least no-one has found a cure yet, and believe me that's not for want of trying!"

"Oh dear, whatever am I to do?"

"Dr. Fothergill will sort out something to relieve the symptoms, though, as I say, so far there isn't any cure."

Mrs. Fortescue-Smythe soon told Mrs.Willoughby-Jones that she had this incurable disease. "Discomfort? No my dear, not really, that wonderful Dr Fothergill gave me something to keep it under control."

Mrs Willoughby-Jones called in at the surgery the following morning. "No, young lady, I do not have an appointment, but I am sure the doctor will fit me in. Tell him I am a friend of Mrs Fortescue-Smythe. I fear I have something more serious than coryza. I will not have Mrs Smythe looking down her nose at me," she added confidentially.

"I'm sure the doctor can help," said Debbie, turning aside to hide her smile, and ushering her into the Doctor.

"Runny nose? Sore throat? It's just a common cold I think," said Tim.

"Common cold! I'll have you know young man there is nothing common about anything I may have. Acute coryza at least, very acute, very very acute!"

"I'm afraid not, Mrs Jones. I can give you the same medicine that I prescribed for your friend."

"Certainly not. You must be able to find something more ... more refined than a common cold. Examine me thoroughly, there must be something. Oh I'll pay, you needn't fear on that score, I have a sufficiency of means thanks to my late husband."

Tim conducted a thorough examination of the wealthy widow. She was overweight, never took any exercise, drank too many gins, and indulged in too many chocolates.

"There is a slight cardiovascular problem, but otherwise you're in fine fettle. You need to adjust your lifestyle a bit, that's all."

"But can't you give me some pills, or something? Cardiovascular, that could be serious couldn't it? "

"Not at this stage, but if it makes you feel easier I'll give you some tablets to keep the blood from clotting and prevent any danger of thrombosis. That will relieve your mind at any rate." He sat at his desk and wrote a prescription for a hundred very mild aspirins.

"Debbie," he called, "make these up for Mrs Willoughby-Jones."

Debbie counted out the hundred small 75 mg tablets of aspirin and labelled the bottle, "Soluble Acetyl Salicylic Acid. One per day with food. It is dangerous to exceed the stated dose. Keep out of reach of children."

"What do I owe the Doctor?"

"Well, Harley Street would cost you a hundred and fifty pounds, but fortunately we're having a sale, so it will only be a hundred."

Mrs Jones wrote a cheque, grasped her bottle of aspirin and left with a satisfied smile. "Cardiovascular! Acetyl Salicylic Acid! That'll show Mrs Smythe. Coryza indeed, Mrs Smythe didn't know what it was to be ill, really ill!"

The two ladies, one with her inverted snobbery, constantly seeking attention, and the other, loud spoken and voluble, soon had everyone aware that at Doctor Fothergill's one could find the rarest ailments.

"Malaria," boomed the Brigadier, "India, you know. Damned mosquitoes everywhere. Can't avoid the little blighters, and not just malaria, yellow fever too, not to mention blackwater fever, now that's really something."

"And have you had blackwater fever, Brigadier?" asked Tim.

"Must have done, with all those damned mosquitoes, must have had it."

"I see. There's no sign of it now."

"Don't be silly, man, everyone knows it gets in the blood and keeps coming back."

"And what did you take for it when you had it?"

"God knows! Some remedy the army quack made up. Some concoction of his own I dare say. Whatever it was, it kept me alive through the war."

"And you want me to give you some of this concoction as you call it, even though there's no sign of blackwater fever?"

"There's no sign, you say, well I want to keep it that way. Dangerous stuff, you know, dangerous stuff. Prevention better than cure, and all that nonsense."

A very small dosage of quinine was prescribed, somewhat against Tim's better judgment, but the Brigadier went away a happy man, having long, long ago recovered from any bouts of malaria which he had had, and yellow fever or blackwater fever, which he had not.

Debbie put another cheque in the practice funds and secretly blessed the snobbishness and the foolishness of the so-called upper classes.

The bridge club, the Women's Institute, the Golf Club, soon the word spread that formerly untalked-about ailments were being readily diagnosed and kept under control by the nice young doctor at the poorer end of the redevelopment. Eventually even the hard-headed, hardworking yuppies got the message. They came in a trickle and then in a flood. Tired, enervated, losing concentration, they felt in need of something, but they didn't know what. Their own high salaried practitioners were helpless in the face of the symptoms, but Tim Fothergill had seen it before. "M.E" he announced. "The trouble is M.E, brought on by hard work, excessive hours at the desk, snatched meals, and general tension." He knew a change of life style was impracticable for these clients, so he prescribed sleeping tablets. A good deep sleep every night would enable them to face the rigours of the day that much better. "It's not a cure," he said, "just a palliative. Try to ease off a bit, but even if you can't, this should help."

It did help. The tension eased, the hectic pace was taken in their stride, and funnily enough, they made even more money, because they made better decisions.

"M.E? No such thing" said one knowledgeable acquaintance in the pub. "I've read about this, there's no evidence that it really exists, all anecdotal."

"Oh really old boy? It isn't anecdotal that I was dead beat and now I'm not, it isn't anecdotal that I was constantly sniffling and coughing, and now I'm not. I'll stick with Fothergill. Anecdotal my arse!"

Time and again this sentiment was repeated by different young entrepreneurs, until, repeated often enough, it became perceived as fact. As time went by the bubble burst, the yuppies became a thing of the past, the retired colonels, brigadiers and commodores, and their haughty, well spoken wives, grew older and less stringent in their demands, but also as time went by, so Tim Fothergill prospered. He moved to better premises, finishing up not quite in Harley Street, but not far away either. His paying clients afforded him a comfortable life style, but he didn't forget his principles. For two days a week his surgery, in the fashionable part of town, continued to cater for the National Health patients for whom he really cared, and Debbie, who was now Mrs Fothergill, continued to be the practice manager.

INDIAN ORPHAN

All my world is shattered
And I am in despair,
Tell me pretty lady
Have you any dreams to spare?
Any old discarded hopes
Which I might hope to share?

You Sir, with your camera,
Am I another scene,
Or can you see my broken life
And all it might have been?

When hunger brings me begging
Will you recall today,
Will you recall this orphan girl,
Or will you turn away?

And if, when I'm a woman,
I approach you in the street,
Will you expect my favours first,
Before I get to eat?

But nothing buys me nothing,
I know that all too well,
But I have no possessions
And there's nothing I can sell,

So you may take your pictures, Sir,
And Lady, you may stare,
But if you cannot help me now
Then why pretend to care?

THE EYE OF THE BUDDHA

"The third eye," said the Guru, "is here," putting his finger to the middle of his forehead. "It is the eye of the spirit, the seat of enlightenment. It has mysterious powers."

"And you want me to do... what?"

"We want you to find a ruby which has been stolen. It is the largest ruby in the world. It has been taken from the forehead of the Buddha at the Tibetan lamasery of Kalithar."

"Why not the police? They have more authority and more resources, why not go to them?"

"It would involve too many. There is bound to be corruption. One investigator, one person we can trust. You were recommended."

Arrangements had already been made for me to be taken to Kalithar, and everything was done with a slick precision which belied the unworldly air adopted by the Guru. The helicopter put down gently on the flat roof of the monastery, and yellow robed monks escorted me to the Lama.

"Welcome. Please sit." He indicated the cushions on the floor. The monks withdrew, and he told me the story. There had been no crime in the monastery for over six generations. Now the ruby was gone, and they didn't know how to deal with it. "Lack of experience, Mr. Jones," he said, "that's why we need you. Come, I'll show you the Buddha."

The statue was forty metres long. It lay on its back with the palms of the hands together expressing greetings, or peace, or meditation. It might have been any of these, but in the present context I guessed it was all three. I knew of only one other reclining Buddha, the one at Kasia, but that was tiny compared with this. In the forehead of the statue there was a depression, ten centimetres across and at least three deep.

"Phew!" I thought, "some ruby!" I didn't fall for all that rubbish about the mystical value of the thing. It was a ruby, the biggest in the world, and priceless. No wonder they wanted it back.

"I need to know something about this place," I said.

"Who had access to the ruby? Who is able to leave the monastery? Where could they go to dispose of it? These are all simple enough questions, but I need the answers."

"True Mr. Jones, they are simple enough questions and we can give you the answers, but we have asked the same questions and the answers have led us nowhere. Everyone in the monastery may go and worship the Buddha, nobody has left since the loss was noticed, and there is nowhere to go without a four day trek across the mountain peaks."

"Absolutely nobody has left?"

"Nobody."

"And there have been no visitors?"

"None, and if there had been, I repeat, nobody has left."

"Then the ruby is still in the monastery."

"So it would seem, but a thorough search has not found it."

He bade me goodnight and I was escorted to a cell. In deference to my layman's standing there was a small heater in the room and an incandescent Tilley lamp.

I was wakened by the chiming of gongs. "Good grief," I thought, "it's the middle of the bloody night." There was the chanting of mantras as the monks left their cells to go to their early morning prayers. I snatched up some clothes and followed them to the large hall which housed the Buddha.

The chanting continued, meaningless to me, but hypnotic in its constant repetition. I felt my mind wandering, and I knew that I would find the ruby, though how or where I couldn't say. Why not? It was what I was good at and what I was being paid for, of course I'd find it. A bunch of Tibetan monks, stuck in the last century or earlier, wasn't going to outwit Quentin Jones.

I made my way out of the incense laden atmosphere, and returned to my cell. Turning back the blanket, I was about to lie down when a huge cobra uncoiled itself from the warm bed and raised itself up to strike. The blanket was in my hand. I took the shock of the strike on the coarse fabric. The second strike was the last. I was ready for it. A quick grab, a sharp twist, and the snake lay dead.

Coincidence? No, it was too pat. I hadn't even started and already someone was out to get me. I searched my memory. Who had been late arriving at the prayers? Who had been missing? It was too soon, I didn't yet know enough about the monastery.

Breakfast was in the large dining hall. I was seated next to the Lama who enquired politely how I had slept. "I am sorry Mr. Jones for your rather Spartan accommodation. We have few luxuries here, but what few we have are at your disposal. I am anxious that your stay should be as comfortable as possible."

"Thank you. May we talk privately?" I told him about the snake, now lying dead beneath my window. "I don't know who was missing from the prayer meeting, or who came late," I said, "but I don't believe that snake came into the bed on its own. Why should anyone want to kill me? I haven't even started my investigation yet."

"Your reputation perhaps goes ahead of you. I wasn't at prayers myself, as you must know, but I will enquire as to who else may have been missing. Please take care, Mr Jones, theft is bad enough, murder would be intolerable."

Later he told me that noone else was missing from the prayers but three monks were late arriving. "But I can't believe it's any of them. They are devout followers, they would never steal the sacred eye, or do harm to a fellow being."

"Nor would any of the others, I dare say, but someone did!"

"True," he sighed. "It is a sad time we have come to."

I spent the day exploring the monastery, trying to absorb the feel of it. I could sense an atmosphere of such serenity that it was difficult to imagine any wrong-doing, but experience had taught me how deceptive appearances can be. That night I slept with my gun under my pillow.

During the night there was a soft thud . Something had fallen on the bed. Another snake I thought, but I had my flashlight and gun handy. I moved rapidly away from the bed, and then the beam caught it. A shang-shang. I had thought they were legend rather than fact, but earlier that day I had learned better. A poisonous tarantula, with a span of nearly thirty centimetres , is not the easiest thing to deal with in the beam from a flashlight. It scurried away but I kept the light on it. I could certainly not afford to have it running around in the dark. In those circumstances it had all the advantages and I had none.

I grabbed my shoe and hammered. It was tough! I gave it three good blows, but then I lost it. I jumped on the bed. Somewhere out there was the shang-shang. It was no time to be wandering about barefoot. I hastily slipped my shoes on, and as quickly as possible I lit the Tilley.

The sharp brilliant light was a relief. I held my revolver by the barrel and carefully looked round. One blow with the butt of the pistol would certainly count for more than any number with the heel of my shoe. No sign. I stood up and started searching. I caught a slight movement at the edge of my vision, and turned to see the injured shang-shang writhing in the corner of the room. A quick blow with the gun butt put an end to it.

I relaxed, only to give a startled jump as a figure walked in. "Are you all right Mr Jones? I heard a disturbance. What is the matter?"

The Lama stood indecisively in the doorway.

"All right now," I replied. "A spider, that's all."

He looked down at the battered carcass. "Shang-shang are dangerous," he said. "They are not common, but deadly. Where did you find it?"

"It dropped on my bed."

He looked up. "Must have been crossing the ceiling and lost its footing. I didn't know there were any in the monastery."

I started to reply but stopped. I had seen some in my wanderings, down in the cellars, about fifteen of the things in a glass fronted cage.

"I doubt if I can sleep now," I said. "Too keyed up. There's a bright moon. I think I'll take a walk along the monastery walls."

"I'll come along, if that's all right. I'm not sleeping well, too worried about this business of the Eye."

We walked along the top of the monastery's outer wall. It

must have been at least two metres thick, sticking up from the mountain like a rock. As we came to the corner of the rectangle I turned and faced the Lama. "Now, suppose you give me the ruby."

He looked surprised. "I don't have the ruby."

"You weren't at the prayer meeting, you were the only one awake when I was dealing with the shang-shang, and you said there weren't any in the monastery. You must know there are ten or fifteen in the cellars. So you see, it must be you who tried to kill me, and you who has the ruby."

He fumbled under his cloak. "I just wanted to frighten you off. I never wanted you here in the first place." When his hand came up it held something heavy. It glinted red in the moonlight as he tried to hit me with it.

I grabbed his hand and we struggled, there on the high wall. With a sudden jerk he lunged at me, but I twisted away. He lost his balance and fell. It seemed to happen in slow motion. He teetered on the edge of the wall. My hand reached out for him, but missed, and slowly, slowly, he toppled. At last there was a thud as he hit the valley, hundreds of metres below.

The monks were reluctant to accept my explanation. They locked me in my cell, but fortunately two of them had been woken by the noise of my attempts to kill the shang-shang. They had seen us on the top of the wall, and they vouched for the fact that I had not attacked the Lama. In fact it had been the other way. I blessed the bright moonlight, for without it I would never have been believed. Plans were made to recover the body of the Lama, and perhaps the ruby too. They would search for it, but it seemed a forlorn hope. I was allowed to return to London.

I had hardly got back to my flat when there was a knock on the door. It was the Guru. With him was a large shaven headed man in yellow robes.

"Well done, Mr Jones, it was clever of you to catch the Lama. No Buddhist would have dreamed of suspecting him, but I knew you would succeed. Now may I have the ruby, please."

"The ruby? It fell down the hill with the Lama. The monks are looking for it."

"Please, Mr Jones, the ruby. I know you have it. Did I not tell you it has mysterious powers? It is the third eye, the all seeing eye of the Buddha." The big man went straight to my case, opened it, and without even searching, took out the leather pouch containing the ruby.

I pulled my gun and trained it on the Guru. "Tell him to put it back."

He nodded to the man, who turned towards me. Casually he tossed the pouch and instinctively I caught it. He was so fast that I never saw it happen, but in that split second my wrist was gripped so tightly that the gun clattered to the floor. The Guru calmly took out the bullets, then handed it back to me.

"The ruby please." Quietly I placed the pouch in his outstretched hand.

"Thank you, Mr. Jones. I shall return it to its proper place. Your fee will be forwarded. Peace be with you."

Was that it I wondered, no recriminations?

Well, I thought, you win some, you lose some. Pity about having to give up the ruby. I didn't believe all that claptrap about its mystical powers, but it was a gorgeous stone, worth an absolute fortune.

That was five months ago. It still hurts to hold a gun in my right hand, but more worrying is the bright red scar in the middle of my forehead. It doesn't allow me to forget what the guru said, "The third eye has mysterious powers".

THE OFFERING

She was sitting on a rock looking out over the valley. Her back was towards me, and she didn't hear me until I was nearly up to her. She turned, not surprised, yet somehow afraid.

"Oh!" A relieved sigh. "I'm glad it's you. It might have been anyone, but it's you!" She rose and threw her arms around me.

I didn't know then what it was all about, but there were so many things on the island I was unaware of. I had seen the red band tied to the tree and gone to investigate it. Nothing much, just a red strip of cloth, loosely tied around the trunk. But further up the hill I saw another, fluttering in the light breeze, so I went to that, and the next, and the next. At the top of the trail, I found her.

"I'm ready," she said.

Ready for what, I wondered. Taking her hand I led her down the trail to the village. As we approached, by the light of a full moon, I saw the fires burning, and food being prepared.

"What's going on?"

"They are preparing the Feast of the Offering," she said. "You will be the chief guest, because you are the one who found me."

I had never heard of this, and I didn't know why she should have been on the hill, but I was happy enough to be honoured and feted. When we came into the circle of light there was a hush. The Chief approached, brushing us with a broom of parakeet feathers, and with a deep obeisance, led me to the dais. I sat down, and she sat beside me.

Drums began to beat with an insidious rhythm, which went on and on. Food was brought to her, then to me, and only after we had tasted ours did the rest of the villagers have theirs. The rhythm of the drums slowly quickened in pace. She rose and went to the centre of the circle, and began to sway sinuously, her arms making graceful, but precise, movements in the air in accordance with the age old customs of her people.

Still swaying, she approached me, and led me to the front

of the dais. As I stood there her movements became more seductive, more suggestive, more provocative, until I finally put my arms around her and lifted her off her feet. The drums grew faster and louder, and a chanting started.

Her head was on my shoulder, her lips to my ear. "Go to the hut," she whispered.

The way was covered in flowers, looking yellow in the firelight, and led to the open door. Inside there was a covering on the floor where I put her down. Someone outside pulled a woven screen across the doorway, and we were alone.

"Love me," she said. "There is only tonight, so love me now."

"Only tonight? I thought you really wanted me, that's what the dance meant, wasn't it?"

"I am the offering. It is the time of the third moon, and each year a maiden is given in sacrifice to the gods. You found me, and I am yours. I'm glad it was you, but in the morning I shall be thrown in the sea. A cut will be made on each breast and the blood will draw the sharks. My death will bring a fine harvest of fish and food from the gods of the sea."

"That's barbaric, I won't let it happen."

She was the first one I met when I landed on the island. She was swimming in the inlet where I beached my boat. She didn't speak English and I didn't speak her language, yet somehow, by signs and facial expressions, we managed to communicate. She helped me put the boat out of sight, and then led me to her people. They made me welcome, but she became my special friend. I learned some words of her language, and she learned some English, and we talked in this mixed up fashion. That was five months ago, and in those five months I had learned to love her.

"It is the custom of our people. It must happen, or the village will starve."

"I won't let you die, you must live."

"Because it is you who found me I want to live, but for that we would have to flee from the village, and they will hunt us down, you as well as me, until they find us. I can't let you die

249

because of me."

"And I can't live without you." I held her and kissed her, whispering pleas and promises to make her change her mind.

She led me to the soft floor covering and we made love. It was then that she said, "All right, I'll come with you, if we can get away. I am marked to die, so I have nothing to lose, but you, you will be risking your life for me."

"I'd risk anything for you." I had loved her from the moment I had first seen her.

We crept out of the back of the reed hut, and quietly out of the village. There were no guards, which surprised me, but there was too much urgency, and need of quiet, for questions. On the beach we took a canoe and paddled slowly round the headland. I was impatient with our slow progress, but she whispered caution, and even the soft sound of the paddles seemed too loud.

We were just rounding the headland when we heard the first cries from the village. "Quick" she said, "they know now." We paddled fast to reach the inlet where I had left my small boat. The motor would outpace any islanders with their primitive canoes and paddles.

We came to the place my boat was hidden. I drew it out of the overhanging leaves and pulled the starter. Nothing. I pulled it again. Still nothing. We could see the first canoe rounding the headland. "Come on, damn you, start!"

It was five months since I left it there. Would it still work? If it didn't then we would die. Still, she was worth dying for, and worth trying to save.

Three more attempts, and then the motor spluttered into life. Ragged and uneven, but working. We set off. There was no chance of secrecy. In the bright moonlight the noise of the motor pinpointed our position. We had to get out of the inlet before they blockaded the opening. When we did reach it it was to find one canoe just arriving. I gunned the engine and went straight for the side of it, seeing with some satisfaction the startled look on the faces of its occupants. At the last minute I swerved and went round the rear of the craft and headed away.

250

The canoe swung round, more rapidly than I thought possible, and joined by others, gave chase. Yet others swerved to cut us off, but we were faster than they, and I headed straight out to sea. There was no point in touching land anywhere that they might find us.

That ruled out any of the nearby islands. We had to go out of reach of the native canoes, which meant not only out running them, but also getting right beyond their range of travel. Thank god for Maya. I'm no navigator, but she was a natural. Without any experience, or expertise, she seemed to know which direction to take. It seemed to me that she must be following the stars, except that she never seemed to look up. She must have had some inbuilt direction finder. At last, when we were running low on fuel, we made landfall. For the last few miles we had been baling steadily, the motor chugging along evenly, but the hull not high enough to prevent taking in water.

The rocky beach was inhospitable, but again it was Maya who acted as guide. We found edible fruits, of a kind I had never seen, and a spring of fresh water. We slept in the open for three days, before we found a cave. In the peculiar hybrid language, part native, part English, which we had developed during my months with her people, we talked of the future.

The future! We couldn't stay here for ever. I needed the things of civilisation, electricity, hospitals, amenities. So I explored, and I found that the rocky island was cut off only at high tide. At the ebb one could wade along a causeway to a large land mass, and at last we found a small town.

From there I was eventually able to make contact. A small steamer took us to Manila, and a larger one brought us back to England.

We live by the sea. Maya needs the sea. She is unhappy if she can't see it and hear it, and plunge herself into its healing waters. Two years have passed, and no disaster has befallen the island. She realises she has not betrayed her people.

She told me once, in her imperfect English, something which I think I must have misunderstood. She said that many generations back, before her great great great grandmother,

251

though she is vague about the actual time, her race came out of the sea. She drew me a picture of her ancestors. It looked very much like our pictures of mermaids.

That's why I think I must have misunderstood.

THE FICTION WRITER

I needed an alibi while I killed her. My stepmother that is. I'd set up the computer to turn itself on and ring Steve's number at six thirty. That would activate the tape recorder and send my message. That message, recorded on the BT answering service, 1571, was my alibi. It gave my phone number and the time. Steve was still on his way back from France, but if I was ringing him from my phone, I could hardly be miles away in Bristol, could I?

I used her own kitchen knife, and I wore rubber gloves, so there weren't any prints. Had to be careful of blood, of course, couldn't get all messed up, could I? An apron, the kitchen apron she kept hanging from a hook prevented any blood getting on me. The apron got bloody of course, but that didn't matter, it was plastic coated, blood wouldn't come through. And there was nothing to connect me with the apron.

I was right. Her kitchen knife was in the drawer, her apron on the hook. I knew it would be, she was obsessively tidy. Stick the knife in her. She screamed of course, but in that isolated cottage there was no-one to hear. Make sure she was dead, and then drive home. That's how I saw it in my mind's eye, that's the way I'd planned it.

It was a good plan, and the bitch deserved to die. Wheedling all Dad's money out of him, and then letting him fade away with Alzheimer's. The money should have been mine, and the house, and the things in it too, but she got the lot. Bloody barmaid, that's all she was, smiling at the customers, flirting with them too, taking their money.

"Have one for yourself, Love."

"Thanks," she'd say, "just a white wine," and pocket the cash.

Dad was lonely. She batted her eyelids at him, and he fell for it. She was pretty enough I guess, in a blowsy sort of way. He was just another customer when I went away. When I returned four months later it was for the wedding. And then the gradual deterioration as the illness took hold.

253

She nursed him with great tenderness, that's what people said, but it's rubbish. She nursed him all right, but it wasn't tenderness, it was greed. I know, you see. I know what she was like. When he died he left everything to her. She acted so surprised, as though she hadn't known. But I knew different!

Well, my plans were made. I'd thought it out to the last detail. I'd recorded the message, I'd set the computer. As soon as the morning at the Writers' Circle ended I was on my way to Bristol. I couldn't really concentrate, and my comments at the Circle were pretty noncommittal. I had other things on my mind. Until Bill started to read his story, that is.

"I needed an alibi while I killed her. My stepmother that is. I'd set up the computer. It turned itself on and rang Steve at six thirty. My message, recorded on the BT answering service....."

I could feel myself sweating, my heart beating faster, my head swimming. Word by word the whole plan was opened up in Bill's story. Was it so obvious? If Bill could write it as a story, it wouldn't take long for the police to rumble my plan. I excused myself. Once in the car I drove fast. No, not to Bristol. I went home. I erased the message for Steve switched off the computer. I was shaking and fumbling with the controls and nearly jumped out of my skin when the phone suddenly jangled.

Let it ring, I didn't want to talk to anyone. Seven rings and the answer phone cut in. "Harry, this is Daisy. I hope you get this message before you set out, but I've just had a call from my sister. She's quite ill, and wants me over there. I can hardly refuse, so the place will be empty if you come. I hope you get this massage in time, but your mobile was turned off. I'll try again later. Don't want you driving all this way for nothing."

Damn her. My bloody stepmother couldn't even stay home when I needed her to. Damned self-centred bitch. Still, no harm done, the plan just wasn't good enough, Bill's story had shown that, but it's not over. I'll find a better plan. That money's really mine, that's what Dad would want. Just need to get rid of her. And I will, just you see!

McCONNIGAN'S WAKE

Patrick McConnigan was a broth of a boy
And it sure was a shame when he happened to die,
But he'd lost his wife Mary a twelve-month or so,
And indeed it was said he'd be happy to go;
So we tried to be cheerful for McConnigan's sake
As we all gathered round at his house for a wake.

There was Shamus and Shaun and Miss Bridie O'Toole,
And the most of the staff from the Catholic school,
When the Protestant vicar walked in, by mistake,
Even he was made welcome with a drink and some cake!

Mahoney, who managed the Workin' Men's Club
Brought gallons of beer, and lashings of grub,
And whiskey there was to be had by the quart,
And we all of us drank rather more than we ought.

Father O'Malley was drunk as a newt,
Pinched someone's bottom and said she was cute,
But he soon sobered up when he found the posterior
He'd pinched was the bum of the Mother Superior!
But Mother forgave him, and she and O'Malley
By the fifteenth 'Hail Mary' was getting quite pally.

Down in the parlour things got interestin'
When we all heard the Protestant Vicar protestin'
That he wasn't party to all the shenanigans
Shamelessly started by Maureen O'Hannigan.
What the Vicar maintained was an innocent hug
Finished up with them both on the fireside rug.

Then, on top of all this, Paddy's sister-in-law, Mabel,
Began a striptease on the dining room table;
She swayed and she twirled as she took off her clothes,
And the more she took off, so the temperature rose;

255

In the end there was even a huffin' and puffin'
From the corpse - which had ought to be dead in the coffin.

I took a quick look at where Patrick lay dead in
The suit he had borrowed from me for his weddin',
And what do I see but the corpse lookin' out
To where Mabel was dancin' and prancin' about,
On his face was a look of most exquisite bliss -
But he should have been dead: there was somethin' amiss.

I told the Headmaster, and Bridie O'Toole,
But they thought I was drunk, or just actin' the fool,
So I phoned Doctor Finnigan, that's what I did,
Then I pushed Paddy down, and I lowered the lid!

Doctor arrived, and before long he stated
That it was as well he'd not yet been cremated.
For Patrick, it seems, had just been in a trance,
But was now fully waked by his sister-in-law's dance.
It appears that the sight of her uncovered torso
Was just like his Mary's, except rather more so.
In all the confusion he quickly proposed,
And Mabel accepted as she put on her clothes.

The doctor confirmed that the corpse wasn't dead
So the funeral was changed to a weddin' instead;
The first of its kind at the Crematorium,
The bride carried flowers, with a card In Memoriam,
And casual observers were taken aback
That the whole wedding party was attired in black.
But those who knew better were touched to the heart
When it came to the bit about 'Death do us part'.
Then vows were exchanged, both for better and worse,
And the newly-weds left - in the back of the hearse!

But the course of events had so radically changed
That the honeymoon couple had nothing arranged,

So the funeral director, as a wedding bequest,
Allowed them a week in the Chapel of Rest.

It sure was a shambles, but make no mistake,
It was a hell of a hooley, was McConnigan's wake!